BROKEN

THE STOLEN SERIES
BOOK TWO

MARLENA FRANK

When *Stolen* was released in January 2019, I wasn't prepared for the journey ahead of me. I knew I wanted to take part in book events, in festivals, in conventions, but I had no idea the incredible places I would go.

I felt like Dorothy just discovering the yellow brick road.

Stolen got me an invite to the Alabama Book Festival. My fellow Parliament House authors invited me to share a booth up in New York City at BookCon. Then again at the Decatur Book Festival in Georgia. Everything started happening so quickly, and I literally squealed when the BookCon invite came in. I had always wanted to visit New York City, but never thought I would. Then I had a reason, a purpose, and my friends and family were at my side to help make it possible.

These days I'm regularly attending events. I'm regularly seeking out shows and ways to talk to new readers. I look back on where I was in January before my book released and shake my head at what all was coming my way. I had no idea, and that's okay.

My mantra this year has been to try to say yes to any opportunity. It certainly hasn't been easy, and there have been many times when I worry I've taken on too much, but then I get an email with a glowing review, or I'm told that I'm a favorite author, or I talk to someone who has been reading my work for years, and I remember: yes, it is worth it.

It is all very worth it.

But I never would have known that if I hadn't tried, if I hadn't taken a chance and been willing to take risks.

It may not feel like it at the time, but sometimes taking risks is the only way we grow.

Marlena Frank
September, 18, 2019

CONTENTS

PART I
RECOVERY

EVERYTHING IS WRONG

Shaleigh

This wasn't how it was supposed to be. She was supposed to be at home, making sure her father was safe and getting to see Kaeja again. She was supposed to be worrying about what her life would be like after she got out of high school. She was supposed to be doing what most teens her age were doing: taking classes, going on dates, or binging on video games.

Instead she was here, in a land where she didn't belong, surrounded by people who saw her as a trespasser.

Teagan had tried to pull her back from the road, had known instantly where they were and the danger she was in, but she didn't listen. She thought they were back at her home, back in the Human World, but they weren't. The Madness had twisted Talek's mind, twisted his intention, and his magic had sent them to his home instead. By the time she fully understood what had happened, it was too late to escape.

Shaleigh walked slowly, the metal chains heavy on her wrists. They looked similar to the ones that Talek wore when he was in the prison cell at High Castle, but they were far heavier than she had expected them to be. Already her shoulders were aching, and she could feel the pain moving down her back.

Teagan was beside her but didn't meet her gaze. His eyes were downcast, and he hadn't spoken since they had been captured. They were being escorted, surrounded by five Faeries, all dressed in leather armor with white skirts and long spears.

Shaleigh had been so shaken by the gleaming human skulls, used as lawn decor in the giant stone archway, that she hadn't realized the Faeries had dropped down from the trees and surrounded them. All she could do was stare at the gleaming white bones.

Shaleigh had seen animal bones before. She spent enough time outside and amid forgotten buildings that she and Kaeja had discovered plenty of them. It just hadn't prepared her for seeing human ones. Nothing could have prepared her for that. All she could focus on was that they had different sizes, meaning some of them had to have been from children. And even though they had walked at least a mile by now, the images still lingered.

She glanced at the guard holding her chains; these guards were nothing like the ones she had seen at High Castle. They had dropped down with barely a sound, moved in formation, and their speed with their spears was intimidating.

They never spoke to her, only to Teagan. And other than clamping the heavy shackles on her arms, they treated her as if she didn't exist.

"Are these truly necessary?" Teagan asked suddenly with a huff, holding up his arms. "I assure you I have no intention of fleeing. It would be fruitless to even try."

The dark-haired guard opposite Teagan arched an eyebrow and gave him an amused smile. "I don't blame you for being frightened. Queen Mab's wrath is something to behold."

"Her wrath?" Teagan asked, a trace of worry on his face. "Why should she be angry with me?"

"Everyone knows what happened at the Garden," the guard replied, keeping his gaze on the path ahead of him. "A magician has been traveling on the wind telling everyone the news. I'm sure our queen will have a few words for you," his gaze shot to Shaleigh, "and most certainly for the Human brat."

Shaleigh narrowed her eyes. "What do you mean?"

The guard exchanged a smirk with the Faerie on the other side of Shaleigh, a tall woman with blonde hair, who gave a deep chuckle. Neither said a word to her though. It felt like high school all over again.

Teagan sighed. "Don't pretend to be deaf, you heard her question. Why should she be of any concern to Queen Mab?"

"Living up in that enormous tower has made your mind soft," the blonde woman retorted and gave Teagan a wide smile, looking past Shaleigh as if she wasn't there.

"You know how she is about Humans trespassing on her land. Knowing she's brought down Madam Cloom proves she's dangerous. If it was up to Sionn and me, we would've taken her head already."

"Easy, Nora, no need to frighten the lamb," Sionn said without a drop of concern on his face. The two exchanged another laugh without saying more.

Shaleigh felt a pit form in her gut. As bad as the Garden was, at least there she had a chance to prove her usefulness - here she didn't even have that luxury.

"It's not my fault!" she blurted out. She lifted her arms in protest, but only rattled the heavy chains instead, earning several glares from the guards. "I didn't know we were even here. How could we have trespassed when we had no control over how we got here?"

Teagan glanced toward her, concern on his face. "Calm down. It will do no good with this group of fools."

One of the guards scowled at them, his grip tightening on his spear. She wanted to tell Teagan that it was dangerous to threaten them, especially since they were surrounded, but she didn't want to risk them overhearing her. She didn't want to make things worse.

Shaleigh felt her eyes burn as tears threatened. Here was another ruler with her own realm and her own unique set of demands. Here was another land where she had no idea what rules existed or how she was supposed to follow them.

Her face flushed as a strange mixture of anger and fear battled within. She wanted to scream in frustration but was afraid they would see that as an attack. Instead a tear streaked down her cheek. Her shoulders and arms were so sore from the weight of the shackles that she didn't have the strength to lift her hand to wipe it away.

Teagan reached over and took her hand in his, giving it a reassuring squeeze. His hand felt cool and dry compared to her own sweaty, trembling fingers. It made her feel a little bit better; at least she wasn't alone.

Shaleigh took a deep breath and tried to calm herself down, even as another tear fell.

She tried to speak, but her throat clenched with the effort it took not to scream or bawl like a baby. Teagan was right though. It wouldn't do any good to try to convince the guards of anything. They clearly didn't want to listen to what she had to say... At least in the Garden she had a voice; here she was worth even less.

"I'm sorry," she whispered.

Teagan looked to the ground, taking a moment to find the right words. "You didn't know what you were doing. Madam Cloom kept..." he squeezed her hand, "no, *we* kept you isolated. That was the plan. I asked far too much from you. It wasn't your fault."

She gave a short laugh as another tear fell. "I knew what I was doing to some extent. Just enough to get us killed. I didn't expect," her throat constricted, "*all* of this to happen."

"You didn't understand the consequences. We were careful not to give you too much information, though in retrospect that was a poor decision. We underestimated our enemies."

He was trying to calm her down, trying to reassure her. Did he really think that was going to help? She was the reason they were trapped here. She was the reason that Mawr and Colin got left behind. She was the reason the High Castle of the Garden fell. If she hadn't been so naive, so blind to the danger, and so willing to help, they wouldn't be here.

"Like Queen Mab?"

Teagan smirked. "Well I wouldn't consider her an enemy exactly..."

Sionn beside him snickered and Teagan glanced anxiously his way before letting go of Shaleigh's hand.

"Perhaps it's best if we hold off on our council for now," this time his voice was lower when he spoke.

She nodded before drawing a deep breath of the humid air, trying to clear her thoughts and the guilt in her heart. She pushed away the thoughts of Colin and Mawr, and of Madam Cloom's mouth disappearing.

Shaleigh shuddered and took another breath in and out. She didn't need to think on that now. She needed to be in the present. She had to collect herself if she wanted to look like more than just a teenager who was way out of her league.

If she had learned anything from Madam Cloom, it was that she needed to keep in mind how she was perceived. She needed to make a good impression - her life might depend on it... again. The guards that surrounded her probably thought she was a meek little pushover and she had to prove them wrong.

Another deep breath and her fingers stopped trembling. She focused on her surroundings to prevent herself from sinking into despair.

The path through the old woods was carefully, oddly maintained. No weeds or underbrush grew on either side, despite the fact that the canopy of trees left big blotches of sunlight. Yet they passed large, red toadstools with white spots on them on either side of the road. They were bigger than any she had seen before, almost coming up to her knees. They were so evenly spaced that she assumed they were like mile markers on the interstate.

'*The exit numbers mark the miles*', her Dad's voice came back to her, as clear as if he had spoken in her ear.

She hadn't allowed herself to think about him yet. Her fingers trembled once again as she remembered him crying in the passenger's seat of the SUV in the garage by himself. That was the last she had seen him. Why had she left him like that? Why hadn't she hugged him and told him it would be okay like she used to? Why was she so full of anger that day?

The tears threatened again and her eyes burned with warning, but she shook her head impatiently.

A cool breeze came by, rustling up a pile of dead leaves as they passed beneath a white, stone structure with square alcoves chiseled into the sides. In each one, a human skull stared out with empty eye sockets. The bone gleamed almost as white as the stone in the late afternoon sunlight.

A shiver went down her spine; her arms broke out into goosebumps. Were these other trespassers? Curious urban explorers like she and Kaeja had been once upon a time? People sent to a mushroom ring like she and Teagan had been? There was no telling who they had been ages ago. All they were now were warnings and trophies, mile markers of their own.

Stumbling, she felt something hard and cold pressed

between her shoulder blades and realized she had lagged behind. The guard hadn't spoken a word to her, only pushed the base of his pike into her shoulder blade and gave it a nudge. She glanced behind to meet his annoyed gaze.

"Sorry," she whispered, and hurried back to Teagan's side, her heavy chains weighing her down. She wasn't sure why she apologized. She was in no hurry to reach Queen Mab and her creepy beheading Faeries.

Teagan reached out to take her hand again as she reached him. Perhaps it was as much to console her as it was to keep her moving.

"Sorry," she muttered. She hated that he felt like he had to hold onto her to keep her from getting hurt. Though maybe he understood the dangers of the guards better than she did. He only gave her a small smile and a nod in reply keeping ahold of her hand.

As they left the archway behind, Shaleigh wondered if the owners of those skulls had gotten the chance to even walk into the city. Knowing how quick and silent their guards had been, she doubted they even knew they were being hunted. If she hadn't had Teagan with her, she probably would have met the same fate.

She could tell they were reaching some civilization, other than disturbing stone pillars and decapitated skulls. The dirt path grew wider with trees that had larger trunks than the ones she had seen before. She noticed the sun must have been close to dipping beyond the horizon, because the beams of light were diagonal across the path. How long had they been walking? For that matter, how long had they been asleep in the fairy ring?

From the corner of her eye, she saw Teagan look up. He had such a sweet smile that it made him look far younger. Were those tears in his dark eyes?

"It's been so long since I've been home."

Shaleigh followed his gaze. Up above them, built into the very branches and trunks of the enormous trees, were houses. They were small by the standards of the ones she had explored back home, with maybe two or three rooms in each, and she could see candles flickering from within.

Doors opened and Faeries looked down at them with their arms crossed; others leaned out their windows.

If they looked at Shaleigh in disgust and annoyance, they looked at Teagan with absolute hatred. One of them even spat onto the ground as they passed. It made an audible splat that had Shaleigh moving a little closer to the guards.

"It may be home," Sionn muttered with a huff, "but don't expect to get a warm welcome. We all know what you did, and now this business with the Garden?" He shook his head in disgust.

The glow that Teagan had in his eyes diminished and he stared down at his feet, once more cowed.

The sadness she saw in his eyes hurt. It reminded her of the throne room with Madam Cloom, when the buildings of the Garden were burning bright below those giant windows, casting shadows throughout the dark room, and Teagan's trembling hands. Shaleigh wasn't always certain if she trusted Teagan or not; he had a bad tendency of doing whatever it took to survive, regardless of who it hurt, but she did pity him now just as she did then. She understood his pain. It couldn't be easy to be hated by your own people.

Shaleigh pursed her lips, realizing that if Teagan was so despised here, she would have to handle the negotiations herself. She wasn't sure how well that would go if the Faeries didn't even want to acknowledge she could speak. They might not care what she had to say, but they all looked as though they wanted to add Teagan's head to some grotesque shrine, and she couldn't let that happen

SHALEIGH COULD TELL they were moving into the city; soon the treetop houses were joined with quaint homes on the ground. They were all made out of wood but rounded like large Chinese lanterns. She wasn't sure how they made the wood bend like that, but each little home housed at least one or two Faeries based on the faces she glimpsed through the windows.

A good crowd had amassed both on the ground and up above them. The more Faeries that joined, the more the crowd stirred like an angry mob - Shaleigh was nervous. They weren't throwing anything yet, but the ones behind her were whispering amongst themselves.

"How *dare* he come back after what he did."

"Did he really bring a *Human* with him?"

"I guess his Garden won't protect him now."

Shaleigh's hands trembled and she clasped them together to keep the chains from betraying her fear. She glanced to Teagan, to find his gaze still on his feet.

Sionn slammed the base of his pike onto the ground

making a ringing sound; Shaleigh jumped. Their escort had come to a complete stop and she turned around, half expecting the mob to run at them. Instead, they had grown quiet, and somehow that made her more nervous.

"This is Mab, the wise Queen of the Land of the Fae." Sionn bowed as the crowd murmured. "My queen, we found these intruders in the forest. We suspect they are from the Garden based on the news we received."

The dirt path they were on came to a junction with four other dirt paths, making a sort of five-pointed star in the road. At the center stood an elaborate throne that looked like it was either sculpted or planted there: the chair grew out of a small mound of dirt and wound upwards; the back of it reached up toward the sky, ending in several sharp wooden spikes.

A green vine wound its way up from the base to the vicious spikes above, bouncing in the breeze. It was covered in tiny white flowers, and occasionally Shaleigh caught their subtle, sweet scent. They smelled light and airy, not like the heavy perfume from the flowers that Madam Cloom kept. It was strange, as they were the first flowers she had seen since waking up amid the ring of mushrooms. They seemed out of place here amid the towering trees, dirt paths, and skull shrines. They seemed too delicate to survive.

Her gaze fell to the throne.

A short, middle-aged woman sat in the chair with long ears and a pale complexion. She had a pink glow on her cheeks and a wide smile on her lips. Shaleigh had expected the Queen of the Fae to be gorgeous, and she was lovely, but... she was nothing like Shaleigh had expected. She wore a simple white gown with flowers that had been stitched into the fabric. Most of the Faeries Shaleigh had seen wore tan colored robes or even leather hide, but the bright white of her dress stood out from all of them.

The queen had the look of a woman who had seen a lot of heartache in her life, yet also had laugh lines along her mouth. She had warm, brown eyes, and looked genuinely happy to see them, which was surprising considering the mob that was merely feet away, still muttering under their breath about their unwanted guests.

Queen Mab waved a hand to the side and the guards stepped away; their heads bowed.

Teagan knelt to the ground, which brought on a new barrage of anger from the crowd. Shaleigh at first wasn't sure if she should follow his lead or not, afraid she would rile up the crowd more, but slowly she knelt as well. The crowd moved in closer, even more enraged, but none of them stepped past the circle of guards that surrounded them.

Kneeling, she realized that the center of the five-pointed star, where the dirt paths met, was stone not dirt. It had an intricate design carved into it that Shaleigh didn't recognize.

"It is good to see you again, Teagan," the queen said with a smile, her voice wavering as though she was close to tears, though she looked grateful. "It has been too long."

"Yes, my queen," he said, looking up to her. "Far too long."

She stood from her chair and came forward with her

arms outstretched. "Kneel not before me, friend. Surely, I deserve a hug, don't I?"

Teagan got to his feet and allowed himself to be embraced. Shaleigh stood as well, not sure what to say or do – just knowing she wanted to keep her head on her shoulders.

Although the crowd went silent as soon as Queen Mab spoke, it was clear just by looking at them that they weren't pleased. Each time Shaleigh stole a glimpse at them, most of them were glaring at Teagan, whispering to each other or trying to get a better look around the still growing crowd, but a few of them had their eyes on Shaleigh. Those were the ones that made her hands shake and forced her to turn back to Queen Mab and Teagan. She kept thinking back to the human skulls she had seen in the alcoves. She wondered how many of them had killed humans.

The queen pulled away and looked at him almost admiringly. "You have done great and terrible things in your time in the Garden. I'm sure even I could learn a few tricks from you."

It was a strange statement for a queen to make, especially when the guards had spoken of how angry she would be. It almost sounded as if she was genuinely praising him. Teagan gave the barest of smiles but wasn't exactly gracious. This negotiation was going to be more difficult than she thought.

At his silence, the queen's gaze narrowed. "You look terrible," she said at last. "What did that horrible magician do to you?"

Teagan looked away from her piercing gaze. His hands

balled into fists and a flush came to his cheeks. "Please, don't," he whispered, his voice barely audible.

"You have nothing to hide from me, you know that." She put a hand on his cheek and gently urged him to look her in the eyes again.

Teagan bit his lip as he turned to look at her, forcing his fists open.

She pursed her lips and narrowed her eyes, quickly looking from his left eye to his right. A hush came over the crowd. Teagan's mouth dropped open and tears went down his cheeks. It only lasted a few seconds, but it felt far longer.

Shaleigh took a step forward, starting to get worried, but finally Queen Mab broke eye contact with him. Teagan let out a shaky breath and wiped at his face, blinking as though to clear the cobwebs.

Queen Mab nodded. "Mmm, you have been through a lot."

Teagan let out another shaky breath. Was she reading his mind? Could she do that? From the crowd one of the Faerie men could no longer keep silent and said, "Are you truly planning to let him return after all he did?"

Queen Mab patted Teagan's cheek affectionately as though he was a child she hadn't seen in ages, then turned to face her people. Shaleigh was amazed at how quickly her kind eyes turned hard. "I have already declared that Teagan and Talek would be welcomed back to their homelands. This was a decision I made decades ago. Or have you all forgotten?"

There were some murmurings before a woman spoke up, "What about the Garden? All those people are dead!"

Shaleigh felt as though she had cold water thrown in her face.

Mawr.

Colin.

"No!" Shaleigh called out, "No, that's not true, is it?" She stepped forward, not sure what the weight on her arms was until she looked down and remembered the shackles. She dragged the chains across the stone ground toward Teagan. "Not everyone," she pleaded.

Teagan stepped closer to her, dragging his own chains, and took her hand in his. His cheeks were stained with tears. The guards didn't stop either one of them. Why should they if she was just going to be beheaded here soon? Any one of the Faeries could chase her down if she ran.

Teagan squeezed her hand. He was trying to calm her, to get her to focus. She knew that, but she could only think of her friends.

"Teagan, they can't be—"

He shook his head in warning.

Shaleigh could feel the anger aimed at her and she glanced to the crowd to see the fury in their eyes. She took a shaky breath and looked to her feet, trying to keep from saying more. Even if her friends were gone, she was still alive. She had to remember that, even if it hurt. If the voices she heard were any indication, she had already said too much.

"How *dare* that Human speak!" one yelled out.

"They're all so arrogant."

"Ought to be slain..."

Shaleigh's mouth went dry as their voices continued.

She drew closer to Teagan's side, gripping his hand tight. The tears she had worked so hard to stop back on the road were threatening again.

The anger from the crowd was relentless, but one statement made her stomach drop - "Those Pello Pines won't leave any of them alive now that the Slumbering Forest has awoken."

Shaleigh felt her bottom lip tremble. She thought of Mawr being so scared behind the library. Had he been killed because he decided to help some stupid Human? She thought of Colin getting so terrified about the kids that day. Was he gone too? He and Shaleigh had finally become friends. What about the children Mawr read aloud to?

A soft hand cupped her chin and she looked up to see Queen Mab's face. Her warm brown eyes were searching, probing. Other than her long, pointed ears she looked more Human than Teagan. At first Shaleigh didn't know what she wanted, then she remembered what the queen had done to Teagan only moments ago. She thought about pulling away, but she felt numb. A part of her just didn't care enough to struggle.

Suddenly she smelled the scent of sage, powerful on the breeze. The knot in her belly relaxed; her mouth didn't feel so dry and her eyes stopped burning.

Queen Mab dragged a thumb across her cheek. Her eyes were kind even as the scent of sage grew stronger to the point Shaleigh feared she would start coughing. Then it was over. The sage dwindled and Queen Mab stepped back, her gaze one of pity.

"Take them to Teagan's home."

"My home?" Teagan blinked. "But my queen..."

She waved a hand to him. "I don't want to hear it, Teagan. I have not been your queen in many years."

Teagan's mouth dropped and he blinked at her. "But..."

She didn't let him finish. "Take them both. It seems I need to remind my people why we are free to do as we wish." She spoke loudly and dropped her hands onto her hips. "It seems I need to remind my people that the Fae will always have a home here. We do not judge what our brothers and sisters do outside of these woods, but we do ensure they will be able to return and recuperate. You will always have a home here for as long as I live. The Fae must remain a family: we remember when others do not, we endure when others do not, we preserve when others do not."

The crowd, which had been so very boisterous moments before, became subdued by her words. The silence was almost eerie. Even the guards, who had begun to walk on either side of Shaleigh and Teagan, had stopped to listen.

Queen Mab walked toward her people, and the crowd parted for her. "I have ruled over the Land of the Fae for many, many millennia." She placed a hand on one man's shoulder, "I have watched many of us fall and many reach great heights." She took one woman's hand briefly. "Sometimes it takes a plummet to the ground in order to learn to fly. Many of you have made horrible mistakes." She looked to Teagan with a dark gaze before turning back to the crowd.

"Many of you have killed." She held up a hand at the murmurs of protest. "Or encouraged it, even if you refuse to admit it to those you love. I know better. I see what you hide and I accept you regardless. I understand and I support you despite it. If you have truly lived, then you have indeed made terrible mistakes in your time."

At this, many of the Fae either avoided her gaze or shifted with discomfort. Shaleigh watched her, both fascinated and awestruck. Queen Mab spoke with such ease and authority that she seemed like a mother to them more than a queen. She was nothing like Madam Cloom.

"Yet I have never prevented your return. I have always kept our realm open and I have welcomed you back with open arms. Each night you light candles in your home to keep away the darkness. I too keep a candle burning, I keep the City of the Fae alight with the hope that you will come home. I keep a safe harbor to which you can return. I do the same for you as I do for Teagan." She had wound her way back through the crowd and stopped to give Teagan a long silent stare causing him to avert his gaze.

"If you do not wish for me to do this, if you think you could lead our people better than I have, then please step forward. I'm happy to give up this position to anyone who wishes to have the weight of this land on their shoulders, the weight of our people on their minds."

The group was quiet. A bird cawed from high overhead. Not a single one of them stepped forward. Shaleigh almost smiled. Queen Mab was impressive, but Shaleigh couldn't help but notice that she hadn't mentioned anything about Humans. She had loosened her grip on Teagan's hand, but she hadn't let go even though the cuffs of her shackles were painful. A part of her wished she could just melt into the ground and let Queen Mab forget she even existed.

"Yet many of you have led, haven't you?" The queen continued, "You have organized groups of mercenaries, advised kings and queens, and helped with the building and sundering of mountains of beauty. You have seen with your own eyes the price of leadership, the pain of death, the blood of wars, and you have returned to me. You have come back, begging for refuge at my side, and I have granted it."

Shaleigh had never seen anyone speak like she did, certainly never in person. She made Dean Hammond look like an amateur with a microphone. It was incredible to see the anger in the crowd transform into something more tangible, more useful.

All Shaleigh could think of was how different Queen Mab's speech was from ones she had heard before. She recalled Madam Cloom in her hot air balloon, mocking Shaleigh as she introduced her to the people of the Garden. Or the way she had insulted Shaleigh the first time they met in her throne room. Queen Mab was very different, and all the talk that Teagan made about leading with fear within the confines of the Garden - how did he ever think that was appropriate when he had seen this woman lead?

One woman spoke up, "But he allowed himself to be in a pact, my queen. Pacts are not permitted!" There were murmurs of agreement within the crowd.

"My queen, please, I can explain," Teagan said hastily, but she held up her hands, silencing him and the crowd.

Queen Mab gave an eerily calm smile. That look,

Shaleigh decided, was most definitely one Madam Cloom used. It sent a shiver down her spine.

"You are right, of course, you are certainly right. We have not permitted pacts since The Night of the Red Moon, but rest assured that Teagan will be dealt with in that regard." She gave a sidelong glare toward Teagan, who immediately went rigid.

"As for the Human, well..." her gaze turned to Shaleigh with just as much venom, "*living* Humans are not permitted within the City of the Fae."

TOGETHER

Colin

Someone was shaking his arm so hard that his whole body shook. He scrunched his brows together in annoyance. Couldn't he get just a few more minutes to sleep? He was so tired.

"Wake up! We need you."

The voice was vaguely familiar, and it made him feel like something was urgent. But he didn't want to wake up. He didn't want to feel the pain in his leg, and sleep was a way better alternative. Something about the frustration he heard in the voice only made him more determined not to respond. He groaned and turned his head to the other side in annoyance.

"Colin, wake up - that's an order!"

His eyes snapped open; he stared into the face of a very cross Captain Briar. She had a bandage on one hand

and the skin around her left eye was swollen from a black eye.

Colin's heart raced in his chest as he fumbled for words, trying to remember what the heck he messed up this time. Surely, he hadn't done that to her face. He would have remembered that.

"I'm sorry, sir," Colin muttered, trying to sit up. A sharp pain flared up in his leg as he unconsciously tried to use it to brace himself, and he hissed before lying back down again. It was an oddly familiar feeling, something he had hoped was only part of a dream. He looked down to see it wrapped in swathes of white cloth, noticing also that his right pant leg had been cut off mid-thigh, exposing far more skin that he wanted in front of Captain Briar.

"Oh wow, I'm so sorry." he didn't know what he was apologizing for, but that was probably the best option. He reached sideways, trying to grab hold of the sheet he had seen.

Captain Briar's glare softened into one that might have been concern. She reached down and pulled the sheet up for him, the faintest smile on her lips. "Here you go."

"Thanks," Colin muttered, covering himself as best he could, then rubbing his fingers anxiously on the rough fabric.

"You were stabbed," she said flatly. "Fortunately, I can mend wounds the old-fashioned way instead of relying on the Healers."

Colin was only half listening. He stared at his wrapped thigh, his heart pounding as he recalled fleeing from Keriam the Magician and the crazed Faerie Talek. He had stolen the magician's staff and he and Mawr had run for it. Talek had attacked them with a blade that was stronger than even Mawr, the stone lion. He had stabbed them both, pinned them together...

They had laid in the pouring rain covered in mud for what felt like hours but was probably only minutes. He feared if he moved, he would have injured them both further. Colin remembered trying to pull out the knife with slick fingers and must have blacked out. Had he been bleeding that badly though? He remembered a brief vision of red water all around him when a flash of lightning struck the stormy sky.

He put a hand to his forehead.

"Colin..."

How could he have forgotten all that? How could he have forgotten Mawr asking him questions, his voice worried and filled with fear. Colin had tried to comfort him, but it wasn't enough.

He swallowed to get his throat to work properly. He had to know if Mawr was alive, but was almost afraid to ask. Captain Briar might know old fashioned ways of fixing up Colin's leg, but nobody alive knew how to fix a Living Statue.

Tears filled his eyes as he stared down at the thin sheet. He wound the fabric tightly around his hand, trying to keep himself from panicking, trying to keep the tears from coming. If Mawr had been killed because of his poor decisions, he would never forgive himself. He was too nice to die because of Colin's infamous stupidity.

"What's wrong, soldier?" Captain Briar asked, her

voice surprisingly gentle despite how bloodthirsty she could be on the battlefield.

Colin let out a shaky laugh. "I'm no soldier, I'm just a Seeker." He grimaced. "But I guess I was trying to play hero too."

She was silent for a moment, then, "People have died for less."

Her words might have been a death toll to his heart; his throat clenched as he fought back a sob. He wiped at his tears, unable to stop them from seeping out. He was back to being that small lost boy wandering the alleyways of the Garden looking for food. Back to that threadbare thief picking fights he couldn't possibly win.

"I didn't mean to get him killed," he said, his voice pitched higher with the effort not to bawl his eyes out. "Talek was so fast and we couldn't go fast enough. I shouldn't have taken that damn wizard's staff."

She put a hand on his shoulder, steady and grounding. "Calm down, now. I'm not following you."

It took an effort to get his voice under control to reply, "I got Mawr killed."

"Really?" she asked with a small smile. "You do realize that Mawr is a Living Statue. I think it would take a bit more than a blade to kill him."

"It wasn't just a blade, it was different. He made it stronger than stone."

There was an annoyed groan from nearby. Colin looked up, to see Madam Cloom with a scarf wrapped around her face, covering her mouth. She stared at him with her gaze full of fire and shook her head in annoyance. Colin blinked. It was bizarre seeing her in plain clothes and he almost didn't recognize her, especially with that scarf.

"Wait," he looked between the two of them, "so Mawr is alive?"

The captain smirked before climbing to her feet.

He struggled into a sitting position. His back was stiff and sore, and he had to stretch it carefully before he looked around to take in his surroundings.

The three of them were alone in a burned-out building that still had the odor of smoke in the air. The floor that he was laying down on was one of the few patches of wood that was still stable. He could see the sky, dressed in gold and oranges, through a giant hole in the roof. If Colin had to guess, he would think that it used to be a storage house judging from the sections that had once been divided off. But whatever goods had once been here were either reduced to partially burned remains in the corners or had already been salvaged. There was only a crate or two of supplies that had been brought in, probably for these two to live off of.

Overall the place was a wreck. They were still in the Garden, at least — or whatever remained of it.

Was it morning or evening? He was almost afraid to ask. It was like he was stuck in some kind of timeless void. He unwrapped his hand which was still balled up in the sheet and realized that the sheets must have been borrowed from the barracks, judging from the number of holes along the edges. Oddly enough it reminded him of being in training, especially with Captain Briar ordering him awake, but things had gotten so much worse than he ever imagined they could.

Captain Briar pulled his attention back to the present, saying, "Madam Cloom and I want you to-"

Madam Cloom elbowed the captain in the arm then threw her hands into the air: she acted like she wasn't able to speak.

Captain Briar rubbed her arm in annoyance, then began again, "Geneva and I want you to approach the Magician and offer your services."

Colin's eyes went wide. "You mean — the guy that I stole the staff from?"

Madam Cloom nodded.

"The guy that burned the Garden to the ground?"

Captain Briar crossed her arms. "Actually, that was due to his Shadow Wolves and Mad Faerie, but yes, close enough."

Colin shook his head and regretted it instantly because the world took a minute to stop turning. He put a hand to his head. "No, I can't do that. You're going to have to get someone else. I can't."

"Why not?"

He gave a nervous laugh. "I don't want to get stabbed again, for one! And I don't want to die. I also don't want to get put into some kind of pact that makes me lose my mind." He flung an arm at Madam Cloom who glared at him. "And I don't even know what he did to her!"

Captain Briar took a step forward, her hand falling to the hilt of her sword which she still wore. He hoped it was just an unconscious move, but it still made him nervous. "There is no one else, Colin. My army is in shambles." She sighed. "Trust me, I'm just as annoyed by it as you are. You weren't my first choice either, but Madam

—" she paused, "but Geneva insists that you're the best person for the job."

Madam Cloom gave a slow, reassuring nod that did nothing for Colin's nerves. He wasn't sure whether to be insulted or not.

"Why me?" he asked. "You must have someone more qualified than me."

The captain turned to Madam Cloom, who nodded again, then pulled out a scroll. "First, you're a Seeker. It's your job to find people, and that's what we need right now. Second, you're friends with Shaleigh, and she trusts you."

As Captain Briar spoke, Madam Cloom watched him with a disconcerting intensity.

"And finally, because you're a friend of Mawr."

He blinked. "What does that have anything to do with it?"

She rolled up the piece of paper. "Because he has already been asked to help find them."

Colin barked a laugh. "Good luck! Mawr's terrified of everything." Neither of them seemed amused, and once again, Colin felt like he was back in training, surrounded by people who wouldn't know a joke if it bit them. He sighed deeply.

"Okay, okay, I'll do it. You two saved my life, after all."

Captain Briar smiled. "Come on, I told Mawr to wait outside." She tossed some clothes on the bed that Colin recognized: a soldier's uniform. "And get dressed," she added as she and Madam Cloom turned away to give him privacy.

Colin pursed his lips to keep from saying something

he would regret. They never doubted once that he would join them; had assumed he'd go along with whatever they asked. He wondered what Shaleigh would do if she was in his situation, but then remembered, that it was following her advice that got him in this situation to begin with...

~

COLIN HAD NEVER SEEN crutches outside of the Human World. It was strange to see them leaning against the wall, waiting for him as he struggled to stand. Captain Briar was quick to get them but handed them over awkwardly. She clearly didn't know how they were supposed to be used, only that they were good for injured legs.

Madam Cloom folded her hands together and watched him with such coldness that eventually he couldn't take it any longer and grumbled, "I really wish you would say something, ma'am. It's starting to really get to me."

She groaned, the corners of her cheeks raising to crinkle her eyes in a smile that must have been hidden by the scarf. He couldn't help but shudder.

He put his hands on the grip of the crutches, instructing Captain Briar on how to adjust them for his height, until they felt comfortable. They were clearly not designed with comfort in mind though because just putting his full weight on them made his armpits ache. He groaned with the realization that he would be using these for days, weeks, possibly even months.

"That looks correct," Captain Briar said with a frown that made her words fall flat.

"Don't give me that, you have no idea how these work."

Her glare was answer enough.

"Where did you even get these anyway?"

She gestured to Madam Cloom before realizing that the woman was apparently mute. "These were being kept over in the Pasture, supposedly no one knew where they came from, but I suspect they merely didn't want to say who retrieved them."

Colin nodded, trying to look shocked about the revelation. He had heard of a black market where magicians would venture to the Human World and retrieve supplies for a price. Word had it that even Seekers had stolen a few times, though that was far riskier with the weight of Master Teagan watching their every move. Or, at least used to be.

He hobbled over to the door, clumsily trying to figure out the best way to adjust his weight to keep from falling on his injured leg and trying to remember to keep that leg off the ground. It was hard trying to forget he had a limb.

He reached for the door handle, but someone grabbed his hand, pushing something into his palm. He nearly toppled before Captain Briar clasped his shoulder to steady him.

"You are jumpy still; I'll give you that!" She laughed, slapping him on the back a little harder than he liked.

He turned to see Madam Cloom eerily close, her keen eyes studying him. In fact, she was so close that he could see the dirt that was smeared on her cheeks and a darkness on the scarf that might have been blood. Her eyes were hollow; she reminded him suddenly of a caged, wild animal.

Colin looked down at the rolled-up parchment she

had pushed into his hand. He went to unroll it, but she slapped his other hand away and shook her head.

"Ow, okay! I'll read it later then." He shoved it into his breast pocket, grateful to Captain Briar for getting him some soldier clothes since his old ones were probably a bloody, muddy mess.

He reached for the door again when Madam Cloom took his hand and gave it a squeeze. Colin gaped at her; were those tears he saw in her eyes? "Madam Cloom, are you okay?"

Captain Briar sighed and gently pulled her back. "She will be. You need to get close to the Magician and, more importantly, get them out of the Garden. Take them on a wild goose chase for all we care, just get them *out*. We can handle the Shadow Wolves while they're gone."

Colin gulped down his nerves and nodded. "Alright, I will. Thanks for the leg, by the way."

Captain Briar cocked her head to the side and arched an eyebrow. "Quit thanking me and get to work!"

He gave a nervous laugh before pushing the door open and stepping out into the daylight.

THE SUNLIGHT STREAMED IN, revealing scores of dust and debris in the air from the fire that had only recently been extinguished. He turned back to look at them; Captain Briar and Madam Cloom looked faded with the sun in his eyes. He noticed then how frail Madam Cloom was, how she twisted her hands together anxiously, how wide her eyes were as she watched him. She was terrified.

Colin's mouth went dry as he pulled the door closed and took a deep breath to steady himself - to get his bearings and figure out what he needed to do. He recognized he was right near High Castle. This had been the storage room he had watched burn to the ground.

It took him a moment to realize that High Castle was gone.

A strange disconnect fell over him and he wondered if, perhaps, he was still asleep and none of this was real. Then he saw the piles of rubble where the Castle had once been, and knew it wasn't a dream. He had lived in that castle for years, worked there, and trained there. The empty patch of sky made his heart hurt.

His eyes burned with fresh tears and his throat clenched. He suddenly didn't know if he wanted to take up Madam Cloom's request. He didn't know if he wanted to find a way to get the Garden back for them. Hadn't they been the ones to get it burned to the ground to begin with?

Just as he was about to turn around and go back inside, already predicting how he would tell them he didn't want to play their game, the ground shook beneath his feet.

His eyes went wide. *The Slumbering Forest*, he thought, *it's awoken.* He turned around to see Mawr bounding up to him - never in his life had he been so happy to see that big, goofy lion.

Colin opened his arms wide for a hug as the stone lion stopped short of colliding with him. He didn't even mind the rough stone grazing his skin as Mawr leaned in close to nuzzle him.

"Mawr, you're alive!" Colin hugged him so tight that Mawr likely would've had trouble breathing if he wasn't a Living Statue.

"Me?" His body rumbled beneath Colin's grip as he started his deep, earth shaking purrs.

Colin couldn't help but smile. The fear and self-doubt melted away. He hadn't gotten his friend killed. He hadn't led him straight into a trap that led to his murder; more tears spilled from his eyes and stained Mawr's stone skin. When he finally pulled away, he could see matching tear streaks under Mawr's eyes beneath his golden spectacles.

"I'm so glad you're alive!"

Mawr purred even harder. "No, I'm glad *you* are! You were far closer to dying than me. I'm made of stone, but you're so fragile. I talked with you as long as I could. I tried to tell you not to pull out the knife, but you wouldn't listen to me. I tried to help you." He nuzzled closer and this time Colin had to flinch away to keep from getting his skin rubbed raw.

"I don't remember any of that," Colin admitted with a sheepish expression. "I don't know what I was thinking. I should've listened to you. You've seen way more battles than I have."

"I know, and I didn't want to lose another friend!" Fresh tears poured down his cheeks, and it took Colin several minutes of soothing, petting, and trying not to get poked in the eye by Mawr's whiskers before the lion finally calmed down.

"So, what's the situation like around here?" Colin asked once Mawr seemed more willing to talk.

Mawr shook his head, glancing around the empty

street as though afraid someone was watching them. "We have to be careful," he said, lowering his voice. "Keriam has taken over the entire Garden and now controls the army. If they found out that Madam..."

Colin shook his head. "Please don't say their names."

"Oh, sorry!" Mawr glanced down and pawed at the ground. "So much has happened. Talek wants me to join them on the hunt for Shaleigh and Teagan. And I was so scared having to go alone, but now you'll be with me. Maybe it won't be so bad."

Colin considered arguing that point but decided against it. His head was swimming with worry. "I guess we should go find the Magician then."

"I mean, I know we should, but I still don't want to."

Colin patted his flank. "We're together, remember?"

Mawr gave a reluctant nod.

"Now where are our two overlords hanging out?"

Colin expected to be taken toward the rubble of High Castle. He had even steeled himself for seeing the desolation of his home firsthand, but instead, Mawr turned away from the remains of High Castle and in the direction of the Marketplace. The buildings were hollowed out shells of what they once were and hardly anyone was on the street. Colin felt his stomach drop as he hobbled along on his crutches, taking in the devastation. Mawr kept his pace slow, never once making him feel rushed.

"I don't see any Shadow Wolves," he muttered as they passed another ravaged building.

"They come in from the forest at night and, now that the gate is gone, they come and go as they please. Sometimes they take any stragglers they find, but mostly they leave people alone."

Colin bit his lip at the realization that his leg was going to make him an easy target come nightfall. He looked up to see the sun was touching the horizon and gulped.

It was as they climbed the hill that led to the library that a beam of sunlight caught Mawr's back just right and exposed what looked like a shadowy spot.

"Hold up," Colin said, gasping for breath. He wiped his forehead on his sleeve, trying not to be annoyed at how difficult it was to walk just a few feet. "What is that?"

Mawr blinked at him for a moment in confusion before realizing that Colin was pointing to his back. "Oh, that."

"Yeah, what happened? Was that when we were stabbed?"

The images of that night came back to him unbidden. He remembered the feeling of Mawr falling to his side, of Colin scrambling to keep from getting crushed while unable to remove his leg from Mawr's back. The dagger had broken into Mawr's stone... Colin's leg was bleeding profusely... *So much blood...*

"That's where he pinned us together," Mawr said looking almost embarrassed as Colin blinked. "Captain — er, our friends were able to find a woman who works with clay. She was able to glaze it so that it wouldn't crack further." He laid down so Colin could see it closer.

The injury looked like a deep V that dug into the stone just behind his shoulder blade. Colin reached up gingerly to feel it, his fingers touching something smooth and cool, very unlike the roughness of the rest of Mawr.

"She filled it with clay to keep the water from pooling in it. So now I have a lovely little patch."

Colin smiled at that. "A battle scar." He met Mawr's surprised gaze. "I guess nobody can call you cowardly now."

Mawr pawed at the ground anxiously. "I don't know about that. I'm not exactly good at fighting battles, I'm far better at running away from them."

Colin laughed, about to disagree, when he saw someone walking down the dirt path from the library. They walked briskly and were dressed completely in crimson.

"Is that - *Talek*?" Colin's heart skipped a beat and a shiver went through him. He couldn't help it, the speed with which the Faerie came toward him made him remember all over again the mad laughter, the chase, and the pain. His leg throbbed with the memory.

It was one thing to be told about them losing the war, it was very different to see Talek walking without resistance down an open patch of road with nothing to fear. The Garden was now in the hands of Keriam the Cruel and his mad Faerie servant, and suddenly Colin had new appreciation for the terrified expression Madam Cloom had given him earlier. It was a look of desperation.

"Maybe he has somewhere to go," Mawr whispered nervously.

"He's who we're here to see, remember?" Colin whispered back.

Talek gave a wicked smile as he approached them. "Ah good, you didn't die after all."

Colin shuddered; his gaze drawn toward the violet eye with swirling black tendrils. He spoke before he even realized it, "No sir, still alive, I'm sorry to say."

Talek looked him up and down, taking in his grungy outfit and his pathetic crutches - Colin had never felt so vulnerable in his entire life. His heart thundered in his chest, but he remembered his training and kept his gaze empty. If Talek decided to kill him now, there was nothing he could do about it.

"Crutches from the Human World! Is that all they could find for you?" Talek smirked.

"They work well enough," Colin said, his mouth going dry.

Poor Mawr was tearing chunks out of the dirt path with his anxious kneading.

Talek leveled him with a steady gaze and a wide smile. "Did you really think my master would let you die?"

Colin blinked a tad too rapidly, betraying his shock. Did they actually know that Captain Briar and Madam Cloom were alive, and just didn't care? Of course, they did. Here he was hobbling down the street with a pair of Human crafted crutches. He wanted to ask, he wanted to know for certain, but he pushed that question down.

"I kind of assumed that was the goal when you turned me into a pincushion."

To Colin's surprise Talek's smile faded slightly as he

replied, "No, he didn't want you dead, little stoatling. He has plans for you and your large friend here."

"Plans?" He tried his best to act shocked, even though he could tell that Talek was seeing right through his charade.

"Oh yes," Talek said, crouching down and laying a hand on Colin's injury.

He sucked in a breath, unable to pretend that the move didn't terrify him.

"Shh," Talek whispered, closing his eyes and knitting his brows.

Colin felt a warmth spread out and encompass his upper leg. It wasn't just warm though, it was soothing, calming. Then he realized that Talek was humming to himself. The song was very different from those that Teagan used to hum, it was faster, arrhythmic, hurried. The soothing warmth that he felt started to feel almost numb. Colin reached out a hand to push at Talek's arm, and the Faerie finally pulled away, blinking.

"What did you do?" The numbness dwindled and Colin realized that his leg didn't hurt anymore.

"I healed you... I think, at least." Talek said, cocking his head to the side. "Try using it."

Colin sighed. On one hand he wasn't sure if he trusted Talek's version of healing, but on the other he really wanted to be able to not use the crutches again. He put out his injured leg and tentatively put weight on it. There was some tingling as though it had fallen asleep and was taking a bit to wake up. He tried walking next.

Mawr came to his side, watching him in case he needed to use his body to brace his fall. Colin took his time, walking slowly, cautiously, ready to feel pain rack up his leg at any moment, but it felt fine.

"Is it okay?" Mawr asked in a terrified voice, glancing anxiously between him and Talek.

"Yeah, I think so," he whispered back then nodded, not really wanting to give Talek the satisfaction of the praise. He was the one who gave him the wound to begin with.

"Good!" Talek beamed.

Colin held up a hand. "That wound was meant to kill. I'm lucky to be alive. So, why didn't you either just let me die, or heal me once you took the Garden if your master had such an interest in me?"

Talek gave a wicked smile again that made the violet in his eye catch the fading light. "I thought it would make a certain Captain feel useful for once. She needs some good motivation before she comes limping back to us. Her dear Madam Cloom won't last much longer without a mouth, and my master is happy to turn a blind eye to her until she finally passes. What good is a leader without a voice?"

Colin felt the blood drain from his face. Madam Cloom... didn't have a mouth? He thought back to the scarf she had wrapped around her face, the way she insisted that Captain Briar speak for her, and the groaning sounds she had made; but mostly, he remembered the pained expression she had given him as he left.

The rolled-up parchment burned within his inside pocket, and it took a force of will to keep him from reading it right there. At the time he thought it was just a list of contacts or something to help him on his mission, but now he understood it would likely be her last words to him. He pushed down the urge. He needed to be cautious.

"You both are needed," Talek's words pulled Colin back from his thoughts. The crimson Faerie turned, his white hair gleaming in the dwindling sunlight. He glanced back to them, impatiently.

Mawr was sitting now, his front paws were maybe half a foot deep in the dirt from his anxious pawing.

"Hey, it's okay," Colin soothed, placing a hand on Mawr's rough shoulder. "We'll be together, remember? We can do this."

Mawr leaned against his hand. "I hope so."

He should have just left it at that, but he couldn't. He never thought he would be angry on Madam Cloom's behalf, but here he was, and anger made him forget his tongue. "Besides, we don't want Shaleigh to have to deal with these two losers alone."

Talek heard and shook his head with a laugh but didn't turn around.

"I miss her," Mawr said, hanging his head low as he walked beside Colin like a scared puppy. "If she was here, she would know what to do."

"She will be soon. You two will help us find her. I must find her," Talek muttered with a tinge of fear in his voice. "She stole my Teagan away from me."

Colin had thought this was some sick power trip for him, but he could hear the tremor enter Talek's voice. This wasn't some grand master plan, at least not on his end, this was personal. He thought about holding his tongue — that's what Master Teagan would want him to do — but that had always been Colin's weakness.

"You really think he's going to want you back after what you did to his Garden?"

He could feel the way Mawr shrank away at his words, but Talek continued forward without even turning back to look at him.

"He was a prisoner. He was not responsible for his horrid actions here."

Colin could barely contain his laughter. Had Talek not seen what his own master had done to this place? Surely, he hadn't missed the burned buildings and severe lack of people. Was he that disconnected from reality?

"Then that Human stole him away from me." He glared over his shoulder. "You two are going to help me get him back."

Yes, Colin decided, he really was that disconnected.

PRETENSE OF POWER

Shaleigh

Shaleigh felt the blood drain out of her face and pool somewhere in her feet. She looked out at the Faeries that surrounded her, and then at Teagan. He looked almost as terrified as she felt.

So many faces were focused on her, many with multi-colored flecks on their cheeks, some with very long, pointed ears. Most had eyes that seemed to gleam brightly with hatred toward her. She had known Madam Cloom's anger, had felt the indifference of the workers in the Pasture, but this level of hatred made her tremble and feel light-headed. Never in her life had so many people wanted her dead.

"I'm going to be killed?" Shaleigh's voice was meek and shaky compared to the easy grace and intensity of Queen Mab's.

The queen laughed and it was a delightful sound. It pulled Shaleigh's lips up into a nervous smile despite how close she felt to either bawling or passing out.

A few of the other Faeries laughed with her, but not Teagan. He stood at Shaleigh's side with that same stricken expression. She could see the gears in his mind working. Surely, he had some plan because at this point she was fresh out of them.

"We shall have to see," Queen Mab said.

More laughter: it started to become more distant, hazier, and it was as though they were all far away from her. Was this more Faerie magic? Then the sky seemed to tilt up overhead. She heard the dragging of chains and someone caught her as her knees folded.

"Can I please have my arms back?" Teagan snapped. "She needs help."

"Go ahead, release them both," Queen Mab's voice lilted over the other voices of the crowd. Shaleigh couldn't hear any laughter now, but her pulse throbbed in her ears and she was freezing. It wasn't that cold outside, right?

Sionn's face appeared before her, sour and disgusted as he unlocked her shackles. As each one fell, she realized how heavy they were. She listened as each of Teagan's shackles dropped, then she tilted her head back to look up at him.

"I'm sorry," she whispered. "I don't know what's wrong with me."

Teagan didn't respond. Instead he lifted her with a grunt, then spoke to Queen Mab with a familiar tinge of anger, "While you joke about her potential demise," he started through clenched teeth, "this child nears collapse. She is exhausted, and rightly so considering what she's been through. She needs rest and nourishment." He looked down at her warmly. "Humans aren't used to being transferred around like that, or to have their minds prodded."

Queen Mab waved away his concern. "There's no need to be so chiding here, Teagan. We all look after ourselves, you know that."

Shaleigh could feel Teagan's rage but he didn't reply.

"If the girl needs rest, then take her to your home. That is where both of you will stay." The queen's smile left her face and to Shaleigh her voice was muffled as though through cotton.

"My home used to be in the trees near the great oaks, I assume it's still there?" Teagan asked, but he was already crouching, preparing to leap up into the branches of the nearest tree. Sionn put a hand on his arm.

"No, it's not," Queen Mab said, and stepped closer, looking to Shaleigh like she stepped out of a cloudy pane of glass. She blinked as the queen crossed her arms and bid him walk with her.

Teagan followed and Shaleigh found she could barely keep her eyes open now. Tiredly, she looked up at the setting sun, seeing it turn the leaves high above them into little fiery clouds of green and orange. Bits of the sky trickled through and Shaleigh listened as well as she could, though all she wanted to do was sleep.

"We had to move Talek's home, your home," Queen Mab stated. Shaleigh turned to see the queen bracing herself as though expecting outrage. "You have to understand how distraught Talek was. You did a terrible wrong to him, you do realize that don't you?"

Teagan glanced down at Shaleigh briefly. She could feel his fingers tighten where he held her. He was angrier than he sounded when he replied, "After being reminded about it by him, I don't understand why I must be continually reminded about it here."

"Because we feared for him, and therefore feared for ourselves." Her voice was cold, distant. "You destroyed him when you abandoned him that day. And now I hear he's made himself even more dangerous."

Shaleigh's mind felt sluggish; her thoughts kept trying to wander away and it annoyed her. She tried to focus her gaze on the homes above them - there must have been hundreds of them. And all of them wanted to kill her, she realized. Every single one of them.

She shuddered and closed her eyes. She felt Teagan adjusting his grip, probably assuming she was uncomfortable.

Teagan sighed again. "Lead the way then."

As they walked, Shaleigh heard other footsteps fall in around them, but didn't bother to open her eyes. It was probably the guards moving in a circle similar to how she and Teagan were brought in. Shaleigh wasn't sure if they were protecting them from the Faeries who lived here or preventing them from leaving.

They all moved as a group based upon the whispers coming in all directions, and Shaleigh opened her eyes to watch the trees above them. She imagined them walking this path along the branches instead of on the ground, floating more than walking from one branch to the next.

Her vision blurred. She had never felt like this before. It was definitely worse than the flu, she decided, because usually people didn't want to kill her when she had that. It was also worse than an injury like a sprained ankle because she relied quite a bit on her vision, and currently her sight would randomly go cloudy and jumbled, like it was pulling in too many signals at once. Her pulse would pound in her ears one minute, and the next be perfectly fine. Sometimes she broke out into gooseflesh for no reason at all.

"What's… wrong with me?" she muttered.

Teagan gave her a worried smile. "Your mind has been overly taxed. You need food and rest."

She scrunched up her eyebrows, trying to make her words not come out so fuzzy. "Sometimes I feel okay though, then I feel cold, then I can't see straight. It's really weird."

"Talek is working with powerful magic, tainted with the Madness," he said, and Shaleigh's vision was clear enough that she noticed Queen Mab's concerned glance. "He had to use quite a lot of it to transfer both of us here. I would never have tried something that powerful because I understood it could damage people in the process." He winced. "As you saw, once he started it, he lost control of it. There was no reversing it once it began. Magic can be as powerful and unpredictable as an ocean wave, which is why you must be cautious and reserved when you use it."

Shaleigh's head rolled, feeling heavier.

"I found it best to use it as sparingly as possible, so that it was easier to control. With the Madness working in him, there's no telling what he'll attempt to do with it."

"And that is precisely why you two will need to stop him," Queen Mab injected with a slow nod.

Teagan gave her a sharp look. "That isn't—"

The queen, however, cut him off, "Ah, here we are! Your new home."

They stopped at a round building that was larger than the others Shaleigh had seen. It had at least four windows, that were really just shuttered window frames, and a cozy front porch. Yellow roses had formed a bush of limbs that almost hid the stone pavers that led up to the door.

Shaleigh breathed in the thick scent of the yellow roses as they passed; it reminded her of the Garden. Though, it felt like much of the Garden was lifted from this place, but perhaps that was by design.

He stepped up the bowed steps to the front door with a frown. "It hasn't been kept up, has it?" Teagan asked with a frown as he readjusted Shaleigh's weight so he could put an arm out to wipe away a few of the spiderwebs that crisscrossed the short walk to the door.

"We assumed neither of you would survive, to be honest. I'm glad you proved me wrong, Teagan."

He turned around to meet the queen's gaze with cold eyes. "Are you? I get the impression you would have preferred Talek back instead of me. Didn't you say I destroyed him? Clearly I'm the party at fault."

She shook her head and turned away, avoiding his question. "I'll leave two of the guards here to make sure neither of you leave. Sionn will be a gopher for you, getting food and whatever else you and the girl need."

Teagan gave her a thin-lipped smile. "You told the others how you welcomed all Faeries back with open arms, but that can hardly be true if we're kept as prisoners."

"I didn't kill you, Teagan, even though they would have adored me for it. And the girl is alive for now. I'm even allowing her to recuperate after getting overwhelmed by our world's magic. Perhaps for once in your life you should be grateful for what you have instead of demanding more than you deserve."

The coldness of Queen Mab's words made Shaleigh realize just how much danger they were in. This land may be beautiful, and the Faeries' rage may have been sated for the time being, but that wouldn't last for long. If even the queen held such disdain for her and Teagan, it was only a matter of time before the other Faeries demanded blood.

Teagan was speechless.

"Sleep well, I'll see you both in the morning."

Most of the guards left with her, but one pair took their positions on either side of the walkway. The third Faerie, their "gopher", Sionn, crossed his arms and snickered after the queen disappeared from view. "So, what would you like, Teagan? Ale to drown in or rope to hang by?"

Teagan gave a deep sigh. "Neither actually. Unspoiled food and untainted water will suffice."

"How specific!" Sionn laughed and the other guards grinned with him.

"Of course," Teagan sounded like he was barely keeping his anger in check. "If you fail to do so, then I'll be happy to report you to Queen Mab. As you told me before, her wrath is something to behold. Do you think she's as fond of you as she is me, little gopher?"

Sionn's smile faded and he quickly turned to walk down the path. Shaleigh wondered if her very presence here made things worse for Teagan. Would Sionn be so vicious if Teagan wasn't carrying a helpless Human child in his arms? Would he and the guards mock him so badly if he wasn't burdened by her weight?

Teagan waited until Sionn was out of sight before turning back to the front door with a curse.

"Teagan, I'm sorry," she said though her voice felt thick.

"Wait until we're inside, please," he whispered as he reached out to turn the doorknob. Shaleigh's shoes scraped against the wood of the door while he leaned in to turn the knob and his arms shook around her. He had been carrying her for at least fifteen minutes, it was no wonder his arms were shaking, but he hadn't once complained.

She still felt light-headed and slightly ill. Queen Mab said she was overwhelmed by their world's magic, but what did that even mean?

The room was dark as the door creaked open. A cold air swept outward, reminding her of the abandoned buildings she had explored back home - back before she was kidnapped, back before she had broken Teagan's bond. It felt like that was somebody else's life, as though she had watched it in a movie instead of lived it.

Teagan reached over to light a candle on a side table that her foot bumped against and light slowly filled the room as the wick caught. The acrid scent of smoke filled her nostrils causing her to remember the chamber she had at High Castle with the fireplace that always seemed to burn. Had it only been earlier today that she had sat there plotting with Colin about how they were going to spree Talek from jail?

As her eyes adjusted to the light, the memory was forgotten as she took in the room. Papers were strewn over the bed and spread out on tables. It looked like someone had thrown everything askew, but there were still some papers pinned to the wall.

"What happened?" she asked, "Was it ransacked?"

"I - I don't know," he said as he carried her further in. He left the door open behind him and she could see the curious gazes of the remaining guards turned toward them. Judging by their expressions, few had been inside this building since Talek left.

Cold fear filled her, something that she hadn't felt in a long time. Perhaps it was the fogginess that filled her brain or the sudden memories that sprung into her mind, but the familiar sensation made her shiver. This room was nothing like her mom's room. It wasn't orderly, it didn't have her clothes laid out for a new day of work, and it didn't smell like flowery perfume, but it *felt* like Mom's room. It felt like a secret that was meant to be hidden. Where something had happened here, and it wasn't meant to be seen.

She reached out with one arm and grabbed hold of the door, causing Teagan to adjust his footing at her sudden movement.

"What are you-?"

She slammed it closed harder than she meant to, and a cloud of dust and leaves swirled briefly on the ground. The candle flame flickered angrily from the table.

Teagan gave her a look. "What was that for?"

"They don't need to see this," she said, painfully aware that she probably wasn't making any sense. Her voice was hoarse, and her pulse throbbed in her ears again. It made her head hurt. "Just put me down."

Teagan sighed and sat her down on a table, then went over to the wooden ledge beside one of the windows and found a cloth to wipe down the spiderwebs that had formed. "Believe it or not, when we shared a home in the trees, we kept it immaculate. It was far smaller than this, and was certainly nothing like High Castle, but it was ours and we were proud of it."

Shaleigh had to put a hand out to keep from toppling off as Teagan cleaned. It was alarming how quickly the dizziness came on and how it wouldn't dissipate fully now. "What's wrong with me?"

A tenseness came over his face, but he only gave her a quick glance. "The world you come from doesn't possess magic. Or at least, I don't believe it does. Humans from your world are prone to illness when overexposed to our world's magic."

She shook her head, instantly regretting it as the world took a moment to catch up. She laid flat down on the table, relaxing on top of the papers that were strewn all over it. She felt better, just a little. "Why didn't I have a problem with the Healers then? They used magic on my leg."

"It wasn't corrupted," Teagan tersely stated. "It was proper magic, not the defiled mess that Talek wields. The good news is that once you recover from this, you'll have a higher tolerance for it. Your body must adjust to it though." In his annoyance, he moved from the table to the bed, cleaning with such clear annoyance that he forgot to return to Shaleigh.

She sighed, at this point she didn't care where she was as long as she was able to lie down, but a bundle of pages was stuffed uncomfortably beneath her elbow and she reached around to pull them out. That's when she finally got a good look at them. From the distance and in the poor candlelight, she had thought they were scribbles or maybe profanity that other Faeries had pushed in through the windows or something. She had assumed this building was like the ones back home, littered with trash and sprinkled with graffiti.

This was different.

She uncurled the closest paper, the stiffness of the pages unwilling to behave. It was a drawing. A beautifully drawn man stared back at her with pure affection in his eyes. She was so stricken with his expression that it took her a moment to recognize the crimson hair and the gold flecks on the cheeks. It was all black and white except for those dashes of color, and Shaleigh felt her pulse pound again in her ears.

"Teagan..." Her voice was barely a whisper and he didn't hear her at first. She cleared her throat and tried again, "Teagan!"

He paused from tearing a blanket from the bed that was filled with holes. "Are you alright?"

"It's you." She stared at him and he didn't move, he just stood there with the blanket clutched in his hands.

For a moment she wondered if she was so sick that she was hallucinating, but then she flipped to another photo.

There he was again, this time staring out of a window that seemed to float beside him, his hair splayed out to the side. And then again, laughing over some joke. "All of these - they're all you..."

He came over and took the photos from her, leaning down to view them in the candlelight. "I don't understand," he said, his voice was calm, but she saw his hands were shaking.

Shaleigh pushed herself up into a sitting position, ignoring the way the room spun and grabbed the candle that Teagan had lit. She held it up to the papers that were pinned to the walls, and the red hair in each one gleamed back.

"Surely, they can't all be you, can they?" She held the candle out over the floor, to the ones scattered on the ground and mixed in with the leaves, to the ones that Teagan had just cleared from the bed, to the others that were strung about the windowsills.

Teagan had a hand over his mouth, his eyes glassy. "I didn't mean-" He sounded on the verge of tears and Shaleigh reached out, taking his free hand in hers. He was trembling, his grip almost painful.

Shaleigh put the candle back and laid down again. Only when the world stopped spinning did she speak, "Did Talek draw these?"

Teagan nodded, a tear sliding down his cheek, but he didn't let go of her hand to wipe it away. "I didn't know it upset him so much. I thought I had given him all the clues, I thought... I thought he understood."

She sighed, trying to find the right words. "He thought you were a captive at the Garden."

"I wasn't a captive!" He pulled his hand away. "I went with Master Cathal willingly. You don't understand how contained this land is here with Queen Mab. Faeries leave Queen Mab's land and it always leads to ruin in some form. Then they return and tell us how terrible it all was and how grateful they are to be back, and it creates this cycle."

He sucked in a harsh breath. "When I left, I had no intention of ever returning for more than a visit. This land is suffocating. I never wanted to be caught in its cycle again." He dragged his fingers through his hair. "Yet here we are. Normally anyone who leaves is seen as disrespectful, but they are usually forgiven." He swallowed harshly. "But to have a whole kingdom fall because of you?" He shook his head and looked to the floor.

"That's why they hate me so much," she whispered, "I'm the reason the Garden fell."

He pursed his lips. "I'm afraid it's more than that. They see Humans as invaders of this world. Humans are seen as an invasive species and are to be killed off to prevent their spread."

Shaleigh gaped. "Invasive? I didn't even ask to be here!"

"They don't care. The only reason you're still alive is likely because they can't decide on whether the falling of the Garden was good or bad."

"That's not true," she said, locking her gaze on him. "They haven't killed me because of you. If I was alone here, I'd be dead right now. You came with me. You're the reason I'm alive."

He gave a sad laugh and rubbed the tears from his

cheeks. "It does no good talking about such things. It's all in the past. We shouldn't dwell on it."

He went back to the bed and flung the rest of the blankets from it revealing a hay stuffed mattress underneath. Shaleigh couldn't help but feel pity for him. To be honest, she felt pity for them both. This was where Talek's sanity first slipped. This place was where Teagan felt so confined that he wanted any excuse to escape.

When a charismatic man like Master Cathal showed up with his big plans and ideas, talking about places that Teagan had never heard of before... Oh yes, she could see exactly how he would be influenced to run away from his lover. Then, it had all fallen apart.

She looked down to another page under her butt and pulled it out. It was a sketch of Teagan holding Talek's hand, they were staring at each other and smiling. Only in artwork could they possibly look so happy. It made her chest ache at the sight of it. It hurt to see what they once were and to know where they were now. She folded it up and slid it into a pocket.

Teagan finally had unearthed the mattress on the frame of the bed. He sucked in a disapproving breath. "You are not sleeping on that. It's simply disgusting at this point. Who knows what all is living in it."

Before Shaleigh could say anything, he stormed to the front door, flung it open, and starting demanding things of the guards. She couldn't make out what they were saying though.

A few minutes later, the guards came in and began taking the old blankets out, the old bed, and even some of the chairs.

"What's going on?" she asked in a daze.

"They're removing all the old things," Teagan said in a clipped tone. "Anything that could be deemed unsanitary or unhealthy for you."

She turned to look at him, standing beside the front door with his arms folded. It was all wrong: he wasn't the High Faerie anymore; he was just Teagan. Even if he was ordering around a couple of guards, that power he so loved was lost and no amount of posing would reclaim it.

"Leave the papers," Shaleigh demanded.

She glanced to one of the guards that had leaned down to collect them from the ground. He shrugged and dropped the stack he had made.

"Shaleigh, there is no need to hang on to such things. They're falling apart and they'll only be in the way."

"I want them."

Teagan stared at her in utter shock. "What?"

"I want them. All of them. You might not have a use for them anymore, but I do."

He scoffed. "What use could you possibly have for them? As kindling?"

"No," she countered, "unlike you, I haven't given up on Talek. I want to learn what happened between you two and I want to help him."

A pained expression came over Teagan as the guards passed him with the mattress. One of them turned to him and added, "We'll send Sionn to fetch a new mattress when he gets back."

Teagan didn't respond, only glared at Shaleigh.

The guards closed the door behind them, and the

candle on the table shuddered at the sudden breeze, casting shadows throughout the room.

"I haven't given up on him," he said in a small voice, all pretense of power lost once more. "I never gave up on him."

"Then why are you trying to forget him?"

Teagan looked away as though searching for the right answer somewhere in the room. "I can't deal with his memory right now. That isn't who he is any longer. That isn't who we are anymore."

"Then what are you exactly? You do love him, don't you? You wanted me to break him out of jail, so I assume you still do!"

He bit his lip and Shaleigh felt her pulse throb painfully in her temple. She rubbed at it and laid back to stare up at the ceiling again. "You don't have to answer that. It's pretty damn obvious really."

The front door opened again and Sionn entered. His voice was filled with sick apathy, "I have the specific food and water choices you requested."

Shaleigh had to move aside as he laid them down on the table as though she wasn't even there. He almost put a plate of what looked like slices of bread down on her hair. She glared at him, but he didn't even glance her way.

Of course, Teagan hadn't even acknowledged his presence. He stood, staring off at a corner of the room, looking like a melancholy statue that had been carefully placed.

"Anything else you need? Still considering that rope I mentioned?" He gave a bitter laugh, but Teagan still didn't look at him.

"Shaleigh needs a proper bed to sleep in. She won't recover properly unless she's able to rest. Queen Mab ordered us to stay here, so I'm assuming she wants her to recover."

"I'm sorry, you want me to bring you an entire mattress?" He laughed at Teagan's curt nod. "This isn't your Garden, Teagan. You're lucky Queen Mab hasn't strung you up or forced you out into the Dark Lands for your actions!"

Teagan bristled. "A mattress, please. Shaleigh needs to recover as Queen Mab requested."

Sionn laughed again even as he stepped out the front door. He was almost through the threshold when Teagan grabbed his arm and spun him around. The guards were calling to each other in warning just as Teagan grabbed the door and moved Sionn's fingers closer, but he stopped the door an inch away.

Sionn screamed and fell to his knees. "Don't, please!" Sionn bawled.

"The girl needs a mattress. Do you think you can procure one for me?"

"Yes, of course!" He hissed and pulled away as soon as Teagan let go of him. Shaleigh could hear his feet on the stone walkway as he ran off.

The guards outside must have backed away because Teagan didn't sound frightened as he called out to them, "Just a misunderstanding, I assure you."

One of the guards said something in response, but Teagan closed the door with a grunt. "Well, that was more difficult that I thought it would be."

"They're going to kill us both. There's nobody here to protect you."

His pride deflated at her words and he sat down in the wooden chair by the window. "I have to. They will walk all over us otherwise." He waved a hand at the door. "You see how Sionn is. Imagine a whole city just like him. Immortality doesn't necessarily bring about wisdom, it just makes you more stubborn and resistant to change—"

Shaleigh wanted to respond, but his words were fading even though his mouth was still moving. The throbbing in her temples was so bad that she could hear only the rushing of blood in her ears.

She pried her eyes open to see Teagan standing over her, his dark eyes clouded with concern, then only darkness.

RESIST

Colin

The place that Colin had once considered a refuge when he had been on the streets was hardly recognizable as the Library of the Garden. The building had partially collapsed, exposing the shelves of books that remained standing to the elements. The ground was littered with books, some scorched, some in the mud, some nothing more than fluttering pages lost to the breeze. It hurt to see it from outside and he didn't know if he could bring himself to go in.

It took him a second to realize that Mawr was no longer at his side. He turned to see his stone friend farther back, staring up at the destroyed structure with a look of immeasurable sadness. Colin stepped back to him, keeping his voice calm, "Mawr, hey, what's wrong"

The lion kept his gaze on the building as if Colin

wasn't there. "I knew it was ruined. They told me it was, but I hadn't seen it yet. I've failed another one, haven't I?"

"Another what? What are you talking about?"

Mawr closed his eyes and lowered his head. "This Library was destroyed just like the one I guarded back in Aife. I can't possibly be a Guardian anymore, maybe I never was one."

Colin stared, realization slowly dawning on him. As painful as it was to see this library destroyed, he couldn't imagine seeing two of them. No wonder Mawr had been so happy that day reading to children. No wonder he had seemed right at home with all of them. That was his purpose, his place.

"Hey look, you did everything you could. We all did." Colin lowered his voice, "We just didn't know what we were dealing with."

"I know," Mawr whispered then gave a shaky sigh. "I didn't just hide in a corner and let it happen this time." He looked to Colin, his golden spectacles sliding down his muzzle. "Does it even matter whether I try or not when the outcome is the same?"

Colin tried to put on an encouraging smile. "It does matter." His mind searched for why he felt it was the right thing to say. He fumbled before finding what he truly felt — "It matters cause even though the library is a wreck, I'm still here, right? You saved my life."

Mawr brightened at that. "You're right. At least I saved someone, even if I couldn't save the library or all my little ones."

Colin winced at his words, but he was right. Colin was alive and there was no telling what happened to all those kids. Were they alive? Were they hidden somewhere like Madam Cloom and Captain Briar? He didn't ask, especially not with Talek just ahead waiting on them.

"You and I really don't belong here," Mawr said suddenly, his gaze back on the ground.

"Wh-what?" Colin asked, not expecting the bluntness.

"We didn't really belong in the Garden; we don't belong here. We don't belong anywhere."

"If we're outcasts, at least we're outcasts together, right? Misery loves company and all that."

Mawr gave him a look. "What a terrible thing to say! Why should misery want to make other people miserable?"

Colin held up his hands and sighed. "Look, it's a saying from the Human World, not one of mine."

"Not all of your precious books have been destroyed, Mawr, the last Guardian of Aife," Keriam the Cruel commented as he stepped out from the gaping hole in the library's side.

He was swathed in a dark violet robe that was almost black, holding his staff tall in one hand and a few books in the other. Colin's stomach flipped. It was his turn now to be scared and he had to take in a deep breath to keep from running back down the path they came from. The staff, Colin was sad to see, was whole and looked completely undamaged from his attempt at stealing it. Mawr may have saved Colin's life, but Colin had nothing good to show for his efforts from that evening.

"Once we have rebuilt the Garden anew," Keriam started, placing his books down on a pile of stone, "you will have more children to read to. Dozens of eager little minds looking forward to meeting you and speaking with you. All of this is merely temporary." He gestured to the library.

To Colin, it was strange seeing the magician in the light of day and without being in a terrible thunderstorm. He moved far quicker than a man who ought to be verging on the ripe age of five hundred. His violet robes looked too clean and perfect, though Colin supposed it would be easy to ask Talek to clean them for him.

Keriam approached them, his voice sticky sweet. "I too love books, my stone friend, and I have a soft spot for children. How can we possibly have a future without them?"

"But you did this," Mawr said, his voice wavering. "The library, the books, the children. They're all gone." He lowered his head, his ears flattening down. "How can this be good?"

"Nature is just as cruel, Mawr," he said with a glint in his eyes. "Wildfires destroy even the oldest forests, but they also make way for new beginnings. The Garden was desperate for a new beginning. You and I, Mawr, we've seen many new beginnings, haven't we?"

Mawr slowly shook his head.

Colin couldn't believe his furry ears. How dare he even pretend that Mawr was his friend? How dare he even try to have anything in common with him.

"One day," Keriam soothed, "once all of these battles and searches are behind us, you will have children who once again look to you for protection. You will read to them of this day and you will tell them stories of what you saw. You will understand then the good that we have done here." He gave a smile, but Colin could see how it didn't reach his eyes.

"I wouldn't lie to children like that," Mawr said in such a simple, honest way that Colin glanced to him in awe. "And I wouldn't want anyone to lie to them like that either."

Colin somehow found the will to speak, though he had no idea from where. All he knew is that this jerk Keriam had somehow gotten Mawr angry, something he couldn't even fathom, and he was not about to let him lash out at his friend just to make a point.

"How dare you pretend to have an ounce of Mawr's decency."

Keriam frowned down at him, but Colin was on a roll.

"He has more good in one stone whisker than you've had your entire life. You have the nerve to tell him about the children he'll guard... have you looked around at all the damage you've done? This was where he read to kids - and you destroyed it! Quit acting like this was caused by some natural disaster or plague. You caused every bit of this. Those were your Shadow Wolves at the gate," Colin said. He pointed a finger at Talek, who was humming to himself as he wandered through the decimated book-shelves, "And it was your magic that destroyed his mind."

Keriam stared at him for a long moment. "For some rodent who was only just brought back to life, you certainly have quite a death wish." He shifted his staff to his other hand, that fake smile still on his lips. Colin's mouth went dry as Keriam stepped closer. "Perhaps I don't need both of you after all. Perhaps I only need Mawr to help us find the girl."

Colin's gaze flicked between Keriam and the violet gem of his staff that had begun to glow.

"If you would like to see tomorrow's sunrise, then you should keep that tongue stilled."

It would be his big mouth that finally did him in. Not Captain Briar, not the Shadow Wolves, and not even Madam Cloom…his own damn mouth would do it.

"Talek," Keriam hissed. "I want you to kill this boy."

"Oh no, please don't!" Mawr gasped. "Please, he doesn't mean anything, he just talks sometimes, that's all."

"*Silence!*"

Mawr went quiet and Colin held his breath.

Talek emerged from the bookshelves with a questioning look. "Really? You want me to kill *him*?"

Keriam rolled his eyes. "You heard me. Get rid of him! I'm already sick of listening to him and we haven't even set out yet."

Talek cocked his head to the side. "No, that makes no sense. Why would we kill him? Teagan went out of his way to create him, and he clearly wanted him to be made into a stoatling, because otherwise he would have reverted back or died by now, right?"

For the first time, Keriam faltered. "You don't know that for certain. You're guessing."

Talek hummed a tune again and gave a mischievous smile. "That tower fell shortly after his pact was broken. The Slumbering Forest awoke almost as quickly. He hasn't lost a single hair since the Garden fell. What's the difference? Teagan *wanted* to transform him, and he didn't want to create that ridiculous castle. Which proves my point," he said and turned to Colin with a knowing expression.

"He was indeed a prisoner here, even if he didn't realize it."

Keriam sighed. "Damn Faerie! You are bound to me, and I order you to kill him."

Talek stepped down through the rubble, the crimson tails of his coat wavering behind him. Colin braced himself.

Mawr stepped forward to stand between them. "I won't let you hurt him!" he cried, his voice wavering. "Please don't!"

Talek held up a hand; Colin winced on reflex. But the Faerie didn't go to them, he went to Keriam. "I will *never* do something that undoes the creations that Teagan wanted. Those belong to my Teagan. You can order me all day to destroy everything else, but those creations that he loved are his children, and I refuse."

Colin gaped at him. Teagan's *children*? He wanted to refute that, but he knew better than to open up his mouth again. He wanted to point out that Teagan wasn't his dad — his real father had died years ago on the streets. He also wanted to remind them that he was trained alongside troops and was a highly skilled Seeker, but he really wasn't sure if that was wise to bring up right this moment. Then he remembered the paper in his pocket that Madam Cloom had given him, and definitely made sure he kept his mouth clamped shut.

Keriam gripped his staff so tightly that Colin thought it might snap. "You are in a pact with me. You cannot deny my commands!"

Talek shrugged and wandered back up into the ruins

of the library. "When are we going to find Teagan? I need to see him."

The magician snarled and struck his staff down on the ground with rage. "Soon, you pathetic thing, soon."

Colin fell to his knees, trembling from head to toe. His stomach was tied into a knot and he let out the breath that he was holding. He gasped a lungful of air, focusing on the cold dirt beneath him. Mawr pushed up against him. He was saying something but Colin was too shaken to hear him. It was only when he felt the sandpaper tongue against his cheek that Colin was pulled from his stupor.

"Are you okay?"

"I'm fine," Colin said with a strained half smile. "It's just that you don't nearly die twice in one day, you know? If this happens a third time, I don't know how many lives I have left."

Mawr rubbed up against him, being as comforting as he could, as Keriam followed Talek into the remains of the library. Colin knew they needed to follow. He barely had his life spared and didn't want to give them a reason to turn on Mawr next.

IT WAS difficult not stepping on books as they followed Keriam into the library. After a few feet in the floor was littered with so many pages and book spines splayed out that it was impossible to step on a bare patch of floor. That was when Mawr stopped.

"You okay?" Colin asked, turning to see Mawr backing up slowly.

"I can't," he said with a tremor in his voice. "So many books... so much knowledge lost. Can I — can I just wait out here?"

"Sure, big guy." Colin gave him a reassuring smile. "I'll let them know you haven't run off." He watched Mawr turn back with his tail between his legs and wished he could follow, but he knew one of them had to keep up with the others, so Colin stepped one foot down on a muddy book and winced. He didn't blame Mawr for turning back.

The normally pristine shelves were marred and covered in dirt and debris. Where normally Colin had found the library to be a comforting place, now it felt broken and desolate. Back when he lived on the streets, he could always trust that the library would open its doors for him for a few hours.

Once when he was just a kid, a couple of Shadow Wolves made their way past the main gate and hunted down anyone they could reach within the Garden. Everybody had bolted up their homes and huddled inside with their families. He and Finn had grabbed the few things they owned and gone to the library. The librarians had let them sleep on the floor for the entire night along with all the other homeless Humans. Colin couldn't help but remember that dark evening listening to the howls of wolves on the wind and being forever thankful for the generosity of the librarians.

It was strange, when he had visited the place with Shaleigh, he had forgotten completely about that cold, fearful night, but now, it felt like it had happened yesterday.

Looking around at the toppled shelves and clawed up front desk, he hoped that nobody had been inside when the wall was torn down and the Shadow Wolves got in. He didn't want to think about those poor homeless Humans, half-asleep and confused, trying to scramble to their feet as the very walls crumbled around them. He didn't want to imagine the librarians screaming and rushing for the gazebo exit, maybe carrying oil lamps and trying to lead the way. Colin didn't see any old blankets amid the ruined books, but that did very little to assuage his fears.

Talek had wandered into the center of the building, finding perhaps the only piece left undamaged in the assault: the statue of Owain the Wise. The cheerful fellow sat on a bench with his hair pulled back in long dreadlocks, surrounded with tall flowers, forever reading to the children on either side of him. He was also forever oblivious to the ruin he sat in.

"Of course, this ridiculous thing would survive," Keriam said with a sigh, tapping the side of the base with his staff. He peered down at the placard. "Owain the *Wise*? Pfah! The only wise thing he ever did was side with that idiot Cathal, and that was more luck than wisdom." He patted the statue on the arm as though he was an old friend. "But it wasn't so wise in the end, was it? It didn't get you what you really wanted? All that work for what? A smile and a word of thanks from the foolish Cathal? What a waste."

Talek stood with his arms folded staring up at the ceiling, his eyes following movement up there as though watching birds. Colin looked up but saw nothing except the husk of what was left of the roof. There was no movement and Colin frowned. Talek continued looking around and started humming to himself. Perhaps this was one of the side effects Talek had inherited from the Madness.

"When are we going to find Teagan?" Talek asked, turning his head slowly to look at Keriam. There was an intensity in his gaze that made Colin uncomfortable.

Keriam gave a long, exhausted sigh. "We have discussed this already. Do we really need to speak of it again with the stoatling here?"

"You promised me that he would be safe. You said I would have him at my side." He stepped toward Keriam; his gaze unwavering. "You said-"

"I know what I said," Keriam spat. "You don't have to remind me. I said a number of things before their pact was destroyed, but circumstances changed." He rubbed a hand against his bearded mouth, watching Talek as though he was a caged animal instead of a trusted ally. "You were the one that sent them home, wherever that may be."

"I know precisely where I sent him, but I can't follow him. The magic won't work right again — why is that?"

"Because your magic is corrupted," Keriam explained through clenched teeth.

"I miss him. I want to see him. You said —"

Keriam slammed a hand down on the head of one of the stone children staring up at Owain. "Damn it, Talek, you are bound to *me* — not that fool!"

Talek leveled a steady gaze at him. "I demand that you let me go to him."

Keriam dragged fingers through his beard.

"If you don't then I will refuse to do your bidding."

The magician laughed, a cold, heartless sound. "How is that even a threat? You already disobey me."

Colin cleared his throat, drawing their attention. His tail twitched nervously. "Couldn't Talek go fetch Teagan and come back? That's the kind of mission I used to be given, you know, back when I was a Seeker."

"Ridiculous," Keriam growled. "I couldn't trust him on his own, certainly not in that Faerie's company. I might as well be cutting the leash."

"Then we go after him together, to the City of the Fae," Talek said with that intense gaze again.

Keriam narrowed his eyes. "That's where you sent him?"

He gave a disturbing smile. "Shaleigh took him from me at the last moment. I intended for him to stay with me." Talek crossed his arms but turned to look off to the side, as though he could see where Teagan was. "I need to see him. I need to be with him."

Keriam sighed. "Then I suppose we're going to the City of the Fae then. It was only a matter of time before we dealt with Queen Mab." He clenched his jaw, saying, "Once we've obtained him though, I expect your absolute allegiance to me, Talek. I'm tired of your excuses and demands."

Talek nodded slowly. "Of course."

Colin shuddered as Keriam's eyes cut towards him.

"You and the Living Statue are coming with us. I want

Shaleigh's friends close at my side, I don't want her building alliances like before."

"I mean, if she's with Teagan in the City of the Fae," Colin started with a shrug, "it's a little late for that."

Talek threw his head back and laughed uncontrollably. The disturbing sound reverberated on the remaining library walls.

Keriam stared at him with a deep frown. Colin could see the gears turning in the magician's head. Was he calculating how much use he would get out of Talek? Was he wondering how long they had before he lost it completely? This pact of theirs couldn't possibly last for too long at the rate it was going.

"Stop that," Keriam growled.

Talek clamped a hand over his mouth, but his shoulders still shook with laughter.

"When we find the girl, I want you to kill her," Keriam ordered in a voice without any emotion. Colin felt a chill go down his spine as Talek's laughter abruptly ended.

"Are you sure?" Talek asked, a rare moment of clarity coming over him. "If we sent her home, to her true home, then she would no longer be a problem."

"For one, you can't be trusted to do that properly," Keriam said and Talek looked away. "And for another, she is too dangerous to be permitted to live. We have taught her how to take down one kingdom, what will stop her from taking down another?"

PART II
CORRUPTION

A PROMISE

Shaleigh

Shaleigh awoke to the sound of music. A flute wavered sweetly on the breeze mixed with the morning sounds of birds. She opened her eyes to see that the shutters were open and bright sunlight filled the room. At first, she thought she was back in the Garden, in her bedroom in High Castle. Then, slowly, she remembered Talek, Madam Cloom, and Queen Mab.

She took a deep breath to let out all the frustration that tried to fill her: she had survived that. She couldn't allow her mind to linger on it anymore. She had to help her friends and she couldn't do that if she was forever wallowing in the past.

The lovely flute lingered with the chorus of birds again and the stress melted away from her mind. It had been too long since she had heard music being played, not used for a magical voice enhancer or for making her invisible, but music for the sake of music. She took in a deep breath of the cool air and let it out again, then allowed herself to look at the room she was in.

She must have been moved to the bed at some point, she could smell fresh cedar where it looked like oils had been rubbed on the sideboards and headboards. Sionn must have arrived with a mattress too, because she was sleeping on a feather stuffed mattress similar to what she had at High Castle. Had Teagan argued for it, or had they had another disagreement while she slept? There was no telling.

The room had looked utterly unwelcoming last night but now looked friendly and inviting with the light of day and the lovely sounds floating in.

She pushed herself into a sitting position but held the blanket closer as a cool breeze swept in from the window. The blanket was made from cloth, not from furs as she had before; at least it didn't have holes in it like the one Teagan had pulled off.

She blinked. The room was completely clean. Everything had been polished, probably with that same cedar oil, and gleamed in the sunlight. For a moment, she wondered what Teagan had done with the pictures, but then she saw them stacked in a corner on the table.

The dizziness she had felt had passed and her stomach now growled in frustration. She noticed across the room on a small end table was a plate of breads and a glass of water. For Shaleigh it was practically a feast.

When she went to get to her feet, she became aware of the fact that she was wearing different clothes. She hoped

Teagan did it because all she wore were her undergarments - at least someone had the decency not to remove everything.

She threw one bare leg over the edge of the bed and touched a toe to the floor. A shiver went through her. The ground, she realized, was made of stone and was far colder than the chilly breeze. Just as she touched one foot to the ground, a pair of flat sandals entered her line of vision. She slid her feet into them and realized quickly they were several sizes too big for her. Shaleigh's stomach grumbled again as she shuffled across the stone floor, heading over to the newly dusted side chair by the front window. Teagan had laid out a simple dress for her on it. She slipped it on; it too was rather large on her, but at least it gave her some warmth.

She was moving around the foot of the bed when she nearly tripped over the pile of blankets on the ground. It was Teagan, she realized with a gasp, sleeping on a pile of hay and wrapped so tightly in blankets that only his crimson hair was visible.

Shaleigh stared at him for a long moment. Was he asleep? Did he have to sleep? It had never occurred to her that he would have to, and for some reason it made him seem more Human. But when had he possibly had time to sleep at High Castle? He seemed to have been awake at all hours, handling everything from preparing the Games, to solving disputes, to cutting flowers. The thought of him squeezing in time to sleep throughout that whole mess made her respect him all the more.

Teagan's clothes were folded neatly on the floor beside him, with the same care that her dress was prepared. He also could have slept on the bed beside Shaleigh, it was certainly big enough for them both to fit, but chose to take the floor on a pile of hay instead of on a proper mattress.

Shaleigh sighed. She appreciated him taking care of her last night, but this wasn't a castle. They were prisoners here and he didn't have to manage and organize everything like he had at High Castle. Trying to constantly be a gentleman or the High Faerie of the Garden would wear him out, and potentially put them at odds with each other.

She moved past him to the front door and turned the knob, wincing as it squeaked.

"Where are you going?" Teagan asked in a tired voice.

She turned around guiltily. "I was going to let you sleep."

He rubbed his eyes and stifled a yawn. "I suppose you must be feeling better if you're trying to sneak out."

That made her bristle. "I wasn't sneaking out. I wanted to look around and see what was here. All I got to see last night were a bunch of spitting Faeries and some irate guards."

Teagan sat up and stretched. The blanket fell and Shaleigh realized he was shirtless. She turned away quickly, feeling her cheeks flush, but Teagan didn't seem to care. "Let me pull some clothes on and I can come with you. I was thinking last night that we might be able to convince Queen Mab to let us stay for a while. You need some time to recuperate."

"Right," Shaleigh said, trying to focus as she avoided his gaze. "We can try."

There was some rustling before Teagan stepped forward to take the handle of the door. He had pulled on a tunic instead of his previous High Faerie clothes, and tied his hair up into a partial updo, allowing long strands to hang down around his face. He still looked tired, but you wouldn't guess it by how eager he was to get moving. Perhaps that was why it was so hard to wrap her mind around him even needing sleep.

"We may need a guard escort but that shouldn't be too difficult." He opened the door and together they stepped out into the bright morning. Shaleigh winced and shielded her eyes for a moment as they adjusted to the light.

"There you are!" a familiar voice called out.

They both turned to see Queen Mab sitting in a chair on the front porch, smiling at them as though she had just told a joke. "Have a seat with me and let's enjoy this beautiful morning." She motioned to the empty chairs beside her.

Shaleigh exchanged a look with Teagan.

"I promise you they won't ensnare you, poison you, or any other such nonsense. All I want is to have a chat, nothing terrible." When they hesitated still, she added, "Not that you have much of a choice in the matter, do you?"

Shaleigh sighed at that reminder and grabbed a piece of bread from inside before walking over. Teagan looked like he wanted to stop her, but Shaleigh ignored him even after he joined her and the queen.

They sat in silence for several minutes watching the branches above them sway in the cool breeze. The air was crisp but invigorating. Shaleigh swallowed down the hard bread, sating her stomach and helping her to think.

Finally, Queen Mab spoke, "What do you think of the house, Teagan? I understand it took some time for you to clean it last night, especially with the girl being ill."

It was odd hearing her talk about Shaleigh's illness as if it wasn't a big concern.

"It's um, larger than I recall. Before there was barely enough room to fit a bed."

Queen Mab chuckled. "Of course, it is. Talek deserved a larger living space after how you treated him."

Teagan blanched, his gaze sliding down to the ground. He had that same hollow expression in his eyes that he had the night before.

The queen waved a hand at the two guards standing watch before the house. "You two are dismissed. I can take care of them for a while. Go get some sleep."

The guards bowed low to her and headed off, keeping their weapons at the ready.

Queen Mab smiled and leaned back in her chair, looking as though she was just a nice lady sitting out on the porch of her home... except for her pointy ears and the golden embroidery on the rim of her plain brown dress. Once the guards had left, she leveled a long-suffering look at Teagan.

"Teagan dear, let me be frank with you. You made an absolute mess of things when you left here. We thought you had been kidnapped at first. We didn't have the magicians delivering messages across the land like we do today, so it took a couple of days for us to figure out what happened. Then to discover that you ran off with that naive Cathal?" She sucked in a breath and shook her head. "He wasn't even a magician of notoriety. Just some young idiot with impossible dreams." She reached over and patted his cheek like a child. A blush spread on his cheeks. "You're quite clever, my dear, but you need to learn how to think."

Teagan came out of his embarrassed haze at her words. "It wasn't like that." His voice grew clipped, "Master Cathal was different."

She gave a wry smile. "He's not your master anymore. If anything, the Garden was your master, and she's very much dead."

Teagan gave a pained look and turned away. "How could you possibly understand? I've been working within a clearly defined set of rules for centuries now. Everything was working perfectly until... this."

She chuckled. "You act like the cause of it all isn't sitting right here." She gestured to Shaleigh who squirmed in her seat. "If it wasn't this child, it would be another who was determined to go home. She was just the lucky one."

"I don't know about that," Shaleigh said with a sigh. "I haven't been lucky at all."

"Nonsense, you're alive, aren't you? That's always cause for celebration. If I have my way, you'll stay that way too."

Shaleigh blinked. "I thought you wanted to kill me."

A little of the humor left the queen's eyes and she gave a solemn nod. "I have to make my people believe you are to be killed. Most of them have no tolerance for your kind, regardless of how dire your situation is or how unwilling you are to be here." She gripped the arms of her wooden chair with long fingers. "I speak as an old queen who's tired of this entire mess."

Shaleigh wasn't sure if she entirely trusted her words, but she at least had to pretend that she did. She nodded and gave a small smile that she hoped looked genuine.

Queen Mab turned back to Teagan. "I'm certainly not your mother, dear, but I'm probably the closest you have to one."

He gave a short chuff of laughter.

"As such, I need you to understand what you did when you left. You left Talek behind without a word or a warning. You left behind a Faerie who had changed his name to be joined with you. You left behind a Faerie who was willing to give up anything to be by your side."

Teagan twirled a bit of hair around one of his fingers. "I didn't know that he would—"

She held up a hand. "Hush. Now listen to me. I've bought you a day to collect yourselves and prepare without getting beheaded, which means you listen when I ask you to."

Teagan nodded.

She let out a shaky breath. "How long were you with Talek exactly?"

"I don't know. I don't remember. It all seemed to go by so quickly."

"Five centuries? Six?" She pressed on, adding, "Do you know what it does to someone when the person they love leaves them like that?"

"Yes," Shaleigh said quietly. Both of them turned to her, surprised. "My father was never the same when my mother left him. I was only a baby at the time, but he never recovered. He told himself that — no, that's not right — he *believed* that she was just at work each day. Or that she was on a business trip. He never wanted to admit the truth. It was too painful for him."

Queen Mab smiled at her with admiration. "You are an observant Human. Perhaps you have more insight into this than I gave you credit for." Her eyes narrowed on Teagan. "To say Talek was devastated is an understatement. He was destroyed. We noted him leaving the city regularly, disappearing off to who knows where. So, we moved him down to the ground level. Then we noticed him wandering through the trees by himself, getting himself into a state and sobbing at all hours." She glanced between each of them. "I've lived long enough to know a Faerie drifting toward the Madness when I see it, so we tried to keep track of him. It was when traders from the south came through that he disappeared. They come twice a year to trade their wares for a good week before moving back down south, scaling along the edge of the Dark Lands." She huffed. "The crazy Faerie knocked one of the women out and stole her clothes. Even the traders themselves hadn't noticed that he was among them, his skill at blending is unmatched."

"That I know very well," Teagan admitted.

A breeze swept past, filled with the scent of campfire. The tree branches creaked above them as the shadows danced upon the ground. Shaleigh breathed it in, letting the cool air flow through her, fill her. It helped her mind to focus.

The queen reached over and pulled Teagan's hand into hers, squeezing it tight. "You need to fix this. This problem is yours to own and to solve. You have made a number of enemies, and they'll all emerge now that you're no longer the feared High Faerie of the Garden." Her eyes cut towards Shaleigh. "You'll need this girl to help you."

"What can I do?" Shaleigh asked. "I want to help my friends, but I don't know any magic."

Queen Mab's eyes gleamed as she leaned closer. She smelled of sage and rosemary. "Ahh, but I hear news from the south. Much news of the Garden and the promise of their latest Chosen Human girl. You are crafty and brave, perhaps foolhardy, but I think he'll need you more than you think."

Shaleigh stared at her, forgetting briefly to breathe. There was a weight to her words that was frightening, a truth to them that shook her from within.

"You cannot help what comes to you. You cannot help what mistakes you've made. All you can do is try your best to learn from them and right them whatever way you can. All you can do is try harder, my child." She sighed. "When you live as long as I have, your memories are strung together with failures and mistakes. It's up to you to figure out what to do with them. Do you let them weigh you down? Or do you pick yourself up and move forward?"

Shaleigh felt tears stinging her eyes. "I'm sorry," she whispered. "I know you're counting on me, but I don't think I'm capable of helping anymore. I'll just make another mistake."

"No, you don't have to apologize to me. I'm an old queen who has only grown more bitter over time. Compared to me, your mistakes are benign and few. A good leader is one who doesn't allow herself to be over-whelmed by mistakes. You pick them up and wear them so that you never forget. That way you can't do it twice."

Shaleigh nodded, wiping her eyes on her arm.

Queen Mab squeezed her shoulder. "I need you to accompany Teagan on this quest, child. He needs you. He may be reluctant to admit it in front of me, but I can tell. He can't handle this alone, and neither can you. So, I need you both to promise each other that you're going to fix the mess you've *both* made."

THE GUILT still weighed so heavily on her that at times Shaleigh was afraid she would crumple under its weight. She wanted to fix what she had caused. She wanted to help her friends, if they were still alive. The thought of them suffering made the sting of tears worse.

Teagan fetched her some water in a squat, ceramic cup and she gulped it down quickly. He nodded at her whis-pered "thanks" and sat back down on the other side of Queen Mab, clearly annoyed.

"I truly don't appreciate being treated like a child, my queen," Teagan said in a measured tone, but Shaleigh could hear the frustration at the edges. "My apologies to Shaleigh, but I don't share her youth. I understand the consequences of my actions. I chose this path fully knowing the dangers and accepting them. I plan to correct them on my own. I don't need to make ridiculous promises, and I don't need Shaleigh's help in order to solve this."

"Wait a minute," Shaleigh said and leaned forward, "I deserve the chance to help! My friends are involved in this."

"You were already ill from being exposed to too much magic. This entire world is filled with magic. It is far too high a risk to bring you with me."

"That's not your choice to make any longer, Teagan. That's my choice. And I choose to help. There's nowhere else for me to go."

"I'm sure we could seek out the Magicians' Sanctuary and find someone to send you home. That's all you really want, isn't it? With the variety of magic, they know, I'm sure one of them must possess that simple power."

Queen Mab's laughter broke up their building argument. It was loud and infectious and Shaleigh found herself smiling even as the fury within flickered. Teagan folded his arms and looked away, but she thought she saw the hint of a smirk on his lips just as he turned.

"My goodness but you've grown haughty, Teagan! Even Talek, for as obsessed and blinded as he was, knew that he needed help to accomplish his goals. Even he was willing to work with others. Surely after two centuries of working among Humans, you aren't still keen on seeing them as worthless."

"That's just it," Shaleigh interrupted, "he didn't work among Humans so much as give them orders." Queen Mab raised her eyebrows. "Sometimes he thought it would be funny to threaten to remove their tongues for talking back. I don't think it was exactly helpful in making him more tolerant."

The queen sighed and patted Teagan's shoulder. "Arrogance is such a disgusting trait."

Teagan turned to her with such wide eyes that it was as if she had slapped him. "*Disgusting...*" he whispered.

"Yes, I know, but it's true. Take this as an opportunity." Queen Mab pushed off her chair then turned to them both. "Neither of you are permitted to leave my land until I get that promise from each of you. I want this fixed. I want the land cleaned of all the mess that Cathal made and whatever new mess you've both caused. I'm tired of having Slumbering Forests and Gardens stuck in spring-time. It isn't natural. It isn't the proper way magic is to be used." She pursed her lips. "Though I imagine you two are going to learn that the hard way."

"What if I refuse?" Teagan asked and Shaleigh stared at him. What was with him suddenly? Why was he so against working with her? One minute he was worried about her health and the next he was refusing to go with her.

Queen Mab smiled. "Then I hope you like that little home, because you're not leaving it anytime soon."

This was just too much. Shaleigh turned to him, "What is wrong with you?" He blinked at her in absolute confusion. "Do you just not like being around me suddenly? I pass out from being teleported to another place and you suddenly see me as too weak to go with you?"

He squinted, "Tele-what? I'm sorry, I'm afraid I don't understand."

"I may be just a weak little *Human*, but I was able to break your two-hundred-year-old pact. I'm pretty sure that proves I'm capable of more than you think."

He shook his head. "No, no, that's not it. I'm simply worried for your safety!"

"My safety?" She got to her feet. "They use human skulls here as decoration and you're worried about me not being safe going with you? I wasn't safe in the Slumbering Forest, I wasn't safe in the Garden, I'm not safe here, and I don't expect to be safe with you."

Teagan frowned.

"Good," Queen Mab said with a smirk. "I'm glad you're at least talking about it. That's a good sign. You two can wander around my city if you wish, the guards will take you anywhere you request." She put a hand to the side of her mouth as though sharing a secret, "Though get used to being spit at regularly. I'm afraid I can't control the anger of my people, and none of them like you two very much." She turned around and headed back down the path, waving at the two new guards on duty who immediately bowed to her.

Shaleigh was already shaking her head when Teagan went to speak. "I don't care what you say, I'm not going around and getting spit at every day because you're too stubborn to work with me."

Teagan sighed. "Look, it's for your own good. I don't know what it will take to fix what happened to the Garden. I don't even know if we'll be able to fix anything. Our going back may just make it worse."

She sighed. It was annoying when he was right. "I can't stay here. They'll probably kill me in a week or two. I'll have better chances wandering the wilderness with you."

Teagan's laughter caught her off guard. It made a cold chill go down the back of her neck as she looked over at him. "If only it was merely wilderness we were dealing with. It would be far easier if that was my only concern. We'll have to move through the Dark Lands, past the Sanctuary, and through woods filled with marauding minotaurs. I could possibly make it on my own, but with a Human at my side? I simply don't know."

"Do you want my honest answer here?" Shaleigh asked, feeling the tears threaten once again. Damn, what was wrong with her? "I would rather die by your side than here among strangers."

He looked down to the faded wood beneath their feet. A cool wind whipped by once more and the branches overhead groaned and swayed.

"Shaleigh, I would take you with me... If you truly believe it is what you want, I would do it." He gave a great sigh. "Only now she wants to have a promise made. Do you know what that means?"

"Not the way you make it sound."

"A promise is usually a simple verbal agreement, but not with the Queen of the Fae. A promise overseen by Queen Mab cannot be broken. It is as binding as servitude until the act is done."

"That's... I don't..." Each sentence that Shaleigh tried to start got lost as though blown away with the wind. "Why would she demand such a thing from us?"

Teagan smirked. "Exactly. I just got out of a pact with a kingdom that I had originally thought would be with a man I loved. I've no intention of joining into another."

Shaleigh cocked her head to the side, "Wait, so you did love Master Cathal, then?"

Teagan took a deep breath and nodded. "Yes, I did. I

knew Talek wouldn't come with me if I left. He didn't see this place as stifling at the time." He glanced back to the house. "I wonder if that changed the longer I was gone."

"Judging by all his drawings, I think that's an understatement. How could you leave him like that, Teagan?"

"I wanted something new, I guess. Maybe it was my youth." He shook his head. "Of course, I could give an array of excuses and I don't think any of them truly fit." He bit his lip, his eyes glassy. "What do you think of Queen Mab then?"

Shaleigh gave a short nod. He wanted to change the subject, of course he did. She stepped off the deck and out onto the grass. The sun had risen just above the tops of the trees now and the wind had picked up. Her gown billowed around her. "She's not as bad as Madam Cloom, but she's close, isn't she?"

Teagan gave a small chuckle. "Queen Mab has had many centuries to practice the art of manipulation and laying traps. Madam Cloom had only begun to learn." He shrugged. "Come, let's walk. Perhaps we can figure a way out of this mess."

Shaleigh nodded, and side by side they walked down the dirt path away from the house. They had barely gotten to the end of the walkway when the guards stepped up behind them. They didn't speak a word, but knowing that they were watching and listening made Shaleigh nervous. Could they even plan with them so close?

She gave Teagan a nervous look as they proceeded.

AN ABOMINATION

Colin

A cold breeze swept through the tall trees and ruffled Colin's fur. They were somewhere in the woods, and although Talek and Keriam led the way, Colin wasn't sure where they were and it bothered him. There were at least twenty troops traveling with them, and they each paused at points to wrap their furs closer around their throats. It was a cold day to travel, but at least it was sunny. Colin, for once, was grateful for his own fur coat, but he still huddled closer to Mawr to use him to help block the wind.

Oddly enough, it hadn't been so bad when they crossed over the river. It was crisp, but the breeze was light from the running water that came down from the mountains as they waited for the drawbridge to be lowered. Colin knew a good bit about the history of the

Garden, but outside of that his knowledge was limited. His geography wasn't that great either, though he felt more confident in his knowledge of the Human World than he did this one. It was his job to know the Human World, after all.

Mawr had been fretting ever since he knew their destination. "The City of the Fae," he whispered, turning to Colin. "There are going to be so many Faeries there, that can't be a safe place to go. They'll all be tricksters."

Colin shuddered against another blast of wind.

"And we're heading through dangerous land - I heard Lieutenant Varg mention that. I have no idea what he means though." Mawr looked nervous but didn't say more… which only made Colin more nervous.

As the trees grew thicker and the sunlight became dappled, Mawr tucked his tail between his legs, and glanced around as though expecting something to leap out at them. Colin tried to keep his senses alert too, but the wind was messing with his sense of smell.

As the soldiers ahead slowed down to cut through some foliage, Colin stepped up closer to Mawr's head so they could talk more discreetly.

"You know more about this place than I do," he admitted. "Where are we? Why is everyone on edge?"

"Minotaur country," Mawr replied, his golden spectacles rattling on his nose from his shaking. "There are bands of them out here, stampeding anyone who gets in their path."

"Minotaurs?" Colin asked, looking around at the trees. "You mean like Graddic? I mean, he's pretty nice."

Mawr shook his head. "Meaner," he said, "Way meaner."

Colin felt a chill go down his back at Mawr's words. He'd never heard him talk about anyone as mean. Colin lowered his voice, "Maybe we can talk to them and get their help. I mean, if they know what happened to the Garden, they might be willing to help us get away."

"We can't leave, it's too dangerous. Especially with a Faerie with the Madness here... Oh no, we can't do that, Colin. I don't know if these minotaurs really liked Madam Cloom or the Garden either, so I can't really say what they would do if we tried to get their help."

Colin dragged his claws through his fur. "There's got to be something. We have to get away so we can warn Shaleigh."

"I know, I just don't know how we can do that. They'll know."

The first warning they had was a flock of blackbirds flying out of a copse of trees and fleeing into the sky with a loud fuss. That was when the horn came. A flush of adrenaline came over Colin in a rush. That horn meant trouble. It also meant to get into a defensive position. And even though he knew what it meant, what to do hadn't been part of his training. The twenty or so troops were changing formation, and Colin envied them knowing exactly where to go. He was absolutely clueless.

"Colin, what is that? What's going on?" Mawr crouched down beside him, burying his nose against his paws.

"It's a defensive military position," Colin said, as the soldiers circled around Keriam and Talek. It was crazy, really, to see these soldiers willing to throw their lives away for such a deplorable leader. Though that was what Captain Briar warned about, hadn't she? They were under occupation. This was the cost of losing. Of course, her family had learned that a long time ago, hadn't they?

"What's that rumbling sound?" Mawr squeaked.

Colin blinked, and then listened harder. He had been so focused on the soldiers that he had ignored the obvious threat.

"That's a stampede."

The roar was getting louder by the second. Colin shifted in an instant from observer to Seeker. They were in a terribly open spot — smack dab in the middle of a clearing with very few trees. The soldiers were having to create a ring around a divot too, which gave them even less of an advantage. There was high ground though, and with Mawr's speed, they might be able to make it. The hairs on the back of his hands stood up on end.

"Mawr, just do as I say, okay?" The poor stone lion just stayed crouched down and trembling. Colin reached over to stroke his mane. "Hey, trust me?"

Mawr gave the barest of nods as he watched Colin with great big eyes. "I don't want to hurt anyone."

Colin leaped gracefully onto Mawr's back. "I can't promise anything. If Shaleigh were here, she'd probably say the same thing."

Mawr gave a sad nod.

Colin pointed to the rocky outcrop up ahead. "I need you to get up to that ledge, okay?"

As Mawr pawed at the ground anxiously, Colin could make out the sound of numerous hooves hitting the ground as the leaves around them rattled.

"Now!" Colin screamed and Mawr took off. Colin nearly slid off but got a good grip on Mawr's stone mane. He heard Lieutenant Varg's shouts as they passed, but paid little mind. If he and Mawr were going to die, he would prefer the magician to kill them rather than being run over.

Just like before when they were racing to get out of the Garden, once Mawr got going, he was incredibly fast and good at maneuvering around the trees. Still it wasn't long before the minotaurs reached them.

Colin had seen the minotaurs in the Garden perform incredible feats of strength, but it was only when about ten of them came into view from the side that he had a true appreciation for their power and speed. They bounded on all fours, charging through saplings and foliage as though the plant life was made of tissue. Even with Mawr's leaping bounds, they had approached the pair of them in hardly any time. They were far faster than any of the Shadow Wolves they had encountered that night in the Garden. It must not have taken them long to realize where they were headed.

The rocky cliff was closer, but they were moving downhill to reach it, which meant it would be a greater leap than Colin had expected. One of the minotaurs ran over, switching to a two-legged run so it could slam into Mawr's side.

Mawr yelped and stumbled but managed to regain his footing to continue. Colin fretted, that was only one... If all ten of them tried, they would never make it.

"Keep going, Mawr," Colin said into Mawr's ear.

"You've got this. You're the fastest lion I know!" It sounded more ridiculous when he said it aloud than it had in his head, but it didn't matter. Mawr needed that encouragement and he went even faster, pushing himself to take larger and larger leaps until there were times when Mawr's feet didn't even touch the ground. It was more like flying than running. The minotaurs were left in the dust.

With a deep cry that vibrated Colin's entire body, Mawr leaped with all his strength. For an instant it looked like they may not make it, but then Mawr's front claws dug into the stone ledge. Colin's grip slipped and for a moment he couldn't find a hold on Mawr's stone body until he latched onto his tail. He yanked unintentionally as he caught himself, but it didn't seem to bother Mawr.

"Are you okay?" Mawr called over his shoulder.

"I'm good," he said breathlessly. He looked below to see that while he thought they were going to be only a few hundred feet up, it was more like a thousand feet. They had even leapt over a deep chasm to reach the rocky outcropping, one that he hadn't seen. Colin felt the blood drain from his face and tightened his grip on Mawr's tail.

Step by step, Mawr pulled them both to the top, and Colin couldn't help but think that this must have been how Shaleigh felt riding on his flying bicycle the day he kidnapped her. How brave she must have been to just let go, he realized, looking down at the distant trees below. This was nothing compared to the distance she fell.

Not for the first time he was reminded not only of Shaleigh's bravery in the face of any opposition, but of his own cowardice. If he had known the drop was so far, would he have pushed Mawr as hard as he did? Would either of them have agreed to make the jump? Probably not.

Once Mawr pulled them to the top, Colin let go of his tail to drop down onto the stony ledge. He meant to fall on his feet, but actually fell onto his hands and knees. He gasped, "I can't believe we just did that."

Mawr plopped down onto his stone belly. "But we made it! I didn't think we could, but somehow I found I could go faster when you believed in me." He leaned over and gently nuzzled Colin's arm.

Colin gave a shaky laugh. "I never knew you could run that fast!"

"Me neither!" Mawr blinked. "I guess I never really tried."

Colin looked down into the clearing to see that the army of twenty soldiers was surrounded. He had only seen maybe five or ten minotaurs aimed at them, but looking at the dark shapes in the distance, he estimated there had to be at least fifty. Those were more than two to one odds, and even with Lieutenant Varg at the helm, he wasn't sure if they would win. The Lieutenant had some big shoes to fill with Captain Briar being out of the picture and it was clear he didn't have half the hold over the soldiers as the Captain did.

"Maybe we should have stayed," Mawr whispered, his voice wavering. "Maybe I could have helped."

Colin took a deep breath. "One alone nearly knocked you to the ground. There was no way you could have taken on all of them."

Mawr scraped his claws against the stone ledge. "I

could have fit more people on my back. I could have saved some of them."

He reached over to rub Mawr's nose. "Hey, don't think like that. They're soldiers, it's their job to protect and defend. Their main concern is Keriam, he's the new ruler of the Garden. You and I are only supposed to take care of ourselves."

Down below a small group of minotaurs approached the circle of soldiers. The solders had their pikes out, aimed at them. Colin swallowed down the lump in his throat. He really didn't want Mawr to have to see bloodshed. The poor guy had been through enough — *he* had already put Mawr through enough.

"Come on, we need to find cover. Once they're done with the soldiers, they'll head this way."

Just as he and Mawr were about to turn away from the confrontation below, a blast of purple light erupted from the center of the soldiers, pushing away everything. Colin instinctively dropped to the ground even as the sound reached them and ricocheted off the stone outcrop. It sounded like an enormous boulder had dropped onto a rocky cliff. Then came a series of great booms followed by the terrified cawing of birds. What was going on down there?

Colin laid close to the ground for a while, listening to the echoes fade, hearing Mawr's spectacles rattle on his stone nose; both of them were shaking from head to toe.

"What was *that*?" Mawr asked, his voice muffled from his muzzle being buried in his paws. Even fully pressed to the ground, he was still about Colin's full height.

Colin clenched his jaw. He wanted to know the same

thing. It took a moment to build up the courage to push up onto his elbows and look down into the trees again.

The clearing had grown. And with it, many trees had been knocked down, pushed outward from the center. From up here, with the tree trunks aimed outward from where they hit the ground - it looked like an enormous eye.

Colin could see the soldiers were slowly getting to their feet, having been pushed forward from the blast, but somehow appeared to not be injured. Dozens of minotaurs however laid scattered on the ground. Almost all of them were motionless, though a few survivors in the distance were darting as fast as they could away from the troops. He could only see shadows of them as they moved through the thicker trees.

Talek stepped out from the center of the soldiers and even from here, Colin could see him shaking with laughter.

"Uh, I think that was Faerie magic."

THE SOLDIERS WERE REGROUPING BELOW, making sure there were no injuries, helping their shaken friends to their feet. Colin could sympathize. Even up here he wished someone was able to pull him to his feet. His legs felt like wet noodles and Mawr was still shaking beside him.

"Why did we come with them?" he whimpered through his paws. "Why didn't we stay at the Garden? I should be trying to put the library together again, not here. I don't belong here."

Mawr's fear gave Colin the motivation to move again. He wrapped an arm around Mawr's muzzle and laid his head on his cheek. "Hey, it's okay. Shhh. We didn't have a choice, okay? If we didn't come with them, for all we know, they would have had us killed. These two are so unpredictable, we don't know where we would be right now otherwise."

Mawr rubbed his face carefully on Colin's to keep from hurting him. "I keep trying not to be pulled into battles like this, Colin, but I keep being pulled into them anyway. I don't know why; I don't want to be here."

"It's not your fault. None of us wanted this to happen. It's really my fault for getting you into this. I should have left you in the castle the night the Shadow Wolves broke through the gate."

"No, I wanted to help. I wanted to help you and Shaleigh. You're my friends, and I've turned my back on enough friends in the past."

Mawr shuddered again and this time Colin could feel his tears on his furry cheek.

He understood Mawr better than he probably knew. He too had failed a friend. There were a hundred different things he could have done to help Finn, but instead he chose to focus on his path as a Seeker.

His transformation was a gift, but Mawr was never given a choice. Colin chose to become a Seeker, but Mawr was created to be a Guardian, even if he hated battle. Colin had read books about the slaughter at the old City of Aife, but it was difficult to even imagine what it must have been like for Mawr.

Colin didn't know what to say to help him, so instead he held him tight and petted his mane. He tried to calm him down until Mawr's crying slowly ceased and eventually the trembling stopped.

"It's never easy seeing these things," Colin said finally. "And it never gets any easier either."

"I know, but it still hurts."

Colin hugged him once more before pulling away. "I'm sorry. I wish I could help more, but I'm not very good at this fighting thing either."

"You got us out of there, that's better than I did." Mawr sniffled. "I just freeze and shake so bad I can't think straight." He sighed. "I'm sorry to be such a bother."

"Please, be a bother," Colin said with a grin. "Then you can help me when I'm a bother next, okay? We'll be bothers together."

That got a chuckle at least and Colin rubbed the lion's nose.

"When you two are done, my master would like you to rejoin the group."

Colin spun around, expecting to see Talek there, but there was nothing. "Where-?" He turned again to see Mawr staring up at the sky; Talek hovering over the gulch, his arms crossed and a wide smile on his lips. He was surrounded in an eerie violet glow that reminded Colin of that blast they had seen below.

Talek gave a disturbing laugh. "Did you two really think you could escape that easily?"

Colin just blinked, unable to think of anything to say.

"We didn't intend to escape, sir, we just didn't want to get trampled," Mawr muttered.

"Did you doubt my master's ability to protect you?"

Colin and Mawr exchanged a glance. Neither of them knew what to say.

"No?" Colin asked in confusion.

Talek arched an eyebrow.

He tried again, "Maybe?"

Talek gave another odd laugh then gestured below. "He's awaiting your return. Shall we?"

Colin looked down to the soldiers and Keriam slowly getting into a walking formation again in the distance. "Sure, but I don't know how we're going to get back down there. We barely found a way up here."

"I'm sure I can assist." Talek hovered closer and patted Colin's head like a dog.

He opened his mouth to protest when his feet left the ground. "What!?" He tilted to the side as he floated into the air, his tail whipping around him as he struggled to keep himself properly balanced.

In the end he hovered sideways and had absolutely no control of how his body shifted. "What did you do?"

"I'm helping you reach the ground again," Talek said simply, turning to Mawr.

Mawr crouched and covered his eyes with his paws. "Oh no, oh no, oh no!"

Talek patted his stone head next and even though Mawr weighed a ton, his body lifted into the air like a feather. "Eep!" he squeaked as he wrapped his paws around his face. "I can't look! I can't!"

"Keep your eyes closed, Mawr," Colin said, sounding far more in control of the situation than he actually felt.

Talek gave a crazed laugh which instantly made Colin very nervous about trusting him to put them back on the ground safely again. "My master wants you with us, and I can't have you two getting hurt. Come."

He floated down toward the clearing with Colin and Mawr floating behind him. Mawr was giving meek little whimpers and Colin was groping helplessly at the air, unable to control how he turned. When they finally reached the ground and were placed onto the grass again, Colin nearly wept. His legs were wet noodles again and it was his turn to shake uncontrollably. Mawr landed exactly how he had been standing before being lifted into the air and gave a great thud when he hit the ground. He blinked and opened his eyes, smiling with relief. "Oh, thank goodness!"

"Yeah," Colin said, trying to get his stomach to quit flip flopping. "Something like that."

Then, Keriam's shoes came into view and his staff slammed down beside Colin's head. He screamed and sat back on his haunches.

The magician leaned down to look him straight in the eye and Colin could count every whisker on his chin. "Try running away from us again, and I won't be so forgiving."

Colin stared at the man for several shocked seconds before finding his tongue again. He looked to Talek for assistance, but the Faerie was silent. "I'm sorry, we were scared and we weren't sure if-"

"Don't doubt me again, little rodent, or you will regret it." He glanced over to Mawr with a glare. "Both of you."

Mawr pawed at the ground but didn't say a word. For once, Colin was grateful. He didn't want this psycho's attention on Mawr. "It was my idea!" he blurted out without even thinking.

Talek came over to stand behind Keriam, a smirk on his lips as though he could see right through Colin. For once he was glad that he had fur on his face to cover any blush he might have. If they were going to get punished though, he wanted it aimed at him, not Mawr. He could take it, he was trained for dangerous situations, and Mawr was just a helpless bystander.

"He wanted to stay and protect the soldiers, but I wanted to try to escape. It was stupid, I know, but I had to try."

Colin braced himself. He expected a scolding, or perhaps a bit of magic to be used against him. That was fine, at least he wouldn't be killed on the spot. Talek had already assured that, but he hadn't expected Keriam to twirl the staff in his hands and smack him across the face. The wooden cage that held the violet gem landed square on his cheek and the flare of pain caught him completely off guard. He fell to the ground, dazed and confused. His ears were ringing, and the world seemed to spin around him.

Keriam crouched down at his side. Colin could smell his rank breath. "Don't you dare try that again or it'll be far worse." He drew so close that Colin could feel the heat of his breath on his ear. "There are many things you can live through, little rodent. Do I make myself clear?"

Colin was only barely able to nod. He tasted blood and could feel the imprint of his teeth in his inner cheek with his tongue. He barely noticed Keriam's footsteps leaving and put his head back down on the ground, trying to get himself together.

It had been a long time, a damn long time since he had been treated like that. He had almost forgotten what it felt like to be hit that hard by someone. With a wooden staff too, it was like getting caned on the streets all over again, wasn't it?

He sighed in frustration. He really needed to learn to keep his mouth shut. If he hadn't said anything, they would've been fine. But as soon as Kerium put his attention on Mawr, Colin couldn't help himself - he had to draw his ire to him instead. Clearly, he hadn't thought it through very well, and now here he was, dazed and bruised and bleeding because of it.

And poor Mawr, he hadn't heard a peep out of him. He had just calmed the poor guy down too.

Someone knelt beside him and sighed. Perhaps it was Lieutenant Varg? Colin squinted and couldn't help but tense at the sight of Talek staring down at him, his violet eye such a stark contrast to his other brown one.

"You shouldn't have angered him," Talek said, his voice unusually calm and somehow more intimidating because of it. "He's looking for an excuse at this point. Lying like that was a very bad idea too. What were you thinking?"

Colin gave a lopsided smile. "I didn't exactly mean to."

Talek glanced up nervously, looking like a child caught awake after hours. Then he placed a hand on Colin's cheek. Colin tried to flinch away, but there was nowhere to go. Was this the true punishment, and Keriam's little smack was just a taste? He squeezed his eyes shut and tried to brace himself this time.

A warmth spread from Talek's fingers and suddenly Colin's fuzzy head grew clearer and the bleeding in his mouth ceased. A crease formed between Colin's brows as he looked up at the Faerie. There was no malice on the Talek's face, simply a surreal calmness.

"Why?" he whispered, aware that Keriam was not far from them and would certainly not be liking this turn of events.

Talek gave a tense smile. "Pretend that you're still hurt. Please."

Colin gave a short nod and Talek got to his feet, reaching a hand down to help him up. While Colin was certainly not nearly as good of an actor as Talek was, he knew what it felt like to get smacked across the mouth, perhaps a little too well. He also knew how long it would last and how it could change his speaking. Mostly his mind was preoccupied with what on earth had gotten into the Faerie to help him, but he couldn't exactly voice anything right now.

Lieutenant Varg was wrangling troops to stack the corpses of the minotaurs. They were going to put them on several bonfires, and Colin was pretty sure it wasn't just because they wanted to clean up the mess they had left behind. No, this was Keriam sending a message to the survivors. A very clear message.

Mawr tried to keep his distance but was clearly very worried for him. Colin wanted to run over and reassure him that he was okay, but Talek put a hand on his shoulder to help steady him... More likely to keep an eye on him a bit closer. It was probably best if Colin didn't bring any attention to Mawr right now.

What was Talek's game though? One minute he was laughing maniacally and killing minotaurs and the next he was healing Colin without his master's approval. Colin wished he had studied Faerie pacts more in his reading. Maybe then he would have a better understanding of what Talek was doing and why he was able to resist the pact when Teagan couldn't.

Keriam surveyed the piles of bodies with a great smile on his lips. Colin realized this might be his only time to try to get information out of Talek. "Why did you help me?" he whispered.

Talek shrugged, "You helped me before, right?" He gave a nervous laugh. "I'm not imagining that, am I? I think you did help me."

Colin gave him a concerned look. Was the Madness affecting his memories too? That didn't bode well. "Yes, I did. I helped you out of the cell with Shaleigh's assistance. You were a prisoner."

He sighed through his nose. "Her again."

"Yes, she helped on Master Teagan's orders."

He brightened at that. "He wanted to help me."

Colin nodded, not quite sure if it was a good idea to talk with him about it, but he had to do something. The Faerie was unhinged and led by a sadistic magician. He had to squeeze in any talks of sanity with him whenever he got the chance. It felt like it was the right thing to do. It felt like something Shaleigh would have done if she was here.

"Shaleigh was worried for you. I know you were just manipulating her, but she really did care about you."

His face shifted between an array of emotions at once: pain, anger, sorrow, and settled on resignation. "I know she did. I betrayed her. Teagan didn't give me a choice though. He," Talek swallowed hard, "hurt me. Then he refused me again after I risked everything for him. If he had just come with me none of this would've happened. That was my last chance, you see. My last chance to help him. My last chance to get him back." He let out a long, shaky breath. "Now he's left me again. I can't have him do this to me. I won't let him."

"Talek!" Keriam called from one of the forming bonfires beside an exhausted Lieutenant Varg. "I need you to help these soldiers stack the bodies for me. We're losing daylight and I want to reach the Dark Lands before night-fall. Do you think you can do that?"

Talek sighed and snapped his fingers. All at once, the minotaur corpses that were laying around on the ground began to shake. It was like an earthquake was occurring, but only the lifeless bodies were affected.

"Talek, what...?" Colin started, unable to think of what to even ask.

Then, one by one, they opened their eyes, and oh how Colin wished they hadn't. Their eyes were rolled up in their sockets, white and unseeing.

Soldiers screamed and ran over to stand near the Lieutenant who stared in utter horror. The dead minotaurs climbed to their feet, some barely able to walk because of how the trees had fallen on top of them. A couple had to drag their bodies with their arms because their spines had been crushed. Some snorted with annoyance at soldiers as they passed. One woman, frozen in fear, nearly got run over by one that wouldn't change its path regardless of who was in front of him. Lieutenant Varg had to rush over to pull her out of the way.

One by one the dead minotaurs approached the pyres and threw themselves onto the fire. There was such a hush over the group that all Colin could hear were the stepping of hooves and dragging of limbs through the undergrowth. Colin got a good look at the last one who flung himself on top of the flames. He had to take a running jump in order to reach it. Then, as the flames rose, his white eyes went wide for a moment before finally closing in a disturbing death slumber.

The silence stretched as the bonfires spit and crackled in the afternoon light.

Talek started chuckling under his breath, but soon the laughter erupted into cackles. All eyes were on him, the Faerie who could raise the dead with the snap of his fingers. In all his years serving Madam Cloom at the Garden, Colin had never seen anything like that. Teagan would have never created such an abomination.

IT WAS NEARLY DUSK, and it felt like they had been walking for ages. Colin's feet hurt, even with all the additional fur and padding on his stoatling feet; he was tired. Yet, still Keriam and Talek ordered them onward. Looking around at the rest of the soldiers, Colin knew that they ought to be hurting, but none of them showed it. They were all resolute, determined to push forward. As much as he wanted to stop and take a rest, he wanted them to push forward too. He knew from studying his maps that they were getting close to the Dark Lands, and he really didn't want to be anywhere near there at night.

Then, the trees started to diminish. It wasn't a sudden cut-off, but rather, they grew farther and farther apart. Next, the birds disappeared. That was the real frightening moment.

The troops stopped for a very short break and that's when he realized he couldn't hear anything. The sun was dipping beneath the horizon and he couldn't even hear the hum of crickets that were common this early in the fall. The air felt wrong here, like it was charged and ready to spark.

Colin flagged down Lieutenant Varg, who removed his helmet and was wiping down the sweat from his beard.

He gave them a tired half-smile as he approached. "I hope you two aren't getting into any more trouble."

Colin's tail swished back and forth as Mawr shuddered. "We're really close now, aren't we?"

He would've preferred to bring up the rear of the progression with Mawr, but after their last failed escape attempt, they were no longer permitted that luxury. Now they walked in the middle, with Lieutenant Varg and a couple of guards between them and Keriam.

Varg's smile faded. "From the Dark Lands?"

Colin nodded.

"They say it spreads," Mawr said in a quiet voice. "In a few decades all of these trees will be swallowed up by it too. It only moves southward, never northward toward the Faerie City."

Colin shuddered. "Did you read much about it? I wasn't sure if the Library at Aife had much information on it."

"Oh yes, there were shelves of research on it. The destruction of Loburg only happened half a century before, so there was plenty of time for people to investigate and write books." He sighed. "I wish more of that research had been transcribed for the Garden Library. I remember some of it, but not in much detail. I wasn't as interested in that. I mostly liked reading about the dragon, Tanwen. This place was too scary."

Colin blinked at him. "So, wait, the Dark Lands were more frightening than a dragon?"

Mawr gave a quick nod that made Colin's stomach drop.

"We're planning to give it a wide berth," Lieutenant Varg assured them, drinking from his waterskin. "We don't want to take any chances here." He sounded confident, but Colin could see the worry behind his eyes. He was tired, his troops were tired, and the weight of leadership had to be heavy on his shoulders. Colin knew he wouldn't want to be in his shoes.

"Wait, if it spreads, how do we know where the boundary line is?" Colin asked.

"By moving cautiously," the Lieutenant said and took a deep breath. "And trusting that our magical *friends* can help us."

Colin bit his lip. That wasn't very reassuring.

Mawr glanced over to Keriam before speaking, "Some

think it's going to take over the land completely one day. Or, at least they used to. I guess what I've read is a few centuries behind." He shivered and his tail flicked back and forth behind him. "If I had known I'd be here, I would have studied more. I never thought I'd need to know."

Colin patted his side absently. "I think I agree with you; I'd rather be reading about this than actually being here."

Soldiers started shouting up ahead. Lieutenant Varg looked forward with wide eyes, then sprinted through the group, pulling his helmet back on as he ran.

"What's going on?" Colin asked, unable to see anything even on his toes.

Mawr lifted his head trying to see. "I don't know," he said, a fearful look in his eyes. Colin scampered up onto Mawr's back so he could see better: it was just the boost he needed.

Something was happening at the very front of the line. Several soldiers were yelling at three soldiers who stood there looking confused, turning in circles as though they couldn't see the others. It looked like they had stepped into a fog, but there was no fog. Instead, long, misty white tendrils covered them. Lieutenant Varg pulled the other soldiers back further. Nobody dared dive in to rescue them.

The three soldiers became more and more difficult to see, though they were calling out to the others, clearly upset and confused. It seemed like they could hear their voices, but they couldn't find their way back to the group. Then a black shadow leaped in front of one and he disappeared completely. Colin got a glimpse of a red eye and almost screamed. Then the second one disappeared, and finally the third. It was as if the three soldiers had never existed to begin with.

"Mawr, did you see that?"

"I wish I hadn't!" he whimpered, trembling and making Colin shake with him. Then the stone lion dropped to the ground. Colin had been standing on his toes to see, and almost lost his balance.

Mawr covered his face with his paws. "I don't want to be here anymore! I don't like this place at all!"

Colin rubbed between his ears to keep him calm, but that wouldn't help the rest of the soldiers.

Shouts were going up and down the line. Some soldiers in the front ran screaming toward the back. Confusion poured through most of them, many not sure what had even happened. Some had been able to see...but weren't sure what they saw. Some thought the three soldiers had deserted, Colin could hear their whispers from where he sat. Others thought they had been killed.

Colin was glad to be on Mawr's back because a group of spooked, well-armed soldiers wasn't exactly the most comforting group to be mixed up in. Soon the soldiers started breaking up, shifting directions, some moving forward to find out what happened, others who knew better running to the back.

One soldier got smacked in the face with Mawr's stone tail and landed flat on his back. Mawr hurriedly wrapped his tail around himself and balled himself inward. "Oh no! I'm so sorry! Colin, is he okay? I didn't mean to hurt anyone!"

The soldier was standing up slowly, a big red welt on his cheek.

"He's fine," Colin said, but his voice was hard to hear over the panicked roar of the soldiers. He huddled further down on Mawr's back, wishing for the first time in ages that he could melt them both into the shadows and disappear.

"*Quiet!*" Keriam the Magician shouted from above, his voice loud and clear. All eyes went upward. Talek and Keriam floated there, outlined in violet, with Talek holding Keriam's arm at his side. "We will be routing farther east in order to accommodate the Dark Lands. If any of you fools plan on deserting, just remember that Talek can hunt you down in an instant! I'll have no hesitation to kill on sight, do you hear me?"

Despite his very stern threat, Talek wasn't even paying attention. His gaze was distracted by the Dark Lands behind them, as though something was drawing his eye. Normally Colin might assume it was just his Madness making him see things that weren't there, but Colin had seen the shadow that wasn't really a shadow, in the fog that wasn't really fog. Perhaps the things that kept distracting Talek were more real than he wanted to admit.

The soldiers were still anxious. There was no denying that, but they at least didn't look ready to bolt. Colin understood. They were trained to defend the Garden or to escort merchants to various Kingdoms, not to face this place. The Dark Lands were a completely different type of enemy, one that they weren't ready for. At least Mawr had studied it, even if his knowledge was outdated, it was better than nothing.

The rest of them had no clue what they were dealing with.

Colin made to get down, but Mawr turned his head to him. "Please don't! Please, I want you to stay if that's okay."

Colin rubbed between the lion's ears again. "Hey, it's alright. I just don't think they want me riding you around again, that's all."

Mawr pawed at the ground. "I just-" he stopped and looked ahead toward the invisible fog. "I don't want us to disappear, but if we do, I'd rather we do it together."

Colin nodded even as a shudder moved down his spine. As terrifying as that thought was, he had to agree. They were already prisoners together; they might as well fade from existence together if that was to be their fate. "Okay, I'll stay for as long as they'll let me."

Mawr gave a relieved smile. "Thank you, Colin. I'm sorry I'm such a burden sometimes."

Colin chuckled. "You're never a burden, okay? You're the one carrying my sorry butt around."

Mawr gave a little laugh at that and Colin smiled. Despite what happened to them, that felt like the key. They had to keep their spirits up. They had to stay positive. They had to keep each other grounded and safe, regardless of what happened.

Lieutenant Varg changed their path, and they diverted further eastward than before. Colin could even make out the distant sounds of birds as they walked, which made him feel far more comfortable. He couldn't help but eye the Dark Lands as they passed it though.

At times he almost thought he could hear those soldiers screaming. The other soldiers didn't catch it and thankfully Mawr didn't either, but his sensitive ears could. It made his blood run cold and he gripped Mawr's stone mane a bit tighter. Once or twice he saw the dark shadow with red eyes within, following the group, watching them, but this time it kept its distance.

As the light faded, they finally moved away from the cursed lands and toward the Faerie City.

"You know," Colin said, his voice heavy with weariness, "at this point I'm not even worried about going to a city full of Faeries. At least we'll be away from that place."

"I don't know, I'm still worried about the Faeries," Mawr said with a shake of his head. "We still have to come back down this way too if we want to get back to the Garden."

Maybe he could convince Keriam and Talek to take a different path, but Colin doubted it.

THE POWER OF KNOWLEDGE

Shaleigh

The sun had climbed over the tops of the trees and the City of the Fae was alive with movement. Violins and flutes filled the air while Shaleigh and Teagan walked through the center of town past Queen Mab's throne, finding a circle of Faeries all clapping together. A trio was playing music, and Shaleigh could only glimpse the swirling of skirts as a man and woman danced inside the circle. She couldn't see much else around the crowd.

"Can we watch?" she asked Teagan, who shook his head.

"I'm afraid they would likely break apart if we even went near them. Normally anyone is permitted to enjoy the festivities, but considering what you are and who I am, I don't think it's a good idea to interrupt them."

Shaleigh noticed they were skirting around the edge of the clearing, as far away from the group as possible. At Teagan's words, a few on the outskirts of the circle had spotted them and glared in their direction. Nobody was spitting on the ground, yet at least, which she hoped was a good sign - it was an improvement from the day before.

She gave a heavy sigh and continued along beside Teagan.

"Don't worry," he said. "Where we're going there won't be anyone to bother us."

She doubted that, especially considering their shadows behind them. They hadn't been able to really talk about the looming promise that Queen Mab had set for them yet because of the two guards. She didn't know what plan Teagan had for shaking them, but she was all for it.

They walked through a few more clearings that weren't nearly as busy as the dancing group from earlier. A few Faeries were moving about carrying baskets of fruit or linens, but they didn't give them a second glance. Perhaps to them, a Human and a Faerie walking around the city wasn't a cause for alarm, at least not with two guards close behind them.

A strong wind blew and Shaleigh caught the crisp scent of rushing water. Soon she could hear it too, rushing just on the edge of the path they followed. They turned twice and went through two more clearings.

The area smelled heavily of honeysuckle which brought back all sorts of memories of places she and Kaeja had explored. It was strange, she had gotten so used to seeing flowers everywhere at the Garden and now there were hardly any. If the seasons worked the same here as they did back home, it was fall now.

"What did the Garden look like in the fall?" she asked, breaking the silence between them.

Teagan glanced to her, "What do you mean?"

"What did it look like when it wasn't springtime?"

He stared forward for a minute, stepping over a patch of rocky earth. "Before Master Cathal, Owain, and I tamed the land, it belonged to the Pello Pines. They ranged from the ruins of Aife to Briar Kingdom, making the land practically inhospitable for anything bigger than a sparrow. In the fall, it was dark, gloomy, foggy, and treacherous."

The idealistic image of a beautiful golden forest with a carpet of leaves that Shaleigh had imagined faded and was replaced with the terrifying scene Teagan described. She thought of the Slumbering Forest that Madam Cloom had pointed out to her from atop the Overlook and shuddered at the memory of the black shadow that hovered over the land. She wondered if the Slumbering Forest had awoken, and then her mind went to Mawr and Colin, wondering if they were even alive. Those were dangerous thoughts though, and she stared at the ground as they walked.

"I also wanted to apologize for my rudeness earlier. That was uncalled for."

Shaleigh breathed in the sweet-scented breeze that blew past before replying, "It's alright. You were probably scared last night when I passed out on you. It makes sense, I guess, but you can see that I'm fine now." She gave a small smile. "And I am coming with you, even if you don't want me to."

He gave a genuine smile and it reminded her of how happy he had been when they were first brought into the City of the Fae. "You are right, of course, we're both responsible. I was foolish to leave Talek like that. I should have handled it all more carefully, but I was excited and headstrong." His eyes grew distant. "To be honest, I don't know why Cathal thought I was worthwhile to be bound to his Garden. I was hardly ready for the job."

"To be honest, I don't think you should have left him at all, but that's just my opinion." She ignored the annoyed glance he gave her. "It's okay, I wasn't ready to lead the Garden either. I just thought I would wait until now to tell you the truth."

Teagan rolled his eyes. "I hate to tell you this, but I already knew the truth. Something about your fighting prowess was a dead giveaway." He was quiet for a moment before he narrowed his eyes. "I was surprised, though. You turned down the chance to go home. I didn't think you were capable of that. The magicians at the Sanctuary truly could grant you that wish, I'm certain of it."

Shaleigh was silent as they started climbing up a short hill, then explained, "I can't run away from the mistakes I've made, no matter how much I want to. I have to pick myself up and continue forward." She paused at the top to catch her breath. "Even if I would love to leave this place and go home, I know I would regret it for the rest of my life. I have to know if Colin and Mawr are safe. I owe them that much after what I did to them."

～

NESTLED at the base of the hill and surrounded with stone columns wrapped in honeysuckle, was what looked like a huge greenhouse. It had to be at least ten times the size of Teagan's home and was larger than any of the other buildings that Shaleigh had seen so far in the City of the Fae. It also had a very different architectural design. The homes she had seen were built of stone and wood: Teagan's home had a stone floor but wooden walls. This one was almost completely made of stone and looked like it had been there for some time from the discoloration of the walls - it almost seemed like it didn't belong. It would have looked more at home with Mawr in Aife before its destruction.

She hurried downhill to reach it while Teagan picked his way down slowly. She couldn't help it, the chance to explore an old building was exciting, especially since she didn't have to deal with an injured leg like in Aife.

The two guards paused briefly, then she heard one call out, "I'll take the Human, you take Teagan."

"Fine by me!"

One of them shuffled down behind her, and she couldn't help but smirk before turning her attention to the building again. It was a grand structure, with all sorts of plants that also didn't seem to belong here. What in the world was it for?

"That is the first Botanic Garden, known as Betha," Teagan said walking down to join her, his guard in tow. "It's beautiful, isn't it?"

"I'm assuming it's not to grow food or anything," she quipped, unable to take her eyes off of it. This was the closest she had come to the urban exploration she loved back home, and she wanted to go inside. Now that she was closer, she could make out some kind of inscription on the large wooden beam that hung over the entrance, but couldn't read the words.

"Millenia ago my kind were the first to make our home here in this land. Then, as Humans slowly were either brought over or stumbled through the hidden portals into our world, we realized the danger that this plant life would have if we didn't conserve it. So, my kind went out and collected plants from all over."

One of the guards joked, "I didn't realize this was going to be a history lesson." The other one laughed, and Shaleigh glared at the two of them. She knew they didn't care because she was just a Human, but she was getting tired of them both.

Teagan continued on as though he hadn't heard them, "Betha is the first of many of these buildings." Teagan smiled. "I thought you would like to see some of the plant life that we have saved from destruction."

"So you brought me down here just to look at a bunch of plants?" The excitement she had was beginning to dwindle. A room full of plants was a lot less interesting.

Teagan arched an eyebrow. "Not just any plants, the ones we deemed most likely to be destroyed. These are the ones that were saved, despite what others thought of them. We saved every last one. Come, there are a couple in particular I want you to see."

He led the way to the front of the building, and as Shaleigh looked up, she could see that what she originally thought were words were actually intricately carved flowers. They looked like bundles of snapdragons that had been carved as though growing out of the beam's base.

Teagan pulled on the main door, which was wooden like the shutters. The hinges squeaked in resistance and a tiny swirl of dust puffed out from the dirt within. Shaleigh peaked around his shoulder to see inside. Long shadows stretched around the limited sunlight. The scents of old, wet leaves, crumpled, dewy grass, and oxidized vegetation struck her quickly. On their own, the scents wouldn't be too bad but having them all blast her at once made her sinuses recoil in confusion; she sneezed.

He turned to smirk at her. "This place can be rather intense at times. Just mind where you step. The roots can trip you." Then, he disappeared into the building, seeming to blend with the shadows.

Perhaps the room full of plants would be more exciting than she expected. Shaleigh stepped over the threshold and had to wait a minute for her eyes to adjust to the limited amount of light.

At first the place looked overgrown, unkempt. However, the more she looked at it, the more she saw the logic of it. The limited sunlight was on purpose. Certain groups of plants had direct sunlight while other batches had indirect light. The stones that divided the types of plants, the ropes that cordoned off zones, and the ledges that divided each group of plants weren't haphazard but planned. They were like little plateaus with steps that led down to each section.

It reminded her of the old cemetery back home that had been there for at least a century - only, instead of using each level for coffins, it was used for dividing up plant life. She understood it, but it still struck her as odd. It felt like an old-fashioned method.

"Are you coming?" Teagan's silky voice pulled her from her thoughts.

"Sure," she muttered, turning to look over her shoulder before she spotted his red hair behind a bush with star-shaped leaves.

"My kind have collected every plant in the land, grown them, and kept them safe for many Human generations."

Shaleigh followed him down one, two, three flights of stairs until they were at the lowest point of the greenhouse. It must have been the only entrance to the place because the guards stayed outside and didn't seem keen to enter. Either that or they didn't want to hear any more history lessons. There was still sunlight here, but the shadows were long and dark making it harder to discern between the different plants. They were more overgrown and the barriers she had seen up above were difficult to find.

"This is the oldest plot of all," Teagan said, his voice filled with reverence. "You might even recognize some of them."

Shaleigh's gaze was transfixed on the far corner of the plateau, where it looked like tall bars were erected. She hadn't seen anything made of metal here and had gotten the impression that anything like that wasn't allowed here in Queen Mab's city.

She approached it slowly, finding it difficult to tell if they were truly bars or not. Were they really just skinny trees?

"So many thought our conservation efforts were a

waste of time, but then so many breeds kept dying off. Some plants would have gone extinct entirely without our efforts."

Shaleigh was only half listening. She reached out to grip one of the bars; the metal was cold and hard in her grip. She looked through the gaps, half expecting a prisoner inside, but there was only a great, hulking shadow of a tree. It was enormous and grazed the roof of the building. The bars, she noted, also carried up to the ceiling.

"Hey Teagan, what is this for?" The words were barely out of her mouth when something dark and wet prickled against her hand. It felt like a bunch of sewing needles were rapidly being stung into her fingers, the pricking felt deeper the further up her hand they went.

"Teagan!" It looked like a simple dark vine, but when she tried to pull her hand away, fresh pain blossomed. The needles, she realized, were hooks that curved inward. There was no way she could get her hand free if all she did was pull.

Teagan was suddenly at her side, holding an axe high into the air. He brought it down hard on the dark, wet limb and the appendage was sliced in two. The shadowy tree shook causing the ground to tremble under her feet. They backed away quickly. More appendages reached for them, but couldn't go farther than the cage's bars. The vines flailed for a full, angry minute before going quiet and still, making it look once again like a passive tree.

"What is that thing?" Shaleigh whispered, still trying to get the vine off. She could feel the hooks deep in her skin. Teagan stepped forward and carefully slipped the vine in the opposite direction, unsnagging each hook out of her now bloody skin one at a time.

"That is a Pello Pine."

Shaleigh stared at the thing with its long bramble limbs dragging on the ground. They looked more like tree moss than limbs: she thought of Mawr hiding from a whole grove of the things and shuddered.

"I warned you about them, but-"

"I wasn't listening," Shaleigh admitted in a terrified whisper.

His expression softened. "It's alright," he said. "These trees originally preyed on small animals and eventually evolved to devour Faeries, Minotaurs, even Humans."

"So, they draw in their prey?"

"Yes, more or less. Especially if you have never encountered them before. You'll be aware of their methods now, though. You'll know what to expect."

It took an effort to pull her gaze away from it. "What to expect — you mean we'll be dealing with more of them?"

"Oh yes," Teagan said and shifted uncomfortably. "With the Slumbering Forest now awake, we'll be facing all of them."

Shaleigh gaped, then looked down at her hand. It wasn't pouring blood, but each little dot had welled up and was glistening in the limited streams of daylight.

"This isn't the only thing I wanted to show you, though. Come to this side."

Shaleigh followed in mute terror, her mind reeling with the new monstrosity she was responsible for awakening: An entire forest of bloodthirsty Pello Pines. What did that mean for those few survivors in the Garden?

She clutched her injured hand to her chest and followed warily.

"You've seen the daegonrúsc, of course."

The plant he motioned to as they walked past was far smaller than the enormous ones, she had seen in the Slumbering Forest. Its tiny black coils were wrapped around a white rose bush, but it must not be as powerful because many of the blossoms and leaves were exposed to sunlight. The rose seemed generally unperturbed. If Shaleigh didn't know any better she would have assumed it was like kudzu, but she had seen just how big the daegonrúsc could get.

Teagan stepped around several large branches from other trees that hadn't been cut back properly. He was moving toward a shadowy corner, an area where the vegetation seemed to die down for some reason. Then in the far corner, she saw it.

The plant didn't even come up to Shaleigh's knee, and unlike the daegonrúsc or the Pello Pines, it was quite lovely. The purple flowers that grew from the dark green of the plant seemed to glow in the darkness with their own violet luminescence. She found herself entranced by it, yet after her experience with the Pello Pine she knew better than to approach it.

"Whoever has ensnared Talek used the Shadow Wolves to their advantage. They found a way to control those fiercely independent beasts, and I know only one way to do that." He motioned towards the plant. "The Scáil flower is extremely rare and it blooms only in the darkest of places. If aggravated, the plant can release a cloud of spores that can disorient a person or leave them susceptible to suggestion. The petals are weaker, but they can also be ground up, mixed with food or water, and when fed to a person is taste-less and odorless. It turns the person into a slave of sorts."

Shaleigh stared at him. "Like a zombie? The voodoo kind that is."

Teagan arched an eyebrow at her. "I'm not sure what you mean by that. Depending on the dosage, a person can become more inclined to be agreeable to even outlandish requests, or pressured into a relationship, or even pushed to treat a person like a deity."

I gaped at him. "You're thinking whoever has bound Talek is controlling the Shadow Wolves that way?"

"Yes," he said, nodding gravely. "Many were slaugh-tered when they broke through the gate of the Garden. Those wolves may occasionally get riled up enough to press their advantage, but risking their lives to invade a city as fortified as the Garden? It would take either an incredible speaker or a decent dosage of Scáil powder in order to sway so many of them to risk their lives. They aren't fools."

Shaleigh shook her head. Teagan was so busy focusing on the Garden that he was missing the bigger picture, and it seemed so obvious to her that she blurted out the words without thinking, "What about Talek?"

Teagan narrowed his eyes. "What do you mean?"

"You just said this stuff could turn someone into a slave. Could Talek's new master have used this on him too?"

Teagan's jaw dropped and in the dim light she could see he hadn't even considered it. "No... no, that couldn't be it. Talek wouldn't be so foolish as to-"

"I mean, he was pretty desperate. If those Shadow Wolves hadn't caused a distraction, he would have been killed."

Teagan put a hand to his mouth and gave a long, desperate stare at the glowing violet petals of the Scáil flower, as though it would force it to share its secrets.

"He couldn't have," he said in a small voice, even as he clutched at the base of his neck. "Talek... he would have known. He couldn't have trusted him to..."

Shaleigh stepped closer and placed a hand on his arm. Part of her couldn't believe that Teagan had known about this plant the whole time and yet had never put it together that Talek could also be controlled by it. Even with all his experience and all of his knowledge, he was still too wrapped up in the Garden to think of the obvious possibilities.

He was shaking and Shaleigh felt bad for mentioning it. As strong as he wanted to seem to his fellow Faeries and to Queen Mab, Teagan was still so fractured on the inside.

She wrapped an arm around him and to her surprise he leaned against her.

"I hadn't even considered," he said in a strained whisper. "I hadn't even considered that as a possibility. Why hadn't I thought of that?"

She rubbed his back, debating on what she ought to say. If she was in his position, she would want the brutal honest truth, no matter what. So that's what she gave him.

"You were wrapped up in yourself," she said and felt a tremor go through him. "You were wrapped up in your Garden and in your power."

He closed his eyes and a tear slid down his cheek, catching in the golden trails along the surface of his caramel skin. "It didn't even cross my mind. Not once. What sort of monster have I become?"

"An enlightened one," she said with a sad smile.

Teagan nodded and wiped at his cheek, taking in a deep breath. "Enlightened, oh yes, I am certainly that." He reached down to grip her hand. "Thank you. I am... sorry you have to put up with me."

"I don't put up with you," she said with a smile. "We help each other out, right?"

He swallowed and nodded, about to say more, but then the door at the far end of Betha opened and the light that poured into the botanical garden was blinding. Shaleigh squinted and shielded her eyes. One of the larger plants on a higher level shrank away from the light and she could have swore she heard it hiss.

"Teagan? Are you still in here?" It was Sionn and he sounded annoyed.

"Yes," he said, wiping away a few stray tears. His voice settled back into its normal tone as he called out, "We're in the back. What's the problem?"

"Queen Mab wants to speak to you both outside. Right now. It's urgent."

Shaleigh glanced to Teagan and saw the concern fall over him. "Urgent?" she asked, careful not to speak too loudly.

"That's not good," Teagan said, his gaze still on the

door. "Come along and watch your step. The queen is not a woman to be kept waiting."

For once, Shaleigh wished she could work with a patient queen. Just somebody that didn't demand her presence on a constant basis would be really nice.

QUEEN MAB WAS PACING as they emerged from Betha. She wore a red, velvet robe, and her hair was pulled back to draw attention to her long ears.

The cool breeze felt wonderful compared to the humid, oxygenated air from inside. Shaleigh hadn't realized how much she had been sweating in there until she emerged. Sionn held the door for them both and motioned them to move faster, an annoyed expression. She was concerned to see they now had five guards in total with them. This couldn't be good.

"There you are," Queen Mab said, her gaze falling on Teagan. There was a crease between her eyebrows that Shaleigh hadn't seen before and she even wrung her hands. "We've received news that Talek and his new master are traveling north, through Minotaur country. I can almost assure you that they're coming here... We cannot admit that we have you both."

Teagan gaped at her, glancing quickly to Shaleigh. "You fear him?"

She pursed her lips. "I don't know how they found out that you were here, but they have. His master has connections that I didn't expect. He's some magician known as Keriam."

Teagan's eyes widened.

Queen Mab continued, "They're taking the trade route up along the edge of the Dark Lands, so that's no longer a safe passage for you to take to leave. You'll need to take a more dangerous route to reach the Garden if you still wish to return there."

"Keriam the Cruel..." Teagan whispered more to himself than to anyone else, but Shaleigh felt the hair on the back of her neck stand up at his words. She knew Talek was a threat, but she hadn't even considered his new master. If their pact was anything like the one between Madam Cloom and Teagan, then Talek would be doing whatever the cruel magician wanted.

Queen Mab stared up at the branches far above them swaying in the wind. Her eyes were glassy with tears. "I had hoped you would both learn something coming here. I had hoped I could keep you safe and protected from those that hunted you. I could handle them if they were alone, but in a pact together with Talek's onset of the Madness? His magic is unpredictable and dangerous." She shook her head and a let out a shaky breath. "There's no way I can protect you from both of them, Teagan. I am so sorry."

"No, my queen, it is my place to apologize. None of this would have happened if I had seen the obvious signs before me. Shaleigh tried to warn me. She tried to tell me what I had become, but I ignored her. Now it seems we will be forced to end this ourselves." His expression was distant, as though he understood just how difficult this would be.

Queen Mab approached Shaleigh and reached out to

take one of her hands. Her skin felt soft despite the lines on her knuckles that spoke of her age. "I am sorry for your role in this, child. You don't deserve to be involved in this mess."

"Maybe not, but I'm just as responsible. I may not have known what I was getting into, but that doesn't mean I'm without fault."

The queen patted her hand, as though reluctant to let her go, a sheen in her eyes. "I believe you are the first and only Human to be permitted to stay in my realm, child. And certainly, the only one who has been allowed to pass through unscathed. Be wise and be cautious. You have such trials ahead of you."

There was that familiar touch in her mind that Shaleigh had felt before. The scent of rosemary and sage drifted over her for a brief moment, and Shaleigh felt her resolve shake slightly at Queen Mab's words. Her lips trembled but she refused to falter before this woman.

The way she spoke, it felt like Shaleigh was going off to her death, and she didn't know how to handle that. So instead of crying, she pulled Queen Mab into a very awkward hug. She heard the guards step forward with concern.

"My queen!" Sionn cried out, but Shaleigh ignored them.

Queen Mab gasped before hugging Shaleigh back, tightly. When she released her, the queen was smiling. She didn't say a word, but in her gaze Shaleigh felt calm and comfort envelop her.

She turned to her guards. "Leave us. I will escort them both to the border."

"But my queen," Sionn protested with disbelief. "You of all people shouldn't be anywhere near the Dark Lands. I think this is a very dangerous idea to entertain."

Her warm brown eyes turned cold. "Do you dare tell me where I should step, Sionn?"

"No, my queen," he choked out.

"I'm well aware of the dangers, far better than you are. Or perhaps you know better than the queen of these lands?"

"No, my queen," his said, his voice wavering. "I'm sorry."

She continued her piercing gaze and Shaleigh wondered if she was pushing into his mind like she had just done to Shaleigh. Only she was fairly certain the queen was doing it in a far less gentle fashion with him. Sionn was trembling now, turning his wide, fearful eyes toward the ground.

Queen Mab seemed satisfied with this. "I don't like the turn of your thoughts, Sionn. I don't like the paths they take. You are relieved of your duties today. Go home. I don't want to see you again until dawn."

He went a shade paler and bowed low, almost falling forward. He turned and walked off at a rapid pace.

She motioned to another guard who carried a large leather sack. The Faerie stepped forward to hand it over to Teagan who put the strap over his head.

"That should be enough to reach your destination, barring any interruptions."

Teagan turned to stare hard at her, clearly concerned, but the queen turned to her guards, ordering, "Now leave us. I want both of them to fully understand what they're walking into." She lifted the hood of her red velvet robe, careful to cover her long ears as she motioned to Shaleigh and Teagan. "Come along. It's not a terribly far walk, but I have much to share with you." She turned to Shaleigh, "Especially you, child. Knowledge is always the most powerful tool."

THE DARK LANDS

Shaleigh

Queen Mab led them far into the woods, away from Betha and the center of the city. She followed no paths and Shaleigh saw no markings to indicate which way they were supposed to go. She didn't even spot any mushroom rings like she had seen when they first entered into this land. The trees though grew thicker, the sunlight dimmer, and even the undergrowth grew sparse.

"You aren't the only person who has made mistakes, Shaleigh," Queen Mab said suddenly. "I've made my share as well, and when you're a queen, your mistakes tend to be far worse than others."

Shaleigh turned toward her as a cold breeze swept by them. Had it gotten colder since they began traveling?

"I'm the reason the Garden was destroyed. Surely your mistakes couldn't be that bad."

She gave a bitter laugh. "You would be surprised."

Shaleigh glanced to Teagan, but he seemed lost in his own thoughts, or at least not interested in talking at the moment.

"There was once a young Faerie named Fineen who was terribly in love. He was a beautiful man with a kind heart and an infectious optimism. The woman of his affection was perhaps the only one to rival his beauty, but she was unfortunately a Human from the Kingdom of Loburg." The queen stepped around a winding root. "At the time, a hatred was brewing for our kind. We were putting many Magicians out of work, and vicious rumors were being spread about us being flighty or untrustworthy. The two lovers were not permitted to be together; there was no safe place for them. One night she rode hard through a rainstorm to see him and grew very ill. When she died, his heart was broken."

"That's terrible," Shaleigh said, not sure why Queen Mab was telling her all of this or what any of it meant.

"It was," she agreed. "His heart was so broken and his mind so torn in two that the Madness descended upon him."

Shaleigh's eyes went wide. She remembered what it had done to Talek. She remembered his violent laughter and the ease with how he had removed Madam Cloom's mouth. "He couldn't have been as powerful as Talek though."

"No, he wasn't, but he was just as dangerous."

The ground had grown barren as they walked, with no

vegetation in sight. The tall trees were now spaced out further and further, but it was just as dark as if the sunlight was being blocked. "What do you mean? If he wasn't in a pact, I don't see why—"

Queen Mab held up a hand, it was pale and stark against her robe. "Child, let me continue. The Madness has its own danger. You see, shortly after the Madness fell upon him came the Night of the Red Moon, or as my people call it, the Night of the Bloody Moon. That was the night my people were slain without cause from sea to sea."

Shaleigh watched her carefully. Captain Briar had referred to that night as a vengeance, as a logical step after a Faerie had burned down Briar Kingdom. Queen Mab saw it very differently.

"I couldn't just let my people be slain without retaliation. They come to me for help, for protection, to be kept safe. I let them find their own destinies, yes, but I was not about to let these fools threaten my people. So, I used Fineen as an example. I shouldn't have, but I did."

Shaleigh stepped around a spindly tree. "What did you do?"

Queen Mab stopped beside the tree and put a hand on the trunk. Flecks of dried bark fell away like dust at her touch. She looked up at the dim sky above them. "I showed them what the Madness could do. Normally we take inflicted Faeries to the Peak of Gwern and allow them to end their lives."

The hairs on Shaleigh's arms stood up at the thought. They assisted them with suicide?

"They are far too dangerous to be permitted to live, you see. The Kingdoms forget this. They forget the deeds we do to keep them safe, to keep all of us safe. So, I reminded them."

"We don't need to discuss this. It won't come to that for Talek," Teagan whispered. He stared at the ground, his eyes desperate and his fingers intertwined.

The queen eyed Teagan. "I'm not talking about Talek, I'm talking about Fineen. The girl needs to understand what has happened before if she hopes to understand the Madness. We must learn about the mistakes of the past – my mistakes – if we hope to not repeat them."

Teagan gave a resigned nod and turned away.

Queen Mab turned back to Shaleigh, her gaze intense. "I led Fineen into Loburg, a city that had made a public proclamation to slay any Faerie that crossed its borders, not so different from the Garden before you destroyed it. I led him to the very center of town and had him wear an eyepatch to hide his Madness from the others. The people all thought I was an old woman." She gave a bitter laugh. "I suppose they weren't wrong."

She stared now at something in the distance. "The only item I gave him was a painting of his dear deceased love. That, I knew, would push him over the edge. The Kingdom acted accordingly. They rallied around him, planning to slay him there on the spot, or incarcerate him. My understanding was that much of the townsfolk had come out to see the foolish Faerie, who was brave enough to enter their city and sit beside their well. Then the Madness reached its zenith: it spread to his other eye. My understanding is that they didn't know the danger he posed. Of course, it was too late for them to flee."

"My queen, please, that is enough," Teagan whispered.

He was standing beside her clutching as his elbows, his words fell out in a rush.

"The girl needs to know," Queen Mab said firmly. "When the Madness took him completely, the Kingdom of Loburg was no more. This was all that remained."

She motioned to the desolation around them. There was no green here because nothing grew. Even the sunlight struggled to reach the ground though there was nothing obviously preventing it. Shaleigh peered ahead of them, only to realize a pattern she had missed before. "The trees," she whispered, looking to either side of her to be certain. "They stop. It's like it creates a perfect edge."

"This was the edge of the eruption," Queen Mab said softly. "This was as far as it reached. All within that space was either destroyed or distorted. None as much as Fineen himself, though. The Madness twisted him into something different, something not of this world or even of yours. Now he is something in between worlds and far more terrible than anything I had imagined."

"You didn't know, did you? You didn't know what would happen to him?"

Queen Mab's eyes shone with tears as she looked at the ruined land, at odds with the gentle smile that came to her lips as she looked at Shaleigh. "Some mistakes cannot be undone, no matter how hard you try, child."

"This is the edge of Fineen's, the Masked King's domain, what we call the Dark Lands," Teagan's voice was steady as he spoke but his eyes were wide.

Shaleigh turned to the empty land. It looked ruined, but not dangerous. She didn't quite understand why they were so nervous, though she guessed they better understood the dangers than she did. This was a place ruined by magic and she worried about the sickness she had before.

"If this place is steeped in magic, will I be able to pass through it?"

Teagan sighed. "If the Masked King wants you to pass through it, no harm will come to you, but that would mean he's curious."

Shaleigh turned to them with a frown. "But he can't hurt you, can he, Teagan? Why would he hurt his own kind?"

Queen Mab laughed. "He is neither Faerie nor Human any longer, child. The Madness has made him its servant with its own designs. He could turn you into a pair of angry crows and you would be grateful for it."

Shaleigh shivered as a cold wind blasted across the empty expanse. Maybe she had made a mistake. Maybe she should have taken up Queen Mab's offer and gone to the Sanctuary: let the magicians there figure out how to send her back home. At least she wouldn't have to worry about living the rest of her life as a pair of birds.

As annoying as school could be, nobody spat on the ground when she walked by there. There were no Shadow Wolves to chase her or masked kings to deal with. If she asked, Queen Mab would probably let her go too.

That was the hardest part. Nobody was forcing her into the Dark Lands, nobody had a spear to her back pushing her in. In fact, Teagan seemed surprised she hadn't chosen to go to the Sanctuary, and instead she was here, standing on the edge of a decision she could not turn away from.

"You don't have to do this, child," Queen Mab's voice

wavered. She sounded close to tears. Shaleigh turned to her, and the queen tapped the side of her head. "I try not to pry, but sometimes my head gets away from me. If you want to leave, if you want to go back home to your family, I'll help you. This doesn't have to be your fight."

"Yes," Teagan added, swallowing hard. "I won't make you come with me if you don't want to. I would rather know that you were safe."

Shaleigh bit her lip. "I don't know."

A part of her warmed at the thought of going home as she starred out into the vast, cold emptiness. She remembered the warmth of her father's arms around her in a tight hug; remembered Kaeja laughing at some bad joke. They both needed her, and that familiar ache in her chest came again at the thought of her father sobbing without her at his side, of Kaeja hunting through the Treehouse for her.

They weren't the only ones waiting for her though. There were others she had let down.

Mawr and Colin were back in the Garden still, or what remained of the place at least. Whatever happened to them was on her shoulders. She had convinced them both to believe in her, to trust her, and she had let them down. Yes, she could blame Talek, Keriam, Madam Cloom, or Teagan, but at the end of the day, she was the one who convinced them. She was the one they trusted to know what was right.

She couldn't turn her back on Dad or Kaeja, she had to get home, but she also couldn't turn her back on her new friends either. They needed her, maybe even more than

Dad did. She was the one to destroy everything, and she was the one to make it right again.

The ache in her chest came on once more, but she forced it away. She had to do this, whether it was dangerous or even deadly, she had to get back to them. She had to set things right for what she had done.

"No, I'll do it. I have too many people relying on me now. They need me."

Queen Mab nodded. "Yes, they do. I hope you can help them."

"Are you sure?" Teagan asked, narrowing his eyes in the most open expression of concern that she had ever seen from him. "I don't mind you at my side, I just want you to be safe."

She reached out and took hold of his warm hand. "I'm sure. Let's get this over with, okay?"

He gave a small nod and together they stepped closer to the tree line. The cold wind blew harder and Shaleigh winced against it. Teagan squeezed her hand.

"We must stay together at all costs," Teagan warned. "Don't let go of me." His hair whipped around his face.

"Stay safe," Queen Mab said from behind them, her voice sounding distant already. "Stay rooted."

"I'm scared," Shaleigh admitted aloud as her eyes welled with tears.

As if summoned by her words, an indistinct shadow emerged on the other side of the boundary. She thought it had a humanoid shape at first until it drew closer. It was an enormous dog. Its black fur moved in the cold wind, leaving shadowy trails behind it. She could hear it panting as though it was right beside her. Then she caught a whiff of its pungent breath. It smelled like rot and nearly made her gag. When it turned its blazing red eyes toward her, Shaleigh froze out of instinct.

"Teagan?" she asked in a dry whisper.

"The Masked King's Black Dogs keep the boundary line protected." He held up a trembling hand to the creature. "Please, we merely wish to pass through. We want no trouble with you."

The dog huffed and licked its muzzle which was dripping with tendrils of saliva. Its red eyes remained locked on them, unblinking. Shaleigh's heart thundered away in her chest.

"Please," Teagan said again, and lowered his hand.

She wasn't sure what was going to happen if the dog didn't let them pass. Would it kill them? Would it do something worse? Judging by how terrified Teagan was, it would definitely be something bad.

Suddenly the Black Dog's body relaxed, and it sat down on its haunches. Its red eyes, however, did not leave them.

Teagan gave out a shaky breath. "Good, we should be safe to pass through."

"Stay safe," Queen Mab repeated. "Stay rooted." It sounded exactly the same as it had before and Shaleigh turned to glance to Teagan, but he merely shook his head.

"Time works differently here. Many worlds and many whens have exits here, portals that can ensnare you. We must be cautious."

They moved farther in through the barrier line and the wind grew so strong that Shaleigh couldn't breathe.

"Stay safe," Queen Mab said once more from behind

them, her voice barely a whisper now. Shaleigh wanted to turn around and scream at her to be quiet. "Stay rooted." Instead she pulled Teagan closer and wrapped her arm around his as they forced their way through the barrier line.

They suddenly found themselves in a windless wasteland.

LOOKING AROUND, Shaleigh knew that nothing could be alive here for miles. The ground was a dull brown and cracked in all directions like shattered glass. What should have been trees looked like black, rotten hands reaching for the sky, breaking through the soil in a last effort at escape. There was no wind here and the stillness along with the silence made the hairs stand up on her arms.

Their ragged breathing sounded coarse and inappropriate in this place. As though just being alive was an insult here.

"Teagan?" Shaleigh whispered.

There was no sunlight, but there also wasn't any nighttime either. The sky was locked in a hazy unknown, like a fog had hidden it. It reflected the dull brown of the earth and made everything feel surreal.

"It's alright," he said. "We can make it through." Once again, the calmness of his voice didn't meet his eyes. He gripped her hand tighter and she got the impression that he was hanging onto her just as much as she was hanging onto him.

"You've never been here, have you?"

"No." He gave her a sympathetic look. "I've only had to pass through the Dark Lands once, and when I stepped through the boundary line I appeared on the other side - exactly where I wanted to be. I've never been... inside before."

"I sure wish you had told me that before we stepped through."

"I don't see why that would have mattered."

Their conversation was cut short when another shadowed shape approached, seeming to float toward them across the cracked wasteland like ink coalescing on water. The ink morphed into another Black Dog, its muzzle narrower than the previous one, but its eyes just as red and just as threatening.

It circled them slowly, each pant so loud that Shaleigh winced at the sound. *This is it,* she thought. *We somehow already made a mistake and this one is going to devour us because of it.*

After circling them once, it froze and cocked its head to the side. It gave a deep sudden chuff that made her and Teagan jump, before it bounded off. She watched as it ran into the distance. At first, she thought they had scared it, but quickly realized it was more likely it was being called: it ran with excitement as though its master had just walked through the front door. A cold chill went down Shaleigh's spine as she realized she could see something in the distance that hadn't been there before.

"What is that?" Teagan asked, squinting in the direction she was looking.

"I was about to ask you the same thing."

It was as dark as the trees but it was far taller than any

of them and seemed to climb up into the sky. Although it was hazy at this distance, she thought she could make out movement.

Teagan shook his head. "We shouldn't go that way. If the Masked King is here, that would be his throne. We must do everything we can to avoid him. Come on," he urged and pulled her in the opposite direction; Shaleigh was happy to follow.

The throne, if that's what it was, freaked her out. There was something about it that made her feel like something dangerous was watching them. It was a feeling she got sometimes in abandoned buildings, a feeling of something dark, cold, and malicious that watched her. A feeling like she was not supposed to be there and was trespassing on someone else's land. Usually she and Kaeja would chalk that mood up to spooks and either adjust their photography plans or just leave the place altogether. They didn't mess with that sort of stuff. Here there was no easy escape.

They walked for several minutes in the opposite direction, but when Shaleigh looked over her shoulder, the throne they wanted to escape was still there. In fact, it was closer.

"Teagan..." Shaleigh pulled at his hand until he turned.

"What? That's not-"

"Let me guess," she started sarcastically, "distance doesn't work the same way here either."

He pursed his lips. "Either that or it's chasing us."

Her eyes widened before she glared. "Why would you even imply that right now?"

"I'm sorry, I don't have an explanation for any of this."

Shaleigh looked to see that the throne was so close that she could now easily make out what looked like a person in gold who sat upon it. The throne was made of the same blackened trees that spotted the earth and looked like they had been thatched together. Even from her distance she could see ends of sticks poking out on the edges and up into the sky. The chair of the throne appeared uneven, uncomfortable, and unpleasant.

Her instinct was to run, but that wouldn't do any good here, would it?

With a deep breath, she turned to the throne. "Come on." This time she pulled Teagan with her and together they approached it.

As they got nearer, Shaleigh's certainty that it was a Human began to dwindle. It was dressed in robes of golden silk that wrapped an emaciated frame, hanging so loose she thought of a decorated Halloween skeleton displayed in a store at the mall. The fabric might have once been very expensive, but now it was worn with rain and dirt. A mask was settled over its face, the same gold color as the rest of its body.

"Is it dead?" Shaleigh asked.

"I'm not sure," Teagan said in a fearful voice. "Let's just keep going."

Just as they were about to pass it, the head turned to look at them, and Shaleigh nearly jumped out of her skin. The mask had a stick attacked to the side as though it was for a masquerade, and the creature held it with one hand, barely keeping it over the face underneath.

"Now is that any way to greet me?" The voice sounded

dry and raspy and made Shaleigh's breathing go up a notch.

Teagan's clammy hand trembled in her grip. As terrified as they were, neither of them were going to let go.

"My apologies," Teagan said breathlessly. Surely his heart was hammering in his chest as loudly as hers was. "We weren't sure if you were—"

The creature, a man, tilted his head to the side, moving the mask along with it. "Alive?" he hissed and the sound came from all around them, not just from him.

Shaleigh turned but saw no one else there. Just the two of them in this wasteland with this disturbing specter. When she looked back, the man was pushing himself to his feet, his knees snapped and creaked as though they hadn't been used in a long time.

"It's been so long," he said with a tinge of excitement. "Since I've had uninvited company. I don't even know how to begin."

"Come on," Teagan whispered to her, pulling her away from the throne. "We have to get away from him. We can't stay here any longer."

Together they began running. Their feet crunched on the ground, noisy from the emptiness all around them.

"Who was that?" she asked, trying to keep up with Teagan's long strides.

"The Masked King."

As if in response to his words, a laughter echoed around them. They stopped and Teagan pulled Shaleigh close again. They turned, trying to see where the laughter was coming from, looking for some kind of an exit, but there was nothing out here. The throne of the Masked

King wasn't even visible anymore, and they hadn't been running that fast. Abruptly, the only sound was their desperate panting.

"I don't think he's going to let us leave, Teagan."

"Ahh," the Masked King's voice echoed. "So that's the Faerie's name. It does sound familiar."

He stopped speaking but the *R* in the last word seemed to extend far longer than it should have and morphed into a distant shriek. Shaleigh glanced to Teagan with wide eyes, hoping to find recognition there, some sense of security, but he was just as confused as she was.

The wailing grew louder. Whatever it was drew closer to them and the shriek began to hurt Shaleigh's ears. She pulled her hand free from Teagan and pushed her palms against her ears, trying her best to drown out the sound. Teagan winced as the shriek turned back to a wail and looped an arm around Shaleigh's before covering his own ears.

Shaleigh spotted something black separate from one of the tree husks. It moved across the ground like a mass of silk blown forward by the wind, only there was no wind. The blackened husks of trees didn't even sway.

She considered running but was afraid that they would get separated. And as terrifying as this thing was that approached them, the idea of being alone here frightened her more.

The black, silky mound grew into a vertical shape and wrapped itself into something like a human shape. A hood appeared and white hair spilled out. Then the face appeared. It was a white, ghastly face, and it was difficult to imagine it ever belonging to a human. The eyes were black holes, the mouth was gaping.

It took a step forward and Shaleigh could hear the shuffle of the silk as it scraped over the dirt. She wasn't sure how that was even possible considering how loud the wailing was even though she still had her ears covered.

She felt someone tug her arm and turned to see Teagan grabbing at her desperately. She had left his side; she had started walking toward it. When had she done that? How had she done that with his arm wrapped around hers?

Teagan was saying something, but she couldn't hear it – there was only the wailing and the shuffling of silk. He had let go of his left ear to grab her, and there was blood trickling down from it. She gasped at the sight and quickly rushed back to his side. She was glad she did because she felt what might have been fingernails brush against her arm right before she moved away.

A tremor went through her as Teagan wrapped an arm around her protectively, keeping his gaze glued to her and not the wailing thing approaching them.

"Please," she said, hearing her own voice reverberate in her head. She wasn't sure if she could be heard over the sound of its wailing. "We don't want to leave; we just want to pass through."

The wailing ended abruptly. She glanced to Teagan to see him releasing his other ear; he nodded to her. Shaleigh stole a glance behind her again to see that the thing had closed its mouth, though its black eyes watched them carefully. She could clearly see it was a woman, or at least it might have been at one time.

"There is no passing through without my permission, and I do not permit it," the Masked King's voice came from everywhere again in its familiar, mocking tone.

Shaleigh swallowed, staring into Teagan's eyes. He shook his head. He thought they might still escape. He thought there was a chance to leave, but Shaleigh knew better. This was the third ruler she was now forced to deal with and knowing that he considered himself the king of this land, then he must have an ego, just like the Faerie Queen, and just like Madam Cloom.

She closed her eyes briefly to gather her strength. If they tried to run again, and that cloaked woman wailed, she doubted she would be able to hear again. Teagan may have already lost his hearing in his left ear, even if the bleeding had stopped.

"We would like an audience with you, Masked King."

Teagan winced at her words and glanced away. His expression hurt more than she had expected. She had to remind herself that she didn't need his approval anymore, she needed to get them out of here.

The cloaked woman backed away and Shaleigh allowed herself to feel a small amount of victory. Then the throne appeared beside them, almost as if it emerged from a fog.

Where they had kept their distance before and couldn't see the detail, Shaleigh could see clearly each piece of scorched wood now.

The scent of burned wood was strong, as though the throne had only just been pieced together. The base of it was thatched together in thick bundles, but the back of the chair was a bunch of pointed black trees that reached up into the sky. It reminded her of Queen Mab's throne, but as though it had been destroyed in a terrible blaze. And where Queen Mab's throne was covered in flowers and almost looked like trees were growing through it, this one seemed to be a throne of death and decay. There was a faint smell beneath the burned wood that wanted to take over her senses, one that she had to push to recognize. It was pungent and repellent, but she couldn't quite figure out what it was.

"Thank you for wrangling them, Ms. Kasey." The Masked King put a hand on the cloaked woman's shoulder and the woman shuddered. Then he approached them.

Teagan still had an arm wrapped around her and Shaleigh was grateful for it now because she forgot to breathe for a moment.

The Masked King's golden robe had tiny intricate details all over. The fabric didn't gleam like it probably once would have; instead, it was dull and dingy. He still held the golden mask to his face, but up close she could see the taut, mummified flesh of his throat as he spoke.

It was hard to believe that he had ever been alive, or even that he still was. From what little she could see of his skin during horrid glimpses behind his mask, he more resembled a corpse than anything living.

"What a strange pair of visitors... The notorious Teagan of the Garden who I've heard so much about." Shaleigh felt Teagan tense when the Masked King put a gloved hand out to caress Teagan's cheek. "A Faerie with a lust for power, who left his lover behind for a certain idealist magician." He tsked. "A Faerie who turned his back on his own kind for a man who filled his bored mind with many promises." He leaned in closer and Shaleigh now knew what the pungent scent was earlier that she couldn't identify - it was the Masked King's decaying body. "Only some of his promises weren't really true, were they?"

Teagan clenched his jaw and the creature gave a low, hissing laugh before he mocked, "He didn't tell you it would involve stealing from your homeland. He didn't tell you that you would be responsible for killing so many Human children."

Teagan shook his head. "No, it wasn't like that!"

"Teagan the Treacherous," the Masked King hissed. "Hated by his people, hated by his kind. Was it worth it?"

Teagan lowered his head, his eyes glassy. "He loved me," he whispered.

"Of course, he did," was the Masked King's reply, his voice rattling with sarcasm. "I'm sure he told you that often."

The creature picked up a tendril of Teagan's red hair to bring between his fingers. "He *coerced* you, didn't he? He changed the binding ritual without you knowing. You wanted to be bound to him, but instead, he bound you to his precious Garden." Teagan brought a hand up to shield his eyes as a sob escaped his lips. "He bound you to eternal servitude and you loved him too much to refuse."

Shaleigh pulled on Teagan's arm. "Don't let him do this to you. He's trying to break you down, but you can't let him!" She glanced to the shrouded woman and remembered her tremble when the Masked King touched her. "I think he's trying to trap us here," she said, no longer caring whether the Masked King heard her. She wasn't about to let either one of them get pulled into this sick game or given a fate like that banshee. "He's trying to hurt you."

Teagan moved his hand away showing his face wet with tears. "But he's right, and that's the worst part. Cathal lied to me." His breath hitched. "At the last moment he changed the binding. I had trusted him with everything. I thought he... no, he *did* love me. But," he shook his head, "I thought he would bind me to *him*, not to the Garden."

The Masked King snarled. "You still believe he loved you after all these years? You struggled to bring his dream to life, even if it meant countless deaths; even if many lived in fear and poverty. You carried on what he began because you fell in love with that power."

Teagan's face hardened. "I didn't do that for me. I did it for the good of many. The Garden was a great kingdom. It was a sanctuary, despite its rules. It helped so many to live and thrive. I went out of my way to ensure the safety of those at my side."

"For those at your side, certainly, but not for everyone. The Humans didn't get such protection, did they?"

Teagan shook his head. "I tried to help them when I could, but it was... difficult."

"Ahh, how noble of you to go out of your way to protect so many. I'm sure you improved countless lives."

Teagan hung his head as the Masked King circled around him, hovering like a vulture ready to sink its bloody beak in. When had she and Teagan even let go? She tried to move closer to him again, but the Masked King intervened and said, "I'm sure the Garden was a great kingdom, but it is no longer that, is it, Shaleigh Mallett?"

"Don't even start," she spat. "If you really cared about the fate of the people in the Garden, then you wouldn't be delaying us. You would grant us speedy passage through your realm. Don't even pretend that those people matter to you."

He laughed; a sinister sound that made her skin go clammy. "I can see how you brought down the Garden with a temperament like that, child. Only, you have your own shadows, don't you? Everyone does, even if they work hard to hide them." He moved fluidly over to her, reminding her of a spider, barely keeping that golden mask over his face. He crouched down to look at her closer and she could see the yellow of his eyes. She recoiled at the stench he brought with him, fresh and startling. She covered her nose as he cocked his head to the side.

"A father... afflicted with his own form of Madness." He grinned. Shaleigh could hear the sound of his skin stretch across his face. "He lives in his own fantasy world and you struggle to help him, but you can't bring yourself to feel any empathy for him, can you? He's a lost cause, just another crazy that you have to deal with."

She narrowed her eyes. "That's not who I am anymore. Maybe you've gotten stale in here without any visitors around to keep you company."

He gave out a raspy laugh and stepped closer. Shaleigh recoiled away from him, but he took up what little space she had left, bringing the mask almost to her nose.

"Please, leave her alone," Teagan said. "She is innocent in all of this."

"Don't worry, I haven't forgotten you, *Master* Teagan." Teagan grew silent and the Masked King focused again on her. "There's a mother too, though she's more distant. Lost, even."

"Stop it," Shaleigh whispered.

"You're conflicted about her, but there's a seed of anger in you. A dark patch you hide away. You hate the woman, don't you?" His words pushed into her mind, more painfully than anything Queen Mab had done, and memories came back to her unbidden.

She was filled with shame when her father bawled uncontrollably at a parent/teacher conference when she was little - her poor teacher watching wide-eyed and pulling out tissues. She had only asked if her mother could make it. Then the memory faded, and suddenly she was a toddler watching Dad as he hung up her mother's freshly pressed dresses on the closet door. He had such a serene expression on his face and told Shaleigh that she would be home soon. Shaleigh had believed it and cried herself to sleep for a week, asking why she hadn't come home yet. Then, that memory faded and she was at Dean Hammond's party, listening as he explained how she was out of town on a work trip for the millionth time.

That familiar anger bubbled up. It was an old feeling, but she recognized it for what it was. It wasn't hatred, it was resentment at her mother for stealing her father from her, but it felt so miniscule now. After everything she had been through, she looked at that anger and that frustration and saw it for what it truly was: a child coping with her father's mental illness.

The memories faded completely and Shaleigh met the gaze of the Masked King with renewed confidence. "No, I don't hate her," she said, even though her mouth was dry and her tongue felt swollen.

The Masked King reached out a hand to her, assuming he had won, assuming she was nothing more than that embarrassed child again, but she wasn't. She was so much more than that.

She slapped the hand away, and it felt like slapping a doll aside because there was so little resistance. Finding more courage than she thought she was capable of, she shoved him back by his shoulders, feeling the frail fabric of his robe crinkle like aged tulle.

He stumbled to keep his footing, and she spotted his bare feet peeking out from beneath his robe, as dead and dry as mummies in the museum. His amusement was gone for just a moment and looking into his yellowed eyes Shaleigh could see past his disturbing visage to the despairing Faerie he had once been.

In that brief moment he reminded her of her father, and she pitied him. Then, the Masked King threw his head back and barked laughter into the empty sky, exposing his throat clumped with pieces of dust and black knots like a plague victim's. The brief moment of pity was gone, and she took a deep breath to steady herself. He was far worse than Dad and she knew in that moment that there was no way she would be able to truly reason with him.

The areas on his shoulders where she had touched him

still bore her palm prints. She looked down at her hands, seeing bits of the fabric stuck there, like dry, decayed tissue paper and rubbed them off on her dress, knowing on some level that it was supposed to frighten her, but not letting it.

"Foolish child! I suppose Queen Mab failed to tell you that anyone who passes into my realm belongs to me." He gave another raspy laugh. "You two are now *my* toys."

"Toys?" Shaleigh asked, feeling anger bubble up again. No, now he was trying to use it against her. She needed to control it. She needed to use it to fuel her - not lash out.

She glanced over to the shrouded woman, determined not to meet the same fate. So instead of yelling at him, she collected herself and folded her arms. "I don't think you need any more toys. I think you have enough already."

Teagan shook his head at her, but Shaleigh didn't break eye contact with the Masked King. This time she was ready for him.

He padded toward her again, his shoulders hunched like a predator, leaning in so close she had to lean away and resist the urge to push him away again. "There's always more room for toys, my dear. Always more room for entertainment."

Shaleigh swallowed the fear that threatened to take hold of her. No, she had to believe in herself. She knew what he really was beneath the facade. "It looks like all your toys do is keep people away. You like to stay alone in here, don't you? You like solitude."

He cocked his head to the side. "What's your point?"

"You don't need toys. You need people who understand you. You need people to talk to."

He gave an annoyed grunt and pulled back allowing her to take a deep breath of clean air. Then, she went for the jugular.

"You like being alone, you clearly don't take care of yourself, and everything around you is dead. The only entertainment you get is out of tormenting others. I'm no doctor, but if you were in the Human World, you would probably have a terrible case of depression."

He narrowed his eyes, but to her amazement, he didn't respond. She wondered how long it had been since someone actually spoke to him instead of screaming in terror. She pressed to see how far he would let her go. "What's your story then, Masked King? From what I heard, I'm not the only one to have destroyed a Kingdom, am I? You got rid of one too, whether you wanted to or not."

Despite the mask hiding his features, she could tell from his eyes that she had hit a nerve. He gave only the slightest flinch and she had to resist smirking.

Instead she gazed right back into those creepy yellowed eyes. "Did you watch them die when it finally happened? I heard you were in the center of town. Did they hurt you before-"

"That's enough," he growled, and Shaleigh's head seemed to vibrate with the sound in warning like a bad case of tinnitus.

The world spun, and she fell to her knees. Startled, warm blood dripped down her nostril and onto her lips, coppery and surreal. Her head was throbbing. What had he even done to her?

Teagan crouched down beside her. "Shaleigh! Are you alright? What happened?"

"...messed with my head," she said sluggishly.

Teagan turned to the creature. "What have you done?!"

The Masked King turned his back to them and jumped effortlessly back up onto his throne. He didn't answer at first as he sat down and let his golden robe flutter down like decomposing butterfly wings. "Your Human is too perceptive for her own good. I'll let her live, for now, simply because this has been... enlightening." His free hand gripped the arm of his throne. "However, if she speaks to me like that again, I won't be so kind."

Teagan helped her to her feet. She was shaky but better. The throbbing in her head had ceased leaving her disoriented like she had just gotten off a rough roller coaster.

"Don't worry," she managed. "You clearly don't want to talk about things that bother you."

Teagan looked at her with wide eyes. It was obvious he wanted to lecture her, but also knew this was neither the time nor the place. Oddly enough it made her want to laugh, but that would only make him worry more. She turned her attention to the Masked King.

"Please, we just want to go back and fix what we screwed up." She stepped forward, wiping the back of her hand across her nose. Oddly enough, the pain helped her focus. "If you could fix what happened, even to those terrible people in Loburg, wouldn't you?"

He looked down at her silently. She noticed the hand that held the golden mask over his face shook. "There were no survivors, but if there had been, I would have personally found each one and murdered them as grue-somely as possible."

Shaleigh felt a chill go through her at his words. Her reply tumbled out before she realized it, "But why? You didn't know them that well, did you? Surely they didn't all deserve that."

"Not everyone deserves second chances, Shaleigh of the Human World. You might not know that yet, but you may understand that one day." He drummed his fingers on a bit of burned wood, dragging a gloved finger over the pointed end. "You are perceptive and that may be your undoing. However, you don't trust as easily as I once did, or as easily as Teagan does. You may survive your journey yet."

She didn't expect to hear praise after digging up such old wounds. She thought she had understood where he was coming from, and probably pushed him too far because of it. At this point he could either kill them both or worse, but at least she had tried. At least she hadn't just sat back and let him destroy Teagan – or herself - piece by piece.

"You are a force of change, Shaleigh Mallett, and you bring it wherever you go. You will be remembered and feared by many." He waved a hand through the air. "I will let you continue on your quest of change and permit you to carry on with your own form of destruction."

Shaleigh blinked at him. What did he mean her "own form of destruction?" Yes, she had brought down the Garden, but she had no intention of causing any *more* harm. She wanted to help save it and to help her friends. What did he mean?

He turned to look down at Teagan. "You are a different story, Teagan. You are as broken inside as I once was." He put a hand to his own heart. "You have been lied to, used, abused, vilified, insulted, and preyed upon. Outside of my realm, you may suffer the same fate all over again. I offer you the chance to escape all of that nonsense and stay here with me."

He waved his hand and the world around them went gray and obtuse before everything turned green and thick foliage surrounded them. Those damn coral colored flowers of Madam Cloom's filled the air with their sweet scent and Shaleigh couldn't help but breathe them in deeply. They made her think of Madam Cloom... and then the way she was groping at her missing mouth on the floor of her own throne room. She winced.

The Masked King was the only constant. Even the shrouded woman had disappeared. He sat like a horrible reminder of the impermanence of this place. Shaleigh could still smell the undercurrents of the burned wooden chair and the Masked King's pungent odor.

"If you want a throne," the Masked King hissed. "I can make it. If you want a gazebo, like this one, it can be done."

Teagan was looking around him in utter shock. He let go of Shaleigh and she saw his hands shaking. There was such a terrible pain in his eyes at the sight of his destroyed creation brought to life in an instant. Was it so different from what his own magic had been? And yet... once again it would be someone else's power, not his own.

"If you want power, I can make you feel like you have it. It's almost as good as having the power yourself, isn't it?" There was an intensity in the Masked King's gaze from atop his throne that made Shaleigh uncomfortable. This wouldn't be without a cost, would it? Was it ever?

She took Teagan's hand in hers, and he looked down at her with a wild expression. It softened after a moment and he squeezed her hand.

Teagan shut his eyes, as though never wanting to see his beautiful creation again. "As tempting as it is, I'm afraid I must decline the offer. I've walked away from that part of my life and nothing will recreate it again. Anything you create would only be partly true, and not truly my masterpiece." Despite the surety in his voice, she saw tears trail down his cheeks.

The world went gray before turning back into the disturbing wasteland again.

"Very well," the Masked King said then gave a sigh. "It was worth showing you the possibility, just so you know what you're giving up."

Teagan flinched at his words.

"I will let you both pass through my realm then, Teagan of the Faeries and Shaleigh Mallett of the Human World. I will let you return to your journey to fix what you both have destroyed." He cocked his head to the side. "But please, let Keriam know that I send my regards. His immortality is not without its cost, and I do expect my payment."

Shaleigh gaped at him. "What are you talking about?"

"Keriam..." Teagan gasped.

"Follow Ms. Kasey. She will show you to safe passage."

The Masked King, along with his throne, glimmered like a heat wave and gave Shaleigh a headache just looking at them before they faded completely. Shaleigh and Teagan stood staring at the empty spot where they had been, both shaking from his final words.

"Did I hear that right?" Shaleigh asked, still trying to find the right words. "Did he admit that he granted immortality to Keriam? Is that the same magician you told me about?"

Teagan nodded. "I'm afraid it is."

~

"IMMORTALITY."

The very thought of it made Shaleigh grow cold. Or perhaps it was the desolate wasteland of the Masked King's realm. She and Teagan followed the shrouded woman, the one called Ms. Kasey. Her name also made Shaleigh uneasy. It was a normal name, one that might fit one of her father's colleagues or the name of a nurse at the dentist office. It didn't suit the wraith who walked ahead of them, her feet moving through the dirt but never making a sound. And she never looked back. Shaleigh couldn't even hear the woman breathing, unlike her and Teagan.

"I had no idea such an ability was even possible," Teagan whispered, keeping his voice low as though the reverent space they were in demanded it. He was gripping Shaleigh's hand tighter than she would have liked, but she wasn't going to complain. Not in this place.

"You sound almost jealous," the words had come without her even meaning to say them aloud, and immediately she regretted them. She glanced over to see the shock fall across his features like melting ice. "I'm sorry," she said, adding quickly, "I didn't mean that. I don't know what I meant really."

He gave a deep sigh. She could still see the patches of wetness on his cheeks from where he had been crying earlier, giving his cheeks a pink flush that his hair only drew attention to. The shame she felt deepened.

"It's alright," he reassured, meeting her gaze. "You know just about all of my mistakes now, I suppose. All my follies that I've tried to keep secret for so long have been unearthed for you. You saw my jealousy before it had even consciously occurred to me."

She shook her head. "Yeah, but it's not fair to you. You may have been hungry for power once, but that shouldn't define you forever."

They went quiet as they followed Ms. Kasey around a lifeless blackened tree. The scent of burned wood was so strong it made Shaleigh sneeze.

"If you had asked me before if I wanted to live in that dreamland of his, wielding absolute power, I would have accepted it without hesitation."

Shaleigh arched an eyebrow at him. "Without hesitation, huh?"

He shrugged. "Alright, I would have had some qualms about it, but standing there in my old gazebo... I didn't realize how much I missed it."

"You can't go back to that life anymore."

He gave a small smile. "I know. I also realized in that moment how much I needed to repair what I had done."

For the first time since they landed in that mushroom ring in the woods, Shaleigh felt like they had finally become a team. It was a relief, especially considering that Teagan had been about to leave her with Queen Mab before, as though that would somehow be any safer than this.

A black shadow moved just out of her vision, letting Shaleigh know the Black Dog was coming. Still, seeing it slink up beside the shrouded woman made a shudder go down her spine.

This was a different Black Dog from the two earlier. This one was scrawny and looked like it had been starved. Its scraggily fur had wavered into tendrils of shadows that trailed behind it. Its skin clung to its ribs and sunken belly. The dog only turned once to look at them, but its red eyes made her forget to breathe. Teagan whispered her name and it pulled her out of the terrified haze she had almost fallen into.

Then the shrouded woman and the dog stopped. The woman pointed forward without a word, her eyes watching them as the Black Dog trotted towards Shaleigh. The scent of decay wafted behind it, reminiscent of the Masked King.

"Is this the exit, or another trick?" Teagan asked the woman, but she merely pointed again. There was nothing special about the land ahead of them. It looked just like all the land behind them: the same burnt lumber look.

Teagan stepped forward like he was going to ask further, but Shaleigh remembered what had happened the last time Ms. Kasey had opened her mouth - Teagan's left ear was still stained with blood.

"It's fine," she said, locking eyes with him. Teagan backed down, though he was clearly anxious. "It could be a trick, but the Masked King gave us his word. This is his land, so we'll have to trust that to be true."

Shaleigh took a deep breath and stepped forward. The Black Dog moved to walk alongside her as Teagan trailed only a step or two behind. He didn't want to lead this time and she couldn't blame him. The Masked King had very nearly taken him to keep in his dreamland.

She just hadn't realized how close he had come to accepting the offer.

The Black Dog was more unnerving as it trotted happily beside her, its shadowy tendrils twitching occasionally. Where the shrouded woman hadn't made a sound when she walked or breathed, the Black Dog panted like a living dog - it just didn't look like it ought to be alive.

A cold wind swept through her, nearly taking her breath away with its strength. She shut her eyes against it on reflex and when she opened them again, the Black Dog was gone. This had to be it. She gripped Teagan's hand tighter and continued forward, the wind whipping around her and making her shiver. Teagan came up beside her as they walked uphill the last few paces and the cold wind finally died down.

They stopped and leaned against a tree trunk on top of the hill, taking in deep breaths and allowing themselves to finally relax. Teagan sat down on the ground with a grunt. "I need a moment, Shaleigh, my apologies."

"That's okay." She sat down beside him. "I need several of them."

He gave a quiet chuckle at her lame joke.

She looked around at the few trees around them.

There weren't many and they mostly looked rather sickly, but at least they were alive. She leaned back against the tree trunk and stared up at the blue sky, that same robin's egg blue that she had grown to love. The sun was setting in the distance and it would soon be nightfall, but she was just glad to see the sky again.

"I think we did pretty well in there, you know that?"

Teagan gave a nervous laugh. "If you say so. We very nearly died. Your tongue nearly got us both killed."

"You were the one that argued with him."

"I didn't argue, I just disagreed with his statements."

Shaleigh went quiet when a pair of red eyes glinted momentarily into view for a second before disappearing again, only a foot away from them. She gaped at Teagan who had clearly seen it too based on his wide eyes.

"Maybe we should keep moving," she said, once again tense and mentally kicking herself for thinking they were safe. Was there a place that was safe in this land? She doubted it.

They both got to their feet, not saying a word.

After putting several trees between them and the Masked King's realm, they soon heard the first bird call and then they both relaxed again.

"Do you think it's safe?" she asked.

"If Queen Mab felt it was safe at around this distance to discuss the Masked King's background, then we should be safe too."

"I know you mentioned they patrolled the boundary line, but I didn't think we would be able to see them outside of it."

Teagan shook his head. "I didn't either. I think I've

discovered renewed respect for the merchants who traverse the outer edge twice a year to bring supplies to the City of the Fae."

She pointed over her shoulder. "They go near *that*? Just to *sell* things?"

Teagan smiled. "My kind are immortal and most of us have some form of funds to our names. I can assure you that we make it worth the trip."

"I don't think you could pay me enough to do that. *Ever*."

Teagan laughed.

Shaleigh thought of walking along the outer edge of that place. Did they have to sleep there overnight? Surely, they would plan to make sure they wouldn't. That would be crazy.

"I'm still amazed," Teagan said as they reached the top of another hill. "To think that Keriam the Clever came to the Masked King of all creatures and asked for immortality, and he actually granted it to him."

"What do you think he wanted in return?"

"I'm not sure. I don't really know what a being like him would want or need to be honest. He clearly doesn't need food or supplies of any kind. I doubt he needs to sleep. He could use a new set of clothes, but I don't think he's interested in that either."

"He wanted entertainment though, he did mention that."

"Yes, but that's so... *medieval*."

Shaleigh couldn't hold back a laugh at that. Teagan said medieval like it was a terrible word, yet here they were living in castles and writing with quills and parchment paper. "You do realize how ironic that is, right?"

Teagan was silent. In fact, she noticed, she didn't even hear his footsteps anymore. She turned quickly, afraid that perhaps they had lost each other somehow, but Teagan stood staring off into the distance and Shaleigh went back to stand at his side.

"What is it?" she whispered.

"Smoke," he hissed. "As though someone has lit many bonfires."

Shaleigh squinted in the direction he was looking, but couldn't see anything but trees.

"I can't see it," he clarified, sounding annoyed. "I can smell it. And it smells... terrible."

Shaleigh felt her stomach drop. "That's not good, is it?"

"No," he said, frowning deeply. "It's strange, I don't know what they're burning."

It wasn't until they had walked another mile before Shaleigh could identify it. It smelled like burned beef.

PART III
HUNTED

OLD MEMORIES

Colin

It was dark by the time they saw the lights of the City of the Fae. The treetops glittered with candlelight which fought against the intense darkness that seemed to linger ever since they skirted the Dark Lands. It was only after seeing a couple of them that Colin realized they were clustered, candlelit homes.

Colin suddenly thought of Master Teagan and wondered if he hated being closed up inside of High Castle all the time. Was that why he went out of his way to make the hallways so wide and curved? Perhaps it was the reason for the eclectic design on the outside too, with all the doors and windows. Maybe it was an homage to where he grew up, high off the ground and in homes out of reach from outsiders.

He could see the Faeries watching from the branches,

standing without a hint of fear on limbs that shouldn't be able to hold their weight. A couple of homes they passed were adorned with flowers. He could spot the crimson or blue petals even from their distance and wondered if maybe Master Teagan had been the one to introduce the flowers to Madam Cloom. Maybe he had offered to plant them in her throne room.

Then there had been the Garden's gazebo, which didn't seem so strange now that Colin had seen where he had come from. If circumstances were different and he wasn't getting dragged along by a vicious magician and a mad Faerie, he wished that he had gotten the chance to visit sooner, maybe with Master Teagan.

Looking at how beautiful everything was, even in the middle of the night, Colin just couldn't fathom why Teagan would've ever wanted to leave it. The place felt like a dream.

He looked ahead to see Talek purposefully keeping his head down and refraining from looking up into the tree branches. Was he embarrassed to be here with a military troop? They couldn't possibly think this was an invasion. There were too few of them. Then again, Talek alone could probably kill a number of them if the fight with the minotaurs earlier was any indication.

Even more strange was that the Faeries weren't shouting at them or making threats, only watching in silence. Colin wasn't quite sure if that was good or bad. He preferred when people told you exactly how they felt about you, rather than stare down at you awkwardly and make you have to guess.

The troop's footsteps, Mawr's lumbering steps, and his

own nervous breathing were the only accompaniment to the chorus of crickets. The silence was intimidating.

"They're watching us, aren't they?" Mawr asked in a whisper.

Colin had begun to understand that his friend had multiple levels of fear, multiple levels of how terrified the poor guy was depending on the level of danger he saw they were in. The only time he had really heard Mawr this terrified before was when he had found him in the corner of his cell back in the Garden and Lieutenant Varg had asked him to measure his head for a new pair of spectacles. That felt like a lifetime ago. Even when they witnessed three soldiers disappear into the Dark Lands or when they were staring down Keriam the Magician, he didn't seem as scared as he did now.

"They're just curious," Colin said, stroking between his ears, a habit he had started doing consistently because it seemed as if Mawr was always on the verge of collapsing into a lump of fear and whimpers. "They're not doing anything, they're just watching. This is their home, remember? They're probably just as scared of us as we are of them."

Mawr glanced back at him. "Do you think so?"

He nodded and gave his warmest smile. "Sure! That's why they're keeping their distance."

Mawr looked ahead and shuddered. "But - but they aren't!"

Colin followed his gaze and saw a group of Faeries moving toward them. There must have been at least twenty and judging by their clothes and the weapons they carried, they were ready for a fight. All except for one. She was a short woman with a crown of flowers and looked nice enough, even with her stern eyes.

The procession came to a stop and the soldiers in front parted so Keriam could step forward. "Queen Mab! I am honored to meet you in person."

Colin noticed that Keriam had this annoying way of talking where the words ought to be respectful, but they came out completely opposite. Currently, he sounded like he was mocking her, and Colin clenched his jaw. That really wasn't the best way to start the meeting.

"Good evening, Keriam the Clever. I don't think I've ever had the pleasure of inviting you to our beautiful city. Yet, you come here with a swarm of Humans at your command. Surely a magician who is so clever doesn't need quite so many bodyguards."

Colin could practically feel the anger that this comment caused in the surrounding soldiers, but they didn't say a word. He was proud of them. He wasn't sure if he would have been able to keep his cool in their shoes.

Keriam gave a cocky laugh and Talek gave out a short chuckle, as though the laughter was infectious. The Faerie stood close behind his master, but kept his arms folded and his eyes averted.

The queen stepped forward and Lieutenant Varg's soldiers in front lifted their arms in preparation. "Please," she said, ignoring the spears aimed at her. "I only wish to speak to my dear Talek."

"He does not obey you any longer, Queen Mab. He has a new master now."

The queen didn't respond or even turn to acknowledge Keriam. Instead she kept her gaze focused on Talek.

It was as though they were the only two in the entire forest. Finally, Talek gave a deep sigh and stepped forward, motioning the soldiers to lower their arms. Queen Mab pulled Talek into a tight embrace, placing her head against his shoulder. It was such a motherly act that it caught Colin off guard.

"I'm glad you've come home, Talek."

Talek pulled away from her, distant and somewhat confused. "I'm not here to stay, my queen. Keriam is my new master now. You know what we seek."

Her kind gaze turned hard as she stepped back from him. "Then you know the rules. Humans are not permitted in the City of the Fae. We haven't permitted Humans here for millennia."

Keriam gave his annoying laugh again. "Now that's not what I heard. I understand that a child of the Human World recently visited your realm and she was not killed." Queen Mab gave him a vicious glance, but Keriam's smug expression didn't fade. "I understand that the pair may still be kept safe in your homeland."

"I can assure you that is not the case."

Keriam shrugged. "If I've learned anything from my dealings with Faeries, it's that their word cannot be trusted."

At this, Colin heard shouts and hisses of dissent from above them in the trees, and from other Faeries watching in the distance that he hadn't even known were there. He wasn't exactly an expert on how to negotiate with queens, but he was pretty sure you weren't supposed to show up in her kingdom and insult her in front of her people.

Despite the outcry though, Queen Mab didn't falter

under his gaze. "As I'm sure you learned in your lengthy time studying in the Sanctuary of Magicians, Keriam, we welcome any other creature to our lands, just not Humans. Anyone in your troop who isn't Human is more than welcome to come search for this supposed child of the Human World if you think I'm lying."

"What about Teagan?" Talek screamed at her and made both Colin and Mawr jump. "Is he here? Are you hiding him as well?"

Queen Mab gave him a pitiful expression. "No, Talek. He's not here. I'm sorry, but your search for him is in vain. I do not harbor him, and I've never kept him here."

"*Liar.*" Talek slapped her across the face, hard enough that she nearly stumbled to the ground, but caught herself at the last moment. The Faeries around Queen Mab rushed forward, so did the soldiers behind Talek. Colin ducked down on Mawr's back, wondering if they had survived passing by the Dark Lands only to be killed here instead.

Then Queen Mab held up a hand and her Faeries came to a halt. Lieutenant Varg held up a fist, calling orders to his soldiers to back down. Keriam had stepped away from Talek in surprise. Despite his threats, he had very little control over his Faerie servant, bound or not.

Talek was oblivious to the battle that had nearly broken out. "He's here," he shouted. "He must be here. I sent him here."

Queen Mab had tears in her eyes. "He's not, but as I said, you are welcome to search."

"I'll find him myself then," Talek snarled as he started to walk toward the guards behind Queen Mab.

"No, no, you'll do no such thing," Keriam said, his voice nearing panic. "You and I will go together."

"No!" Queen Mab said with a shout.

Colin gripped hold of Mawr's mane, slightly afraid she would shoot sparks out from her fingertips.

"Keriam the Clever, you may be a magician, meaning that you have magic within you, but you are still a Human."

Keriam's mouth dropped open in outrage.

"As such, I'm afraid I cannot permit you to enter our lands."

"Why — I —" Keriam sputtered.

"However, I will permit that furry creature back there to go with him. Perhaps he can help."

Colin pushed himself up from Mawr's back and pointed to himself with one clawed finger. "Me?"

She nodded.

He slid down and Mawr gave him one last concerned nuzzle that scraped at his elbow before he made his way to the front. Queen Mab was smiling down at him, but Keriam was so irate he looked like he might shoot fire from his staff at any moment.

Colin scratched the back of his neck. "Uh, do you want me to go with him, sir?"

"Yes," Keriam snapped. "You're a Seeker, it's your job to find things, is it not? Go with him. Return back as quickly as possible." Colin stepped closer to Talek, but Keriam grabbed his arm and yanked him back so that he almost fell over.

Keriam hissed into his ear, "Bring him back here and

don't let him run off. If he does, your stone friend dies, do you understand me?"

Colin sucked in a breath, hardly believing what he was hearing. He was a Seeker, not a caretaker. How was he supposed to make sure that Talek came back? He had no power over him. He glanced away only to see Queen Mab giving him a sympathetic look. A strange scent of sage wafted strongly over him before it disappeared. Keriam shook him again and he winced at the pain in his arm.

"Alright, yes, okay! Can you let go of me now?"

"Good!" Keriam growled, and practically threw him forward.

Colin rubbed at his arm nervously, glancing back to catch Mawr's expression. He looked terrified and Colin felt terrible. He walked up to Talek, who looked like he hadn't even noticed what had happened because he was so maddeningly desperate to find Teagan.

"You have until dawn!" Keriam shouted. "The rest of them will camp here for now. However, if I need you here, Talek, you must drop everything and come at once. Understood?"

It seemed to take an effort for Talek to pull his gaze away from the path ahead, but he looked back to his master and nodded. "Understood."

"Good. Then make it quick."

Before Colin knew what was happening, Talek picked him up with both arms, and rose into the air. They were surrounded with that violet light — the same color that bled through on his eye – then suddenly they shot through the trees like an arrow.

Colin couldn't even find a breath to scream.

~

COLIN DUG his claws into Talek's shoulders as they shot off. He didn't mean too, but could Talek really blame him? He had barely realized they were flying into the air before they had flown off into the woods. He tried to keep his eyes open, but the wind made them water so bad he couldn't see anything.

"Talek, can we — can we slow down a bit?" He had to scream the words into the Faerie's ear because he could barely even hear himself.

"We only have until dawn. That's hardly any time at all to search through the entire City. He could be anywhere."

"Well if you —" he gulped down a deep breath and tried again. "I'm a Seeker, I can help you find him. Please, just slow down!"

With a grunt of annoyance, Talek slowed. They hovered amid what must have been hundreds of small, candlelit homes. At this angle, the ones in the distance could have been flickering fireflies. Colin's head spun with the lights and his body was cold all over. His fur was prickly in places and he had to force himself to uncurl his claws. It took an effort; some stoat instincts were hard to let go.

The Faerie didn't seem to even notice. His eyes were wide; his gaze desperate. Colin couldn't figure out if he was on the verge of tears or wanting to kill somebody. Maybe both. Realizing that he was in a rather dangerous position, he pushed his fear aside and tried to think like a Seeker.

"Okay, first of all, instead of zooming around the

entire forest looking for him and wasting time, let's try thinking through this instead. Can you help me do that?"

Talek wasn't paying attention. He was looking all around them, the desperation in his gaze growing more extreme by the moment.

"Hey, look at me!"

The command got his attention, but he looked at him as though surprised that he was there. Colin was beginning to think his mind was more gone than he let on. It was like the Madness was unraveling his ability to reason.

"Think," Colin insisted. "Where would he go if he were here?"

"If he were here?"

Colin resisted the urge to grind his teeth. "Yes, we're trying to figure out where he would be hiding. So, let's track down where he would likely go, alright?"

Talek nodded slowly, clearly still frantic, but focusing on questions seemed to help. That was at least a step in the right direction.

"You knew him better than anyone else in this place. If anybody knew where he would go, you would."

The Faerie froze and looked off into the woods. "He would go home. He would have to. If Queen Mab found him, he would have to find a place to stay, and that's where she would put him."

Before Colin could say a word, they flew off again, and the sudden acceleration pushed the breath out of his lungs.

When they stopped to hover down to the ground, Talek thankfully let go of him. Colin had honestly never been so glad to reach the ground in his life. Though he didn't have long to gain his footing. Talek wasn't at all bothered by their accelerated tour of Faerie City and walked briskly toward the front door before Colin could blink.

The building was round and notably bigger than the ones he had seen in the branches earlier. It was also really cute. Yellow roses had overtaken the pathway that led up to the front porch that even had a few chairs on it. Colin half expected Teagan to walk out to greet them, but the shutters were open, and it was dark inside. Talek seemed determined at first to walk in, but stopped at the door, not even raising his hand to touch the doorknob. He froze as though terrified of what he would find.

Colin stepped up quietly to his side. "This is home, right?"

Talek gave a stiff nod.

"And you think Teagan would go here?"

Another nod.

Colin rubbed his hands together nervously. "Is that why we're not going inside?"

"I don't know if I'm ready," he whispered and shook his head. Colin could see the fear in his eyes, which actually made Colin relax a bit. He much preferred that to potential bloodshed.

"If he was here, then he might have seen..." Talek stopped and looked down to his feet. "I guess I'm afraid of what I'll find."

Colin sighed and reached for the doorknob. "There's only one way to find out." The knob squeaked as he turned it and the hinges complained when he pushed the door open.

Inside was dark. Other than the moonlight that came in from the open windows, it was hard to see anything. At least it didn't take long for Colin's eyes to grow accustomed to the darkness, and what he saw made his heart sink. There was a bed big enough for two people in the corner, but more importantly, it looked like someone had slept on the floor. Talek was still standing in the doorway, staring at his feet, and Colin bit his lip. Teagan *had* been here. Suddenly he was afraid of what Talek would do when he realized it too.

He turned quickly to Talek; his palms raised. "You know what? Maybe this is too difficult for you right now. Maybe it's too soon. If you want, I can take a look around and—"

"No," Talek said, stepping in without looking up. He glanced to the table and the candle flickered to life. "I have to see it. Even if I don't want to."

Of course, the first thing Talek would see was the bed on the floor. It was clear evidence that two people slept here, and even more proof that both Shaleigh and Teagan had been here. Who else would have stayed in their house? Plus, there was the overwhelming scent of cedar oil which was a huge giveaway. Only Teagan would have insisted on rubbing down every piece of wood in the room with that. If it was a squatter or if the place was abandoned, Colin doubted it would have been taken care of nearly as well.

Talek shuffled past him, trailing his fingers on the clean, oiled table, his hands trembling. "This place holds so many memories," he whispered. "We were so happy before..."

Colin cocked his head to the side, "Until what?"

The Faerie stopped in front of the makeshift bed on the floor and made a soft sound as though something inside of him broke at the sight of it and dropped heavily to his knees, dragging his hands over the sheets. "Until he left me," he sobbed, pulling one of the blankets to his face and holding it there, rocking back and forth as his tears fell.

Most people might have been shocked to hear that, Colin knew, but he wasn't surprised. He had seen how callous Master Teagan could be at times. It made his own flesh crawl when he did things like that, but usually it was for a good reason. Usually he had to for the good of the Garden or he was given orders to do it.

Here there wasn't an excuse, and that made him uncomfortable. By all appearances, Master Teagan just decided to abandon his ex-boyfriend without even an excuse or a note. Even for him, that was pretty damn cruel.

Talek pulled more blankets to his face and Colin didn't know what to do. His instincts said he should comfort him, but he was hesitant. With the Madness in Talek, any interaction was like walking on broken glass, and he was afraid of pushing him when he was so fragile. He couldn't just stand there, though. It felt invasive and rude.

"You really miss him, don't you?"

Talek shook his head, pulling away from the blankets so he could speak, "I don't just miss him. I *need* him."

Colin put a hand on his shoulder and could feel him trembling as though he would shatter to pieces at any moment. "I'm sorry. I miss him too, you know. As much of an ass as he could be, he believed in me when nobody else did."

Lifting his hand, Colin marveled, as he did sometimes, at the fur that covered him. It used to be that he couldn't get used to the idea of being a *stoatling*, as Master Teagan called it, but now it was difficult to remember what he used to look like at all. Was his hair brown or dark blonde? Did he have freckles?

"He gave me a gift that I can never repay him for. Just because he liked me. And now I know that he did it himself, not on the orders of Madam Cloom. It makes me feel... I don't know, special. I'd never really felt like that before."

Talek looked up at him with red eyes and blotchy cheeks, but he was smiling. "He liked you. Even though he knew you so very briefly, he wanted to help you. He saw potential in you." His smile faded. "I miss that. I miss him staring at me with anything other than disgust and revulsion."

Colin shook his head. "I don't think it's that. I think he was afraid for you, and now..." he trailed off, not knowing if he ought to finish the statement, but Talek finished it for him.

"Now he's afraid *of* me," he said with a shaky voice. "I know. I saw the fear in his eyes; that's why he ran off with that girl from the Human World." There was anger in his words that made the fur stick up on Colin's neck in warning. He backed away, not sure if this was his cue to leave or not. Talek stared down at the sheets in silence.

Carefully Colin backed into the corner of the table, and a pile of papers fell over. He reached out to straighten them, expecting them to be documents, papers, perhaps even old records. He wasn't expecting sketches; certainly not adorable sketches of Master Teagan.

He flipped through them, suddenly fully understanding the pain that Talek was going through. They hadn't just been together, they had been head-over-heels in love... for *centuries*.

He found one where Master Teagan was laughing over a joke and couldn't help but smile as well. Colin really did miss him and hadn't realized how much until now. He missed his guidance and his ability to know exactly what to do regardless of what they were dealing with. If he was here, he would probably wrap his arms around Talek and calm him down. He would tell Colin to step outside and give them some privacy. He would negotiate with Queen Mab and organize some kind of safe house. The only person he couldn't work around was Keriam the damn Magician.

"Are these yours?" He flipped the laughing picture of Teagan around and Talek rolled his eyes.

"Those are from another lifetime ago. Another existence. Back when my heart was still whole, and it wasn't bleeding everywhere." He sniffed. "They ought to be destroyed."

"I don't think so. I think they're cute. You're very good."

Talek didn't respond. Apparently, he wasn't in the mood for compliments.

"May I keep one?"

The Faerie shrugged. "I don't care. Just leave me for a bit. I need to think. I need to figure out how to feel again."

Colin bit his lip, wishing he could say more, but knowing he shouldn't. He folded the picture of Teagan up and put it into one of his many pockets, then glanced to Talek as he headed for the door.

What could possibly have made Teagan abandon him like that, after spending several lifetimes with him? It was difficult to admit, but maybe he didn't know Master Teagan as well as he thought he did. Maybe when Teagan gave all those excuses for why he was doing horrible things like ordering executions and requesting he steal people from the Human World... No, it wasn't stealing people, it was *kidnapping* people, like Shaleigh had said.

Maybe it wasn't all Madam Cloom demanding it like Colin always thought. Maybe there was more of Master Teagan in those decisions than he liked to admit. He closed his eyes briefly and felt that familiar weight of guilt sweep over him. Maybe he was also more guilty than he liked to think. Maybe they all were.

He stepped out onto the porch and took in a deep breath of the cold air. Tears threatened, but Colin wiped his eyes with the back of his hand. He had learned that his fur was very useful for wiping away tears — another of Teagan's gifts that he probably hadn't considered.

The guilt still sat in him like a coldness that wouldn't leave, but he didn't try to ignore it like he normally would. He allowed it to stay. He deserved it to some extent and understood that now - regardless of who was giving orders - he was still complicit.

He needed to help Shaleigh get back home. He needed to help the Garden get back on its feet. He needed to try to undo all the wrongs that he had assisted in. It might take some time, but he was determined to find a way.

He also needed to try to fix this mess between Teagan and Talek. He got the impression they were both good people underneath, but damn did they need to sit down and have a real talk — not in jail cells and not in arenas, but as equals. He just wasn't sure if it was even possible any longer.

Another blast of wind blew and Colin felt his fur ruffle all over his body. He breathed it in, let it fill his lungs, let it fill him up. He wasn't going to keep being the scared little rodent anymore, he was going to stand up for himself and for his friends. Even if it meant feeling Keriam's wrath on occasion, it was worth it.

For now, he gave Talek the privacy he deserved, and steeled himself for what would come next. Once Talek got his crying out of the way, he wasn't sure what the Faerie would do. His rage was just under the surface and with the Madness in him there was no telling how he'd react next.

They had proof now that both Shaleigh and Teagan had been here, and that Queen Mab had covered for them. Seeing how crafty she seemed to be, the queen probably knew exactly where they were and was purposely buying them time. He wasn't sure how Talek or Keriam would handle that, but he refused to be on the sidelines any longer. He would do whatever it took to help his friends.

It was still a few hours before dawn when Talek carried Colin back to the troops. He hadn't said a word when he came out of the house and, for a moment, didn't even seem to see Colin.

What scared Colin the most was his expression. He looked like he was broken inside, like he had given up the last shred of decency and humanity that he possessed. Colin had to grab Talek's arm for him to remember to bring Colin with him, and even then, he hadn't said a word the whole time. It gave Colin more chills than the cold wind.

"There they are," Colin said aloud as Talek flew. He seemed to have not noticed, then, in an instant, dive-bombed. Colin held on for dear life as the ground careened up to greet them and bit back a scream as Talek stilled a good distance from the ground.

"I must do this alone," he said, his gaze fixed on some-thing in the distance.

"Wait, what?"

Colin felt Talek's hand grip the scruff on the back of his neck and pry him off as if Colin had no more strength than a kitten. Colin flailed, scratching at the Faerie's skin right before Talek dropped him. Colin's eyes went wide as gravity took hold.

"Wait!" he screamed, but Talek had already flown on.

His animal instincts took over and even though he hit the ground hard, he forced himself to roll to take the momentum of the impact. He finally flopped onto the ground, face in the dirt. He just stared at the base of the trees, his eyes wide and breathing fast. The world took a few minutes to still and his mind took just as long to figure out what just happened. He didn't even know that he was able to do that. Was that in his training? He didn't think so. They never covered what to do when flung out onto the ground like a heap of trash.

With shaky arms he pushed himself up, his mind still whirling. Then he felt something rough brush against his cheek. It took a moment for him to realize it was a big stone tongue lapping at him.

With a grin, he held up a hand. "It's okay, you can stop that, I'm fine."

"Are you sure?" Mawr said, his golden-rimmed eyes studying him with absolute worry.

Colin barked a laugh. "Not really, but you grooming me isn't going to help." He pushed himself up to a seated position and stared up into the trees, for some reason expecting Talek to still be hovering there. "Where did he go?"

Mawr looked off to the side. "He's...fighting with Queen Mab."

"What!? Come on, we have to get over there!" Colin tried to get to his feet, but his body wouldn't obey, and with a sigh he climbed back up onto Mawr's back.

"I told you, I don't know where they are!" Queen Mab's fury pulled Colin back to his senses the closer they got to the fighting. He looked up to see that Talek had her pinned against a tree. Her Faerie soldiers surrounded the two of them but were several steps back. Talek had one hand on her throat as though he could snap her neck if he wanted to and honestly at this point Colin believed he could.

"Yes, you do," Talek insisted. "You have to. You're a plotter, a schemer, you always have been."

"Normally yes, but not this time. I just want my children to be safe."

Her words must have affected him because he shook his head, and Colin could see tears in his eyes. "No."

She reached a hand up to his cheek. "I've only ever wanted you to be happy, Talek. That's all. I've wanted you and Teagan both to-"

She didn't have a chance to finish her words. Talek threw her so hard that she only looked like a blur. She hit the trunk of a big tree hard and fell in a heap to the ground. Colin wasn't sure if she was alive or not. Several of the Faeries went to her side, but those that had circled Talek moved closer, their spears out and aimed for his throat.

He smiled. "Oh please, what do you plan to do with those?"

Colin watched in terror as the tips of the spears bent and turned. Black rings appeared from the tip of the spears down to the base of the shafts. Two large, yellow eyes appeared next, then a long-split tongue emerged. The heads turned triangular in shape and Colin realized that they became the largest copperhead snakes he had ever seen. He also was pretty sure he had only ever seen them in the Human World. The Faerie solders scattered, and even some of Lieutenant Varg's troops were panicking.

Talek walked back to Keriam and the snakes gathered near him.

Keriam looked more annoyed than anything as he asked, "Was that really necessary?"

Talek shrugged. He said over the shrieks from the Faerie soldiers, "My queen and I had a matter to discuss. They had no part in it."

"And how do you propose to get the information out of her now? We still are no closer to knowing where they went. Damn you, Talek!"

"I know where they went," Talek stated simply. "I wasn't entirely sure at first but then I did what Colin suggested and stopped to think - something I admittedly haven't been doing very well lately." His eyes cut to Colin as he gave a little laugh that made Mawr paw at the ground anxiously. "I realized that if Queen Mab couldn't keep him safe, where else could he possibly go? Not to the Dark Lands, and it certainly wouldn't be safe to go to the Garden. So where would it be? Who else would take him in that hates you enough to do it, Master?" Talek gave him a knowing smile and Keriam shook his head in outrage.

"No, they wouldn't. They wouldn't dare."

"Who are we talking about?" Colin asked, pushing himself up so he could sit properly on Mawr's back again even if he still hurt from head to toe.

"Keriam's dear old friends back at the Sanctuary, where every Magician is trained."

Keriam paced back and forth, stabbing at the ground with his staff as though the dirt itself was responsible for his wrath. "All of those pathetic old men who weren't willing to raise a single finger to help me. All those idiots who sit in that gilded tower. How *dare* they protect known fugitives."

"Teagan would go there. I know he would." Talek looked off into the distance and reached a hand out as though stroking Teagan's cheek. "I know his beautiful, demented mind so well. He's a plotter too, you see. Just like you and just like Queen Mab, only he's desperate. He'll appeal to their sense of order and decorum. He'll appear to have everything in control," he paused, his hand turning into a fist. "Only he'll be desperate inside, scared. That's how we'll find him. That's how we reach him."

"Him and that girl." Keriam nodded. "Good, good. I'm impressed, Talek. I thought you were just wasting our time here visiting old memories and old friends." He smirked over to where Queen Mab lay broken on the ground; she hadn't moved - if she wasn't dead, she was very badly injured. Colin knew better than to try to offer help, though. He had to choose his next actions carefully.

"Lieutenant! We're moving out. Plan a path to the Sanctuary."

"Yes sir! We should be able to completely avoid the Dark Lands this time too, so that will certainly make it easier."

One of the Faeries approached Keriam, looking very nervous and frequently looking behind him at the other Faeries gathered around their queen. "Um, excuse me. Sir?"

Talek narrowed his eyes at him, and the other Faerie slinked back a bit. "What is it?"

"I, um, have some information on where they went — Teagan and that disgusting girl from the Human World."

Keriam smiled and patted Talek on the shoulder. "You can handle this one I think."

Talek approached the Faerie, a grimace on his face. "What do you want, Sionn?"

"I, ah, helped them while they were here on the queen's orders. I didn't want to, mind you. We had to bring a new mattress and I had to fetch bread and water, it was ridiculous! I'm a soldier, not some kind of stupid nurse maid, you know what I mean, Talek?"

Talek crossed his arms. "You certainly sound like you're wasting my time right now."

"Oh, yes, well, the queen got wind that you were coming this way and had them go through the Dark Lands."

Talek narrowed his eyes, "Through it?"

"Yes! I was shocked too; she clearly must be losing her mind to give such an order." He laughed at his own joke, but Talek didn't join him, so he just trailed off awkwardly. "I just, I thought you would find it useful to know. I don't know if they got out, I don't even know if they survived! It is the Dark-"

Talek grabbed his throat and lifted him off the ground. "You think my Teagan died in the Dark Lands? Is that what you're telling me?"

Sionn clawed as his throat, his eyes bulging. Mawr backed away from them, and Colin had to rub between his ears to keep him from darting away.

"You think that's funny? You think that's entertaining to me?"

The Faerie's face was turning purple, but he gave a short shake of his head and mouthed *"no"* over and over. Talek held him for a moment more before dropping him to the ground. He collapsed to the dirt in a horrible coughing fit.

"Colin," Mawr whimpered, hunching down to the ground. The poor guy was shaking from head to toe.

"I know," Colin swallowed down the lump in his throat. "We'll be okay, don't worry." He sure wished he believed his own words.

Talek turned to his master, "Maybe we should head to the Dark Lands then?"

"No, I don't think so. He wouldn't have kept them." Keriam smiled. "You see, the Masked King is a friend of mine."

Even Talek was taken aback by that. "A *friend?*"

"Oh yes, maybe one day I'll tell you all about it." He slipped an arm around Talek's and they walked off following the procession who urged Mawr to walk in front of them.

Mawr was so close to the ground that he was almost dragging his belly as he inched forward. Colin had to keep encouraging him to keep him moving. He really didn't want them to attract Talek's attention right now.

Behind them Colin could hear Sionn still wheezing on the ground.

UNINVITED GUESTS

Shaleigh

It wasn't long before Shaleigh and Teagan could both see the smoke trails that carried a horrible smell that permeated throughout the forest. Shaleigh counted five trails in all and the closer they got the thicker the smoke and the stronger the scent of burned beef became. By the time they could see the flickering fire, Shaleigh had pulled the sleeve of her dress up to cover her nose.

"We shouldn't be here!" she hissed, tugging at Teagan's arm. "If there are bonfires, that could mean soldiers."

Teagan scanned the clearing with concern. "I don't think anyone is here. Not anymore, that is." He tried to move forward, but Shaleigh held his arm.

"Just because you can't see them doesn't mean they aren't there." She thought back to all the trash fires she and Kaeja had seen when exploring abandoned buildings. Usually it was just a homeless person looking for warmth wherever they could find it, but sometimes it was someone who didn't want to be found. Regardless, it was best to leave the person alone or at least give them a wide berth.

Far above, large black birds circled like vultures, but their red plumage didn't look like any vultures she knew. Fallen trees made the clearing look far more exposed than it ought to be, and Shaleigh could see the numerous fires burning hot and high into the air. They were setup well, so nothing else should catch on fire, but she wondered at how long they had been burning. These weren't for warmth, these looked as if they were a warning, forming a circle in the large clearing to keep others at bay.

"I really don't like this, Teagan."

Teagan gently removed her hand from his arm. "I need to find out what happened here. These woods belong to the minotaurs. While they might not be the most welcoming of groups, this could be evidence that Keriam passed through here and we need to know where they've gone if we plan to avoid them. If we can, we need to understand their plan."

Reluctantly Shaleigh nodded. She didn't really care if it was Keriam's work or not. She wanted to get out of there, but they were trying to work as a team and Teagan knew this land better than she did. He understood how to work with the minotaurs in the Garden, maybe he knew how to deal with them here too.

Remembering quite clearly the panic she had felt when Graddic had gotten in her face at the carriage during the

Games, she stayed close as Teagan led the way, doing her best to keep the smell at bay and to keep her nerves calm.

They approached the closest fire slowly, and even from a distance they could hear the crackling as the wood at the bottom gave way. Her steps slowed, what she had originally thought was a misshapen tree limb hanging outside of the fire was actually an arm. Her eyes widened as she realized that that wasn't the only body in the pile — these weren't just casual fires out here, they were funeral pyres.

She rushed forward and grabbed Teagan's tunic, pulling him so hard that he nearly fell backward. "We need to go, now!" she cried.

"Calm down," he said with alarm. "We need to see what happened here."

"Those aren't just fires, Teagan, they're funeral pyres! Those are bodies!"

His eyes went wide and his mouth dropped open. He took a step back but kept staring at the fire. "But... so many of them..." he whispered, backing away another step.

What used to have been bodies shifted in one black glob together, toppling a few fiery bits to the ground.

From behind one of the other fires, a minotaur emerged and kicked dirt over the scattered flames. Shaleigh hadn't even seen him there.

"Oh dear," Teagan whispered, freezing in place.

Another minotaur joined the first in kicking out the flames, this one wearing a dress. Both of them looked upset, like they had been crying. Shaleigh's mouth went dry. What had happened here? Who had died, and how? She wished she hadn't listened to Teagan's advice for them to approach. She guessed neither of them would be very happy to see a Human and a Faerie watching them mourn.

Then, the woman minotaur looked up and locked eyes with her. The sadness shifted immediately from shock to outrage, and Shaleigh's heart skipped a beat. Both of the minotaurs stepped toward them and Shaleigh could see that the fur on their cheeks was matted from crying.

"My apologies, madam," Teagan bowed low to them. "We mean no harm and we don't mean to intrude, but..." he gestured to the flames, "what happened?"

As he spoke, Shaleigh saw more faces appear from around the other fires. There must have been ten or more minotaurs, all standing vigil over the flames. She looked closer into the fire and saw a metal ring on the ground, less than a foot away from the pyre. It was the same kind of nose ring that Graddic wore, only silver. She inched closer to Teagan: it was obvious now that they were mourning the death of what had to have been dozens of minotaurs.

Teagan felt her approach and glanced back to her with concern.

"Some crazy soldiers trespassed on our lands," the woman said. "They carried weapons with them, ready for battle. They were led by a magician with horrifying magic." She shook her head. "He slaughtered all of them. Both of my boys were killed. What for? They were just protecting our land. They were innocents."

The other minotaur put his arm around her. He had silver hairs around his nose and mouth. He didn't have the sadness though that the woman did. No, he looked angry.

"I'm very sorry for your loss," Teagan said, sounding more stoic than Shaleigh would have liked. "You said the soldiers were led by a magician? Did there happen to be a Faerie with him?"

Shaleigh felt the atmosphere shift at his words. The silver-haired minotaur noticed Teagan's ears and then eyed Shaleigh in suspicion. She didn't like the way his gaze shifted over them, getting the feeling he wasn't making the best conclusions.

She took Teagan's hand in hers. "We should go," she said, pulling him away.

"I was trying to get information." Shaleigh ignored him and kept gently pulling him away from the pyres. This time Teagan didn't resist, but he did continue the conversation with the pair of minotaurs.

"My apologies," he said and gave an awkward laugh. "She's in a hurry."

Shaleigh clenched her jaw to keep from speaking. There was something in the way he said it that reminded her of the condescending way that her father would speak to her at parties. It made her instantly seem unreliable or eccentric. But this wasn't one of Dad's social events and something about this made her very anxious. Maybe it was due to the additional minotaurs she kept seeing appear around the pyres, or maybe it was the way the silver-haired minotaur eyed them both, or maybe it was the shift that happened in the conversation…either way, she couldn't ignore her instincts anymore.

"There was a Faerie," the woman said, hurrying toward them. Shaleigh watched her closely. "The Faerie killed them all. My mother said he made their corpses get to their feet and walk to the pyres. That's impossible though, right? That's outright madness!" She was crying again, her hands balling up into fists beside her. "Corpses don't walk. My boys wouldn't do that if they were really dead, would they? They wouldn't do that!" She fell to her knees, covered her eyes, and sobbed.

Shaleigh's heart ached for the woman, but she was also terrified by her words. Had Talek made the dead walk? Did he really have that much power?

Teagan glanced back to Shaleigh, this time with terrified eyes himself. "I think you're right. Let's go," he whispered.

They headed off to the side, moving further into the woods, but the pyres emitted so much light that there was no easy way for them to hide from the gazes that had already spotted them. A group of five minotaurs stepped towards them, blocking their path. Unlike the woman, they hadn't been crying and looked angrier than the silver-haired minotaur had been.

A burly minotaur in front had several long scars across his chest where his fur hadn't grown back in; he snorted into the evening air. "The purple-eyed Faerie was in a pact with that magician, that's how they did it. It was all magic, all a damn game to your kind, wasn't it? A crazy magician and a Faerie with the Madness, that's all it took to take out half my tribe."

Shaleigh exchanged a glance with Teagan. Neither of them knew what to say.

"My boys are in that pile," the woman behind them screamed and Shaleigh jumped. The silver-haired minotaur was holding her, trying to calm her down, but she pushed him, stomping her hooves into the ground. "My beautiful boys!"

The burly minotaur snorted again and cocked his head to the side. "Now look at how lucky we are. We find a Faerie hiding with a little Human in the woods, asking about all this. I bet you know them, don't you? I bet you're the real reason my tribe was slain, aren't you?"

"I'm afraid you have mistaken us for someone else," Teagan said, his voice stern despite the way he tightened his grip on Shaleigh's hand. "Just because I am a Faerie doesn't mean I know every one of my kind in the land."

He grinned. "No, that I get. But somehow... if a minotaur was out here having killed some rich fool in the Garden, or was making trouble with the Faeries up north, I don't think you would care." He moved closer. "Right now? I don't think we should either."

Teagan stood a bit straighter. "I am deeply sorry for your loss, but we had nothing to do with it, I assure you. Please, we want no trouble today."

"Maybe not," said another female minotaur who stepped forward beside the burly one. Shaleigh realized she was missing her right eye and shuddered. "But maybe if we burn your body on a pyre, alongside my sister's boys, maybe that's just the message we need." She cracked her neck. "Maybe you shouldn't have come this way, Faerie."

With that, all five of the minotaurs lunged at them.

Before Shaleigh could even scream Teagan yanked on her arm so hard that her shoulder ached. Suddenly she was in the air, her feet dangling beneath her. Teagan held her arm still and it took her a moment to realize that he had jumped into the trees to get to safety.

"Give me your other arm!" he cried out.

Shaleigh just looked at him, stunned and terrified.

Beneath them the one-eyed woman shouted, "You think the trees will help you? These trees belong to us! As do any trespassers foolish enough to interrupt our mourning."

"Especially nosy Faeries!" someone shouted.

Boom!

The tree shook all around them. Teagan pulled her up into his arms and prepared for another jump.

"Can't you just fly us out of here?"

Boom!

The tree shook again and creaked, leaning to one side. The world went diagonal right before Teagan leaped to another tree.

"I can't fly!" he muttered after landing.

"Yes, you can! You flew me down at the Games!"

Boom!

This tree shook more violently than the first and Teagan put a hand on the trunk to keep from falling.

"I can't fly without being in a pact," he snapped. "I can jump higher than Humans, but I can't fly."

"Damn it, Teagan, why did you lie to me then?"

He looked at her with wide, frightened eyes. "I wanted you to respect me!"

Boom!

This tree began to fall and Teagan jumped again. "I can't have this argument now. I have to concentrate if we're to get out of this alive. Hold on."

Shaleigh took a deep breath and locked her hands together behind Teagan's neck before they jumped again.

"Our only chance is speed," he whispered. Then he took off.

It was almost like a dance the way he leaped from branch to branch, moving from tree to tree with incredible grace and ease. Behind them she could see the dark shapes of the minotaurs shoving through the undergrowth and tearing through saplings. There were more than the original five now and they had broken off into two groups, moving in strategic waves. One was putting pressure behind them while another group was trying to speed ahead and cut them off.

"Take a left - a left!" she urged, squeezing his shoulder.

"Okay!" he gasped, leaping suddenly to the left as the tree he had almost jumped to was torn down without warning. It took a moment for Teagan to catch his footing though because the branch he had jumped on wasn't as strong as the others he had chosen. It was the added weight, Shaleigh realized, that was throwing him off.

"What should we do?" she asked, unable to keep her voice from quivering.

"I know a place," he said, continuing his leaps. "It's not far from here, but it's going to be tricky getting there like this. Keep an eye on them for me. I don't like how close we came to being brought down."

Shaleigh shivered and situated herself into a better position to be a proper lookout. Three more times the minotaurs tried to intercept them, but Shaleigh was able to give enough warning in time.

Then a third group emerged, almost seeming to have been waiting for them the entire chase. There was no time to give a warning as suddenly the tree was going down. Shaleigh felt needles scrape her bare legs; a branch smacked against her face just under her left eye - so close that her eye teared up instantly.

She winced, feeling Teagan's arms grip hard.

Jump by jump, he climbed. Shaleigh saw they were in a nearby tree, but it wouldn't be good enough. While it was huge, it had been an obvious choice for Teagan to go for since the branches held their combined weight the best. It would also take down several other trees along the way and the minotaurs were already working to bring it down. Teagan had to get them away from it – now.

"Teagan, we have to keep moving!"

She gripped hold of his tunic, now soaked through with sweat. He was getting tired, breathing hard around her grip, and it took him a moment to regain his footing. They were running out of time.

"Teagan, please!"

With a loud grunt he made a huge leap over an empty gap, and Shaleigh felt a shift around them mid-air. It was like passing through a doorway into a differ-ence space. It had the same sort of trees, the same sort of ground, but it was different somehow. They landed with a crash as the branch beneath them broke, then the next and the next. Finally, Teagan landed in the crook between two branches, right on his rear, and he cried out.

Shaleigh held tight and breathed deep for a minute, holding Teagan as the scent of sap filled her nostrils.

Teagan shuddered.

"Are you okay?" she whispered.

Teagan's eyes were still closed and his face held in a grimace. "Yes, I think so. Just very badly bruised."

"We need to keep moving," she urged, scanning the ground for the minotaurs. She saw them, but noticed they weren't moving. They had crowded right beside the gap of empty space that Teagan had jumped through. They were watching them, but for some reason they didn't approach. That only put Shaleigh more on edge.

"You think they will protect you," the one-eyed woman called out to them, pawing a hoof impatiently at the ground. "But you are mistaken, Faerie. They hate your kind just like they hate us. Almost as much as they hate anything from the Human World."

Shaleigh took a deep breath and wiped at her swollen eye.

The woman laughed, "Good luck!" The group of them began laughing and Shaleigh couldn't take it anymore. She held onto the trunk of the tree as she dislodged herself from Teagan, who still hadn't gotten to his feet.

"Are you sure you're alright?"

Teagan nodded. "More or less." With her help he got to his feet, though it took an effort for him to straighten up completely. "Oh, wow." He rubbed his backside and winced. Unlike Shaleigh, he didn't need to hold onto the tree to keep his balance. He was perfectly fine walking on a branch as if he was walking on the ground. It was kind of unnerving.

"They're not following us," she said a bit more panicked than she intended.

"Of course they're not. This land doesn't belong to them and there is magic in place to prevent them from crossing the boundary."

"Who does it belong to then? They said that whoever it is won't protect us. You heard them."

He held up a hand to her. "I heard them, Shaleigh, calm down."

She fought down the impulse of anger she felt and took a moment to breathe. He was right, she was too worked up and anxious. "I mean, I'd be a lot calmer if you had just listened to me. Then we wouldn't have been chased through the treetops."

He chuckled sadly. "Yes, I know. That was entirely my mistake and I'm sorry. Perhaps I ought to listen to you more often instead of assuming that I know what's best."

"Bingo."

He cocked his head to the side and Shaleigh rolled her eyes. "I mean yes, that's exactly my point."

He nodded and motioned for her to climb into his arms again, then dropped them down to the ground. She squirmed out of his arms immediately, mostly because she could tell that he was hurting more than he let on and carrying her around wasn't helping. But it also because felt really good to have her feet on solid ground again.

She pulled a few stray needles out of the skin of her legs with a hiss. They were scraped pretty badly and really stung, but at least nothing was broken. She was pulling off a leaf that had stuck to the blood on her face when she saw Teagan had a hand pressed to his lower back, clearly still in a lot of pain.

"You sure nothing's broken?"

He gave a sad smile. "I hope not. I doubt I'll find much medical help here."

She frowned and looked around. "I don't think the supplies Queen Mab gave us survived either."

"Ah yes, that's what I felt pinch my shoulder when we nearly fell that first time." He pursed his lips. "Things just keep getting better."

Shaleigh sighed. "So, who owns this land? I hope they don't also want to chase us through the trees."

Teagan stretched his neck and arms. "Ah yes, my apologies. This path leads to the Sanctuary, and this land is all owned by the council of magicians who live there."

It took Shaleigh a moment to recall where she had heard of that place before. "That's where magicians come from, right?"

"Well, it's where they are trained. Every magician who is able to control their magic must be trained, and the Sanctuary is really the best place to do that. They offer free services to anyone who shows potential and serve as a sanctuary for any magician seeking refuge there."

Shaleigh looked over and realized that the gap they jumped over must have been the boundary line: a clear path marked in the grass that disappeared off in both directions. It was well maintained even though there were no markers anywhere.

"And you think these magicians will help us undo what happened at the Garden?"

Teagan laughed. "Oh, that is very doubtful. They are painfully apathetic about such things."

She narrowed her eyes. "Then you think they'll give us refuge?"

"That is highly improbable too. Those minotaurs weren't lying about the fact that they dislike our kind."

"So why the heck did you bring us here?" She had a hard time keeping the anger out of her voice and likely failed by the disapproving glance Teagan gave her.

"This is perhaps the safest place we can be for protection from Keriam and Talek. The Council will be aware of such untamed magic and will hopefully want to prevent it from destroying the land. They also may take an interest in us since we survived Talek's magic relatively unscathed. But mostly, well," he gave a sheepish grin, "I was running out of branches."

Shaleigh couldn't help but laugh at that. It was an admittedly good excuse.

INTO A CAGE

Shaleigh

It didn't take long for Teagan and Shaleigh to spot the Sanctuary in the distance. It was impossible to miss it.

To Shaleigh, it looked like someone had taken a threaded, cone-shaped drill and run the building up through the ground. It was completely black, but since the sun had set, it was difficult to tell if it was made of metal or not. Shaleigh would've expected a place that trained magicians to be more welcoming, but this place was the exact opposite. It was surrounded with rocky hills on all sides, as though the earth had been upended when it was built.

It was like a place that was more fit to live in nightmares than one she went to for safety.

"That's the Sanctuary?"

Teagan nodded then grimaced, still clearly in pain though he refused to admit it.

They crested a hill and Shaleigh saw that, ahead of them, the path sloped downward to a bridge that led to the entrance. Already she was regretting their decision to come here, but Teagan was right, where else were they supposed to go?

The woods were filled with angry minotaurs, the Dark Lands was where the Masked King ruled, and she didn't think it was a good idea to return to the Garden when it was just the two of them; especially not now that Teagan was injured. They needed a safe space to retreat to, and even though the Sanctuary looked more like a prison than a place of protection, they weren't really in a position to be picky.

"It doesn't look like much of a sanctuary, does it?" Shaleigh asked, leaning on one of the trees. They had to pause for Teagan to catch his breath.

"No, it really doesn't," Teagan said between deep breaths. "It's almost a mockery to call it such."

"And you said this is a school?"

"Yes, of sorts. It's more of a training ground, a place where magicians of all ages can learn to refine and, hopefully, master their skills. Few are able to reach the mastery level though." Teagan gave a small smile and his gaze grew distant. "Master Cathal was one of the few I've met who accomplished that."

"I thought he chose that title because of the Garden, you know, like a king."

He shook his head. "That was a title he earned here. He was even offered the chance to sit on the Council at one point, but he turned it down. Master Cathal had bigger plans."

Shaleigh couldn't help but remember the bait and switch maneuver Cathal had done on Teagan centuries ago by making him get into a pact with the Garden instead of with Cathal, himself. The magician certainly did have big plans, and they weren't exactly ethical – at least to her.

"I have no idea who is on the Council these days, but hopefully we can appeal to them. We'll find them at the top floor. Only members of the Council and their assistants are permitted up there."

He pointed to the top floor, just beneath the pointed peak, and Shaleigh could just make out windows. She shook her head. "Why do all these people with magic like to build such unsafe structures?"

Teagan blinked. "Are you critiquing my own creations?"

"Yes, actually, I am," Shaleigh said and couldn't hold back a snicker at Teagan's outraged expression as they started down the hill. She kept a slower pace for him so he wouldn't be winded by the time they reached the bottom. "The Garden Castle wouldn't have fallen if it had been built properly, you know. Sometimes the boring, old-fashioned Human ways have their benefits."

"Yes, but they don't attract attention. For example," he held out a hand toward the Sanctuary, "clearly the message I see here is that they don't want visitors."

"Which is exactly what we hope to be."

"Well, yes, but that's why we have to prove we're not

just some random travelers. We need to give them a reason to let us through the gates."

They drew quiet as they approached the gate where two people waited in long robes with thick belts. It was the same attire Shaleigh remembered from when she had seen them wandering the streets of the Marketplace in the Garden before. Only these two were carrying staffs that looked very similar to Keriam's.

It made her uncomfortable; she slowed her pace and moved closer to Teagan just to be safe. She looked to him for any sign of warning, but his demeanor had completely changed. He wasn't holding onto his lower back. In fact, he had sped up as they walked downhill and smiled at the two magicians. If she didn't know any better, she never would've guessed that he was injured - his old familiar mask from the Garden was firmly in place.

"Good evening," Teagan called out and Shaleigh couldn't help but notice that the two guards gripped their staffs. Once again, her instincts were screaming at her that they shouldn't be there, but she ignored them. They had no other alternative. If the magicians here turned them away, where could they possibly hide? She hoped this at least turned out better than the ordeal with the angry minotaurs.

The taller magician squinted at them with suspicion. "Names?"

Teagan blinked in surprise. "I beg your pardon?"

"I need your names. Who are you and from where do you hail?"

The shorter magician was a woman with a dark complexion and had dark ringlets. She tilted her staff so that the top of it, a golden gem, was aimed in their direction. "You heard him. No one passes without giving their names!"

Teagan and Shaleigh exchanged a worried glance. Should they give aliases? Should they pretend to be someone they weren't? Was it worth even trying to pretend?

She took a deep breath and stepped forward. "I'm Shaleigh Mallett from the Human Wor—"

"Quiet, Human," the woman snapped, keeping her eyes on Teagan. "We don't care about where you're from. Give us your information, Faerie, or else you'll both be turned away."

Teagan gave a nervous laugh. "I'm — sorry, I merely wanted to allow her to go first."

The golden gem began to glow in the cradle of the staff with its own inner light. Shaleigh took a step back, not wanting to get hit with magic and be incapacitated again.

Teagan held up his hands. "Please, calm down, I mean no harm. My name is Teagan, and this is my companion. We hail from the Garden."

The taller magician cocked his head to the side. "Teagan, as in the High Faerie of the Garden?"

He nodded enthusiastically and Shaleigh could practically hear his ego rattling around.

"We were notified that you were killed when the Garden fell."

Teagan gave a wide smile to hide his wince. "I can assure you that I am quite alive." He clasped his hands together as though it proved his point.

The woman brought her staff back and the golden gem stopped glowing. "You believe him?" the woman asked of the other magician, looking like she would very much like to still have an excuse to use magic on them.

"Not really. He isn't dressed as the High Faerie. Maybe we should inform Queen Mab that one of her own has gone roaming again."

Teagan jumped in, "I'm afraid I have no further proof other than my words. I have no documentation proving who I am, only my presence."

"Why are you here?" the woman asked.

"We seek sanctuary within your walls. We seek the counsel of your wise and experienced leaders. We seek guidance, direction, and— "

"Protection," the man finished with snide frustration. "Just spit it out, you damn Faerie. Are you afraid your kind are going to hunt you down now that your pact with Madam Cloom is gone? We all knew it was just a matter of time before that Garden fell. Eternal spring…ha."

Teagan shuffled, clearly insulted but not sure what to say. He was losing his advantage after seeming to have had control over the situation just a moment ago, but in a flash, it was lost.

Once again, Shaleigh was reminded of the fact that Teagan was used to his Garden and his guards who gave him absolute respect. Now he was nothing more than a whimsical, wandering Faerie who didn't know how to get to the point.

Shaleigh stepped forward, determined not to be dismissed again. "As Teagan stated —"

The taller magician barked a laugh. "Yes, whatever,

'High' Faerie." He turned around to lean against the wall of the gate again. "High Faerie indeed! I say send them away, Laurel."

The woman, however, gave Shaleigh a look as though she might still be swayed. Although she hadn't put away her staff like the taller magician had.

"Yes, we seek your protection," Shaleigh admitted, locking her eyes desperately with the woman. "We have information about Keriam the Magician. He's the one who brought down the Garden. He's also bound a mad Faerie as his servant. However, we'll only share the information if—"

"Wait, did you say a *mad* Faerie?" the woman asked, her eyes going wide. Her words made the tall magician step forward again, actually looking like he was interested in what Shaleigh had to say.

"Yes," she stated, mentally pleading they wouldn't send them away. Finally, they understood the weight of the situation, or at least she hoped so.

Teagan put a hand on her shoulder and nodded for her to continue. For the first time since she had fallen into this world from that ridiculous flying bicycle, Shaleigh felt like she not only had control over the situation but she also had a voice. Even back at home she rarely felt like this.

She took a deep breath before she continued, "However, we'll only share the information we have if your leaders give us protection from the magician and his Faerie." She felt Teagan's hand flinch at her words.

The guards stepped back to discuss what to do and Shaleigh let out a big, nervous breath.

"You did well," Teagan whispered with a sad smile.

She knew she had upset him when she called Talek *his* Faerie, but if she had learned anything from the tricky politics of Madam Cloom, Queen Mab, and now the Masked King, it was that she needed to choose the right language in order to be taken seriously.

She hadn't done that in the Garden until she was standing face to face with Madam Cloom herself. Queen Mab and her Faerie soldiers, like Sionn, would never see her as anything more than a vermin who didn't deserve even a clean bed to sleep on. Finally, there was the Masked King…

She glanced at Teagan, taking in his closed expression. She doubted he would have lost himself completely in the Dark Lands, but she also wasn't sure if he would have been able to keep his mind if she hadn't been there to ground him. Teagan's weakness was his addiction to power, just as Talek had told her down in the dungeons of the Garden. She hadn't truly understood until the Dark Lands just how deep that addiction went. He honestly had considered living in a complete fantasy world with a king who could twist people into strange creatures if it meant gaining back that beloved power.

Between the minotaurs, and now these guards, the fact that he still tried to wield it unnerved her and she didn't know how to tell him.

The woman stepped forward again pulling her from her thoughts. "I will escort you to the Council of the Wise. They'll decide what to do with you. Follow me, please."

Teagan beamed at her and motioned for her to lead. Shaleigh was happy to follow and couldn't help but be

proud of how far she had come: she could now help negotiate at Teagan's side, something she never thought herself
capable of back home.

The woman led them through the outer gate and
down the path that wound up to the front of the giant
black spiral that climbed into the sky. Now that they were
closer to it, the design of the building made it look like it
was lopsided – it had to be an optical illusion brought on
by the spirals. Looking up at it made Shaleigh dizzy so she
kept her gaze fixed on their surroundings instead.

They were walking past what she at first thought were
well cared for trees and bushes, but soon realized they
were gardens. The trees bore fruit that the men and
women in cloaks were harvesting. For some reason it
took her by surprise after seeing the destitution of the
Pasture within the Garden.

These people weren't slaves or servants; they were
dressed like the guards. She would have thought they
could use magic to harvest the trees instead, but none of
them were wielding staffs. Was it part of their training?

It was clear that unexpected visitors were a rare occasion - she could see them whisper as they passed but
couldn't make out what they said. She wondered what
was most shocking: the fact that Teagan was a Faerie, that
she was from the Human World, or that the two of them
had rather accidentally brought down one of the most
powerful kingdoms in the land.

The woman who led them glanced back with a
knowing smile that instantly made Shaleigh feel guilty
even though she hadn't said a word.

She whispered to Teagan, trying not to be rude, but

unable to keep from asking, "How exactly does this place work?"

"As I said, anyone with magical abilities are permitted to train here and then—"

"No, I know that part. But... what kind of abilities do they have here?"

His eyes narrowed. "I don't understand what you're asking."

"I mean, are they trained in how to wield fire or ice or something? Are they trained in how to talk to animals? What can they do?"

"Ah, you're asking what specialties this school has."

"*Yes*, that's it."

He clasped his hands behind his back. "The Sanctuary specializes in all of them. Anyone with magical abilities are permitted here, so they support any type of magic. They teach students dedication and rigor, but also how to hone their power and control it." He gave a small reminiscent smile. "Master Cathal, for example, had many abilities, but magic was always a last resort. He thought that battles could be won with words and that, if done properly, negotiations should never lead to bloodshed."

Shaleigh considered this as they neared the front of the spiral building. "So why was there a war with the Pello Pines?"

Teagan shrugged. "Because the trees were addicted to feasting on blood and refused to live like normal trees again. You saw the one back in Bertha. It lives on sunlight and water, but it still tries to attack anything with blood in its veins. They are quite greedy creatures."

Shaleigh considered for a moment, then lowered her

voice. "Do you think those Pello Pines are attacking the Garden right now?"

Teagan frowned and pursed his lips, but spoke in a hushed voice, "Each day the daegonrúsc gets weaker and the Pello Pines get stronger. I honestly have no idea how much time we have, if any." There was a worry in his eyes that made a pit of concern form in her stomach. She had no idea how many days it had been since she cut the ribbon. Between waking up in the forest with Teagan to traveling through the Dark Lands, they could already be out of time.

Shaleigh wasn't able to continue down those dark thoughts because they came to a pair of black metal doors, each with four overlapping silver rings etched into the wood like an endless chain. Now that Shaleigh was close enough, she could see that the entire building was made out of that same metal. The taller guard pulled a door open, clearly struggling with the weight of it.

Glancing to Teagan, Shaleigh met his concerned expression with one of her own. He was probably thinking exactly what she was: they were walking into a cage.

"Do the Council of the Wise not take visitors outdoors?" Teagan asked, the worry in his voice unmistakable. This was a very different place than the houses in the trees back in the City of the Fae or the Masked King's throne.

"No," the woman said with a tight smile. "And if you want our protection, you'll have to abide by our rules, Teagan."

~

THE WOMAN LED them through the large metal doors, using her staff as a walking stick. Inside the sound reverberated up the metal walls and Shaleigh jumped.

"Are you alright?" Teagan asked, his voice low.

"Yeah, just jumpy. I don't like this place."

"Neither do I."

But what choice did they have? That was the unspoken question between them as Shaleigh gripped her elbows closer to her chest. The staff rapped again and again on the metal floor. She hoped she would eventually get used to it, but wasn't sure if she could.

The air felt noticeably warmer inside compared to the cool wind of the evening, though it also smelled stale. Shaleigh doubted they opened up any windows to let the wind in very often. This place was clearly meant to contain, not to embrace the outdoors.

They came to stand at the edge of a large, circular room with a blazing fire in the center that would have taken up at least three fireplaces back home. It looked like a fire pit with a chimney that was built above it that extended up the center of the building. There were benches and tables everywhere with people reading books longer than her outstretched hand.

She wasn't sure how they could concentrate with the random slamming of staffs on the metal because their guide wasn't the only one doing it. It had to be some sort of training method to get them to concentrate. Shaleigh knew it was a test she would never be able to pass.

Then there was the staircase. The silver steps wound

up the outer edge of the spiral, crawling out into doors that likely led to more rooms. She craned her neck back trying to see all of them at once. There must have been hundreds of them. If the outside of the Sanctuary was intimidating, the inside was like a fractal, ever continuing upwards and into the sky.

"Welcome to the Sanctuary," the woman with the black ringlets said with a smile. "My name is Laurel by the way, I don't know if we were properly introduced. Did I tell you that my specialty was in telepathy?"

Shaleigh's mouth dropped open.

Teagan cocked his head to the side. "I'm sorry, but I'm not familiar with that school of magic."

"It means she can read our minds." Shaleigh sighed. "And she's probably been doing that ever since she saw us."

Laurel smiled brightly. "This kid from the Human World sure does know a lot."

"Wait, so what were you going to do to us with your staff?" Shaleigh asked, knowing she probably wouldn't like the answer.

"I was going to make you forget we ever existed, at least for a few days. Let you wander around the woods for a bit."

Shaleigh thought of them wandering back toward the minotaurs without any memory of being attacked by them. "I'm really glad you didn't do that!"

The woman's smile turned into a frown. "Yeah, me too... the minotaurs, are they really that upset?"

It was Shaleigh's turn to give a knowing smile. "I'm sorry, but that information is for the leaders."

"She means the Council," Teagan added, giving Shaleigh a wink. She almost got it right, but he did seem to appreciate her taking the lead for a little while.

"I hope you all are up for a climb today," Laurel said. "If you want to speak to the Council of the Wise, they are at the top of the staircase."

Shaleigh stared up to the dizzying height of the spiral again. "Why would they want to sit way up there? Doesn't it take them forever to get back down?"

Laurel laughed and patted Shaleigh's head as though she was a dog and had done something silly. Shaleigh's mouth dropped and she had to refrain herself from slapping the magician. She was aware that her hair probably wasn't in the best condition between their unexpected trip to the Faerie city and their travels through the Dark Lands, but that didn't mean that anybody had the right to touch her hair without her permission.

The words fell out of her mouth before she even realized it, "Excuse you."

Laurel's smile faded to awkward embarrassment, and Shaleigh hoped that she saw exactly how freaking rude she had been.

"I think you're going to regret reading my mind at some point."

Laurel shook her head. "If you aren't up for the climb, I can have one of my friends —"

"There's no need," Teagan interrupted. "I can make that climb without hardly any effort. Outrunning minotaurs was honestly far more challenging than a simple stairwell." He held out his arms to Shaleigh. "Would you join me again?"

Shaleigh met his eyes in shock, wanting to smack him for even considering doing that, but he knew she couldn't. She had already lost her temper once and that was pushing it. Instead, she kept her voice low, "Are you sure you're up for that? You were hurt pretty bad earlier."

He gave a fake smile as though he hadn't been out of breath earlier over a simple hill and rubbing his back like it was killing him. That really wasn't a big surprise considering it was Teagan.

She sighed. "Okay, but if you drop me, you're going to regret it."

He picked her up with a laugh and made sure she was secure before leaping to the stairwell. One magician gaped and dropped the rolled-up parchments he was carrying. Another dropped her book on the ground with a resounding *boom* that echoed up and down the spiral building.

Shaleigh didn't have long to watch their reactions because soon Teagan leaped to a higher set of stairs, then a higher one. She could feel the air getting warmer as they rose and occasionally doors would open as curious onlookers poked their heads out only to be shocked as a red-headed Faerie and a grinning Human landed and leaped again. One hapless young magician, wearing a grey cloak who had clearly been asleep, walked out onto the stairwell — right in Teagan's way as he was about to land.

Shaleigh gripped Teagan's arm, but the Faerie landed on the metal railing instead of the stairwell. The poor magician let out a yelp of fright before falling to the ground.

"Sorry!" Shaleigh called out to him; he blinked with only mute, wide-eyed shock.

Soon the coil shaped building was narrow enough that Teagan could easily have jumped from one side to the next, but instead he stopped and put Shaleigh down. It was then that she noticed that he was breathing hard. He put a hand on the railing as Shaleigh found her footing on the stairs.

"Are you alright?"

"Yes," he breathed, swallowing as he gulped down air. "Just a bit winded." He rubbed his back again, and Shaleigh gave him the best impersonation of an outraged Kaeja that she could muster.

"You're still injured. Badly. I knew you were and yet you still insisted on that stupidity. What is wrong with you? I have legs, you know, two of them!"

He smiled at her, standing up a bit straighter. "Yes, but you couldn't handle the stairs at the High Castle. You couldn't possibly handle these."

She narrowed her eyes at him. "You were in a Faerie pact at the time, you know. That's why they didn't bother you. Don't act like you're all high and mighty now. You shouldn't have pushed yourself. That was a really bad idea."

Teagan rolled his eyes. "I don't think it's that bad. You're making this out to be a far bigger issue than it is."

A door creaked open behind them and Shaleigh turned in frustration. "We're good, thanks for checking on us." A woman stared at her wide-eyed, not saying a word, but Shaleigh ignored her and pulled the door closed again. She held the handle for a moment, not really wanting to deal with another person to ogle them or to see them arguing. They needed to talk and she was tired of every person around wanting to watch or get involved.

"Can you walk okay? How bad is it?" she asked, still holding the handle despite the angry calls on the other side of the door.

Teagan laughed. "I can walk well enough. Though, maybe we can take a slower pace?"

"Please," she said then they began climbing the stairs side by side.

The woman from behind the door came out as they walked away shouting, "How dare you! Such an impudent child."

Shaleigh grinned and bit her lip to keep from laughing; Teagan shook his head.

"What in the world has gotten into you?" he asked as they took a moment to let him catch his breath before starting on the next level.

She shrugged. "I don't know, I just didn't want them to see you struggling. I don't think that's a good idea here. I'm also tired of you having to hide when you're injured. You did that enough in the Garden," she paused, before adding, "plus, it was fun."

Teagan smiled. "Why do you think I did that back in the Garden? As you said, I was in a Faerie pact. I didn't feel strain or injuries like you and I do now. It was a very different situation."

"I don't think so." She dragged her fingers across the cold metal railing. "I know you don't like to talk about it, but I think you hurt a lot around that time." He gave her a concerned look but didn't respond. "If everything had been as fantastic as you keep saying it was, then why did the Masked King take you apart like that?"

Teagan pursed his lips.

"We both know the truth. You can fake it for them if you want, or if you feel like we're in danger, but you don't have to do that for me. I don't need the fake you; I need the *real* you. I like him way better anyway."

Teagan gave her a genuine smile and took a moment to figure out what to say. She thought she saw tears in his eyes, but it was hard to tell in the dim light. "Thank you," he whispered. "That means a lot to me actually. More than you probably know."

They climbed the next two levels in silence until, once again, they had to take a break. It wasn't just for Teagan that time, Shaleigh's legs were burning. She leaned forward to rub on her quads to try to get them to loosen up while Teagan leaned his back against the wall and took deep breaths.

"Why they heck would they build a place like this?" she grumbled.

"From my experience, leaders like to be housed higher up than the people they lead. It makes them feel powerful."

She smirked, knowing she shouldn't ask, but unable to help herself, "Is that why your people live in trees?"

He arched an eyebrow. "No, that's not at all the reason. It's far easier to make the best use of space when you build vertically instead of horizontally."

She nodded in mock agreement.

He sighed. "You're suggesting that not every building method is a power play."

"Maybe," she said and shrugged. "You're the one that immediately talked about power. I was meaning the stairway more than the height. You would think that a bunch of magicians could build an elevator if you all had one at the Games."

He chuckled. "That was my own design based on what I had seen your people do in the Human World. It was fairly basic by comparison, but quite functional as you saw."

"I didn't bring it up as an excuse for you to brag about your creations," she teased as she started climbing again. Teagan joined her.

"No, but you did ask."

Shaleigh paused to look at him. "I was hoping you knew the reasoning behind it instead of just comparing them to Madam Cloom and your Garden again."

"Ah, I see," he said then went silent for a moment as they climbed. "I understand that they do it as a sort of meditation. The repetitive, strenuous activity is seen as forcing the mind to be elsewhere, and therefore to focus attention on anything other than how much your legs hurt."

She shook her head as they got to the next level. "I don't think it's working. That's *all* I can think about."

The rest of the climb was done in silence. Both of them had to stop to breathe before they reached the end. At least now they were at the very top center of the edifice, where the top of the chimney reached the roof.

Shaleigh knocked at the door that they stood before. It squeaked open and a short young woman in a brown robe that was clearly too big for her poked her head out. She had dark skin with a pinkish complexion and very short hair. She stared at them both with wide, curious eyes.

"Are you expected?" she asked in a soft voice.

"I don't think so," Shaleigh said. "However, the guards told us that in order to speak to the Council of the Wise we needed to—"

"Ah yes, that was probably Laurel. She notified us that you were being sent up."

Shaleigh blinked at her. That hadn't been that long ago. How had they gotten notice so quickly? She was pretty sure she would have noticed if someone had passed them on the stairwell, and if the woman had expected them, why had she even asked? There didn't look to be any other visitors here, at least none that she could see. She couldn't help but be reminded of the Healers back in the Garden with their stuffy attitudes.

"Come in, please. The Council will meet with you shortly." It took the short woman some effort to pull back the large wooden door, but she didn't complain. There was another short set of steps and Shaleigh couldn't repress a groan at the sight of them.

"Come along," Teagan encouraged before he started up them. "We went up that many, we can do a few more." Shaleigh shook her head but followed. He was very good at feigning health when there was an audience. Perhaps him not being bothered by the stairs at High Castle wasn't his Faerie pact after all, maybe it was just his pride.

The few steps opened up to a large circular room with windows on all sides. It reminded Shaleigh of the Overlook, where Madam Cloom was able to look out at all ends of the Garden.

In the distance she could see the fires of the pyres that she and Teagan had escaped from, still burning brightly against the darkness. Even at night she could spot the plumes of smoke against the clear sky. She hadn't realized though the distance they had traveled before, but now saw how far they had run through the treetops.

Someone cleared their throat and she turned, noticing a crowd of people standing near the window, also overlooking the pyres in the distance. They reminded her of a bunch of rubberneckers back home, only without the cell phones held up to take photos.

"Excuse me, Council members?" The short woman stepped forward, having to hold up her robe so she didn't trip over it as she approached them.

One of the people turned around, an older man with a thick white and gray beard. He looked back to Teagan and Shaleigh, snorted a laugh and gave them a sneer, then turned away to whisper to the person on his left. He acted as though staring at burning bodies in the distance was far more important than anything they had to say.

"You have visitors," the woman tried again, shifting her weight from one leg to the next.

"Oh?" the same man asked with a huff, and Shaleigh couldn't tell if it was a scoffing sound or a gruff laugh. Either way, she already didn't like the attitude of this Council.

"You do realize those aren't bonfires in the distance, right?" Shaleigh asked, drawing several pairs of eyes, but beyond caring.

Teagan pursed his lips and placed a hand on her shoulder – she just wasn't sure if that was meant to encourage her to continue or to get her to stop. Either way, her legs were burning and Teagan was in pain, even if he didn't want to admit it. Somewhere near the Garden the Pello Pines were slowly waking up, and the longer they waited to speak, the more time they wasted.

"Those are burning corpses you're all watching."

THE PURPOSE OF KNOWLEDGE

Shaleigh

The group broke up into murmurs of concern and frustration, probably at Shaleigh for speaking out of turn. All of them had to be at least eighty years old and they were all in a fluster at her words. Surely, they hadn't just sat there for a day, staring at those pyres in the distance and not actually going to look at them. Surely, they weren't that disconnected from something that close to their borders.

She had thought she was stating the obvious, but that clearly wasn't the case. And as much as she despised Madam Cloom, at least she knew what was happening around the Garden. She didn't just watch and speculate, she acted.

Teagan thought all those steps were supposed to be a meditation, but Shaleigh saw what they really were: a barrier to keep the terrified Council safe; an extra obstacle to keep the precious Council from having to deal with the students down below, an extra preventative step to keep any guests at bay, and another layer of distance to prevent any naysayers an audience.

Then, she had walked in and broke through their protective barrier. If she had any hope that they would find swift aid here, it was quickly dwindling.

The short woman who had answered the door blinked her big eyes in shock, clearly trying to find a way to excuse herself from the tense room. She turned to hurry out the door but one of the women on the council called out to her, "Daphne! Aren't you going to tell us who these visitors are, you daft woman?"

She stopped and turned back, her voice cracking and sounding near tears as she said, "I'm sorry, I-I-"

Shaleigh couldn't help but feel sorry for her. She wouldn't want to have to work for the Council either.

"There's no need," Teagan interrupted. Even his patience had reached its limit, it seemed. "I can assure you that we are both fully capable of introducing ourselves." He placed a hand to his chest and said, "I am Teagan, once the High Faerie of the Garden and assistant to Master Cathal in the Battle of the Pello Pines." He gestured to Shaleigh, a smirk on the edge of his lips. "And this is Shaleigh Mallet, my Human companion."

"Ha! Human companion," spat the old man with the thick beard who had glared at them before. He climbed into one of the cushioned chairs in the room. The seat creaked under his frail frame. "Is that what you call a Human who made the respectable Garden fall to flame and Shadow Wolves? Your *companion?*" He barked out a dry laugh.

Shaleigh felt her mouth go dry. Teagan glanced to her and gave a silent apology with his gaze. The old man's words were true and she knew it. She couldn't let that define her, not when Teagan needed medical assistance. Perhaps it was the fact that her thighs were still burning from climbing those last few floors, or that Teagan's hand had drifted down to his back, or that this was the fourth place that she had to prove her competence, but Shaleigh was tired of playing nice.

"If you call a land that regularly kidnaps people from the Human World and makes them fight in battles or work the fields until they're dead a *"respectable* land," then I don't know if we can have a proper discussion here."

The arguing ceased. The old man with the beard glared at her so hard she thought his eyes might turn red at any moment. It was better than being laughed at though. She was tired of that.

Teagan gave a nervous laugh. "What she means is—"

Shaleigh cut him off, "What I mean is that we have information on the crazed magician behind all of this and the mad Faerie he's in a pact with. Now, we can either work together to try to stop them, or we can sit here and exchange insults all night." She frowned. "Also, Teagan needs medical aid, but we were told we first had to climb a bunch of stairs first before we could even get that." She took a deep breath. The room was so quiet she could hear Daphne's nervous breathing behind her. Even Teagan wasn't sure what to say.

"Now, are you all going to help us or are you going to

turn us away? And if you do plan to turn us away, know that when they come to kill me, I will let every magician in this place know that it was the Council that didn't want to take responsibility for one of your own wayward members."

The old man leaned forward, his lean fingers gripping the cushy armrests with a force that made his hands tremble. "What do you mean by that, exactly?"

Shaleigh met his stern gaze. "He's a magician, isn't he? That means he was trained here like all the others."

There was a stillness in the room that lasted longer than Shaleigh liked until the old man sat back in his chair and gave a long sigh. Despite his frail body, Shaleigh could tell he was the leader in the group. There was a reason he was the only one to address her so far, and the others all looked to him for direction. He reminded her of some of the older tenured professors at the university, the ones who had been doing research for twenty something years and had graduate students clamoring to be in their labs. The ones who were so quick witted, you had to take great leaps to keep up mentally.

The group before her might have been called a Council of Elders, but the old man glaring at them from across the room, as though he was placating children, was the true decision maker. He was the one she had to convince to help them. He was the one she had to prove herself to.

"For such a young child of the Human World, you certainly have learned much about this land in your sheltered time here." The old man's voice rumbled with authority, then he gave the tiniest smile and the edges of his eyes crinkled. "Especially regarding tricky nego-tiations."

Shaleigh held her hands out. "Look, I know you don't want us here. I know you see us as a threat that could bring a dangerous enemy here, but you have to under-stand that you all are partially responsible for that enemy."

The old man lifted up his hand and Shaleigh went quiet as though she was in school. She wondered at herself for going silent so easily.

"Daphne, please take my fellow Council members downstairs so I can speak with these two... visitors alone."

Daphne blinked a few times in confusion and Shaleigh inwardly frowned. So, this wasn't a normal request.

The other Council members didn't argue, but they looked concerned as they passed and Shaleigh started to doubt her earlier assumptions. Maybe this old man wasn't the true leader and decision maker as she thought; maybe he was some sort of executioner. No, she couldn't second-guess herself. She had to keep her self-assurance if she wanted to be taken seriously.

The room was eerily quiet again with all the others gone and for the first time Shaleigh could hear the wind whipping around the tower outside. She could also feel the slight vertigo that the building gave as it swayed in the wind.

Teagan closed his eyes for a moment to gather himself. He would normally never even show a hint of weakness to someone like this, yet it was clear he was struggling. Shaleigh had to stay focused not only for herself but for him too. She put an arm on his shoulder and he leaned heavily against her.

"I guess there are plenty of seats free now, aren't there?" she asked out loud. Without a glance to the old man, she led Teagan up to sit on one of the plush seats. After Teagan sat down, letting out a shaky sigh, the tension in the room grew.

Finally, she turned to the old man, but he was no longer glaring at them. Instead, he looked concerned and slightly outraged. "My name is Druce and I am the Speaker of the Council of Elders here at the Sanctuary."

"Pleased to meet you, I guess," she said impatiently.

He smiled slightly. "Tell me, do you know why this place is called the Sanctuary?"

"Well it's clearly not out of a desire to aid the wounded."

Teagan sighed. "Shaleigh..."

Druce gave a laugh. "No, she has a good point. We don't aid the wounded, not without reason. Our knowledge is vast and our magic is powerful, but we do this for the beauty of knowledge itself. Our libraries are stocked with the most precious books in all the land."

Shaleigh remembered the molding library of Aife with its gorgeous high ceilings and walls upon walls of books. She wondered if Druce the Speaker of the Council of Elders had ever climbed down from his high horse to go explore any other library besides his own. She really doubted it.

"Our experts could bring down any kingdom they wish, destroy any land they encountered, take any place they wanted, but they don't. They understand that there is a balance that is needed. They understand that such power is to be contained. It is to be gathered, to be admired, to be studied, not to be used except in what-ever small amounts are needed for survival. My point, young lady," he said aiming a crooked finger in her direction, "is that this magician could not have come from within our walls. That simply isn't possible. You say that we are somehow responsible for this mess that happened in the Garden, for the pyres of supposed bodies that burn in the distance, but our values don't permit such atrocities."

Shaleigh crossed her arms. "I thought that all magicians had to be trained here. I thought that in order to master their magic they had to come here."

"Of course, they must, but that doesn't mean that they do." He gave her a thin smile, clearly relishing that he knew something that she didn't, and Shaleigh had to clench her teeth in order to keep from saying something she shouldn't. "There are some ridiculous magicians who decide that our way of life isn't for them. These crazed youths decide to teach themselves how to wield the magic they possess and I'm afraid that they aren't graced with our guidance and values. They, in turn, can do all sorts of disturbing acts, but we cannot be held accountable. We cannot be blamed for every so-called magician's mistakes."

Shaleigh ran a hand through her hair, noting with annoyance that a twig had gotten stuck in one of her fraying twists. "So, you're saying that because this magician didn't come here to train, that you're washing your hands of anything he's done?" As she spoke his smile grew wider. From the corner of her eye, she saw Teagan shaking his head. "You aren't going to help us, and you're not going to try to stop him. Instead, you're just going to sit here while he forces a Faerie to lose his mind and succumb to the Madness."

"Yes, the Madness." A deep furrow appeared between his brows. "That is very unfortunate. Faeries are susceptible to that illness and are quite volatile I understand when it reaches the tipping point."

"This is all fascinating to learn about," Teagan said, sounding less out of breath, "but I can assure you that Keriam was in fact a student here. He studied alongside Flidais, Breena, Owain, and of course, my dear Cathal. He learned your so-called values and turned away from them purposefully. He was, in fact, the first to ever try to use a magic elixir to force an entire village to become his slaves, if I recall correctly."

"Keriam was *not* one of ours," Druce growled. "He might have attended the Sanctuary, he might have pretended to be one of us, but he was *not* one of our apprentices. That man only had eyes on destruction and domination."

Teagan cocked his head to the side. "But he did attend, and he did succeed while in these walls. You cannot deny that, even if you do refuse to admit he was granted mastery here."

Druce's face went bright red and Shaleigh prepared to shove him back if he tried anything. "Keriam is dead. That happened centuries ago."

"No, he's not." Shaleigh said. "He's alive and he's made a pact with a Faerie named Talek. We think he found immortality with the Masked King, but we're not sure."

A shudder went through the elder magician and he

leaned back heavily in his creaky chair. "That *thing* is involved in this too?"

"Please," Shaleigh said urgently, "we need your help. I know they're looking for us and I don't know what they'll do if they find us."

Druce wiped at his whiskers on the side of his mouth in thought. "They'll kill you if you're lucky," he said and shook his head. "If he's that determined to find you though, he probably won't do that."

"Talek wants me back," Teagan admitted, his gaze on the distant pyres. "He'll do anything to get me back. He's possibly more trouble than he's worth for Keriam, but once the pact is in place, they're both stuck."

Druce got to his feet with a groan, both knees popping. "Keriam is working with unstable magic at this point. Dabbling with immortality, making deals with the Masked King. It's honestly no wonder his Faerie pact was tainted with Madness. His immortality has likely made his magic unstable too. If the Faerie was also unstable... there's no telling when the blast will come, and it would be best if he is as isolated as possible when it does."

"The blast..." Shaleigh whispered, remembering all too well the wasteland of the Dark Lands and the red-eyed black dogs who guarded the perimeter. She thought of the banshee woman, Ms. Kasey, and shuddered.

Druce put his hands on his hips and stared down at Teagan, who had slumped further into the chair. "We can't assist with this, and I do apologize for that. If they were to come here, we simply have too many apprentices and magicians working here for it to be safe. I wish I could say we could fend them off, but even our combined forces are no match for a Faerie pact."

Teagan hung his head. "I was afraid of that. We honestly have no alternatives at this point."

The elder turned to Shaleigh, "What about the Human World? If you fled there perhaps, they would follow and then the explosion of magic would be a Human problem, not ours."

"Are you seriously asking if we want to blow up a bunch of Humans instead of magicians? We don't even have magic over there! We would be defenseless."

Druce gave a disturbing smile. "Why not? It's certainly not the first time mistakes of our land were pushed out there. Where do you think the first minotaur was sent?"

Teagan waved a hand. "That's simply out of the question. We can't corrupt other lands with our mistakes."

"Then I suppose we can at least make sure you're both healed up before we send you out to meet your fates."

Shaleigh glared as Druce shuffled toward the door. "And none of you could, oh I don't know, come with us? Help us out?"

"And waste our valuable time and resources on a wayward magician and some crazed Faerie? I think not! It would be too risky. If our entire Sanctuary wouldn't stand a chance against them, why do you think a handful would? Honestly, you are such a young, naive thing."

Shaleigh gaped at him as he reached for the door.

"I'll send Daphne in with a few of our magicians that specialize in healing. They'll get you up and moving faster than any Faerie magic could." The door closed and the sound echoed through the empty room.

"'A young, naive *thing?*' Did you hear that? I hope he falls down those stairs!"

Teagan laughed. "We are in the Sanctuary, led by probably the most arrogant leaders in all the land. Of course, the head of their council is going to talk down to you. They talk down to everyone."

Shaleigh took his hand and squeezed when she saw him wipe away a tear. "At least they're going to get you patched up. That's honestly what I wanted most."

"Not just that, they're going to send up magicians to do it. You realize how rare that is? I know it probably doesn't seem like much of a victory to you, but it is."

"Maybe I can convince them to give us some supplies for the road before they kick us out?"

Before he could respond, the door opened again. This time four men and women in long, blue robes walked in. Shaleigh left Teagan's side and tried to introduce herself, but they brushed past her and went to Teagan, where they crouched down and spoke in whispers.

Teagan gave a whimpered cry, but she couldn't see anything because they were surrounding him, and their robes obscured everything.

"What are you doing to him?"

Silence.

"Teagan, are you okay?"

More silence.

Shaleigh's heart thudded in her temples; she wrung her hands together. Unable to wait, she approached slowly. She could see that Teagan's shirt had been lifted up and that they had their hands on his abdomen.

Before she could see too much though, one of the

women put a hand out and glanced her way with a stern expression. "Stay back, please. We need space."

Shaleigh backed away quickly. They reminded her of EMTs from home, working quickly and as efficiently as possible. Perhaps whatever they were doing to Teagan was uncomfortable to look at and they didn't want her to see it. She felt a hand on her shoulder and turned to see Daphne.

"He'll be alright," she reassured and smiled, blinking rapidly. "They're good at what they do even if they are a little intimidating."

Shaleigh watched her for a moment, remembering how close she was earlier to breaking down in tears. "I'm sorry for how they treat you."

She glanced away. "Oh no, I deserve it. I'm fortunate to still be here. I'm not very good with my magical skills, so they gave me this job to teach me how to be more disciplined. I'm afraid I'm not very good at it either."

Shaleigh watched her carefully. "You're probably better than you give yourself credit for. The Council is just full of jerks."

Dalphne gave a small smile before pushing it away and clearing her throat. "Anyway, you don't have to worry about your friend. This group knows what they're doing. They're sent in to handle the most serious injuries."

Shaleigh arched her eyebrows. "So, this is their job here?"

"Something like that. They're the best in the entire Sanctuary, and some of the busiest magicians here, to be honest. It's amazing how many ways people can injure themselves. Between the woods, the minotaurs, and the Sanctuary repairs, there are always people needing help."

So Druce wasn't being entirely honest with them then. He had said that magicians only studied there for the sake of gathering knowledge, but they appeared to have an emergency healing team on hand for grave injuries. She wondered what other lies he had peppered into their little talk.

After a few more difficult minutes of waiting, the magicians helped Teagan to his feet as he pulled his shirt down. Shaleigh was only able to briefly glimpse where the bruising had been, and where she suspected he had been bleeding internally. Now she couldn't even see any dark blemish on his skin.

"Thanks," she said as they passed, but the magicians left without looking her way, talking amongst themselves in hushed whispers. She gave a heavy sigh and went to Teagan. "How do you feel?"

"Tired, but much better." He stretched gingerly with a hand on his back. "Good as new in fact. Though, I must say that the Healers in the Garden were much more adept at preventing pain." He touched his side. "I can tell they're still learning the craft."

Shaleigh smiled. It had to be frustrating for him having to deal with those magicians when he used to be able to heal wounds easily on his own. That familiar guilt tried to rise up again, but she pushed it back down. It was best that the Garden was gone, she reminded herself, even if it did have some perks like perfected healing.

"If you two will follow me, I'll show you to the exit," Daphne said with a polite smile.

"Um..." Shaleigh glanced to Teagan before turning back to her. "Druce said that we could also get some supplies to take with us."

"Really?" She blinked. "I don't recall him mentioning that, but he was in quite a hurry to leave."

Shaleigh grinned. "Okay, he didn't really, but I was hoping we could get something. Those minotaurs out there were brutal. I was going to ask Druce about it, but he was too busy insulting me." It was a risky move, but Shaleigh hoped that their talk earlier had put her on Daphne's good side. Plus, she had met enough abused assistants at the university parties back home to know one when she saw one.

Sure enough, a spark entered Daphne's eyes. "Was he? Well that does sound familiar. Let's go see what we can find. We have more supplies than we can use in the Sanctuary, but the Elders believe that everything should be stockpiled, just like their precious knowledge." She fake laughed and Shaleigh joined in.

As Daphne turned for the door, Shaleigh gave a very pointed look toward Teagan. It seemed there was quite a lot about the Sanctuary and its leaders that weren't what they seemed. Maybe it was best that they were leaving.

INSTEAD OF HAVING to take the many stairs down to the bottom of the building, they discovered that the Elders had a convenient magical lift. It was through one of the doors that Shaleigh had assumed belonged to another magician. The lift looked like it was fashioned in the style of an elevator from the Human World, but they clearly didn't completely understand how it worked. She was amused to see little decorative circles were carved on the interior wall where buttons would normally go.

She grinned at Teagan as they stepped on and she pressed a few of the fake buttons for show. "It's good to see so much creativity on display here."

Teagan rolled his eyes.

Daphne blinked at her, oblivious to the sarcasm. "Oh yes, the Elders are very proud of this. Others have tried to replicate it, but resisting gravity is a difficult talent to master."

The lift didn't groan, grumble, or rattle as the door closed and it began to descend. Shaleigh wasn't quite sure how they made it lower because there was no lever like the lift she had used at the Games. It was mostly made of metal, but tiny slots on either side of the wooden door allowed her to look out, and it was daunting to see so many levels pass by, especially when she wasn't sure how it even worked. Even roller coaster rides weren't all smoke and mirrors.

As they slowly descended, Shaleigh wondered: what was the point of having so much technology, knowledge, and supplies at their fingertips if they weren't going to use them to help anyone? The Council didn't even want the lift to be used to help their own apprentices. Instead, the Elders hoarded their knowledge and perks for themselves only and left the others to suffer. She wondered if the healing magicians who came upstairs earlier had to climb the steps to reach them or if they were permitted to use the lift... then she saw them, grouped together on one of the stair landings, stopping to catch their breath and rest their legs.

Shaleigh clenched her jaw; it took every ounce of control she had not to curse.

She thought of Queen Mab in the City of the Fae. She was a completely different leader compared to the power-hungry Madam Cloom and the arrogant, aloof Council of Elders at the Sanctuary. Queen Mab was the most feared of all the leaders Shaleigh had met, even by leaders outside of her realm. It was probably due to her psychic abilities and the dedication of her people, but despite it all she was still the best leader. She supported her people regardless of the mistakes they made. Yes, she had wiped out an entire city once and she condoned the murder of Humans, but her heart seemed to be in the right place.

Shaleigh sighed, closing her eyes. For once, she could understand why Master Cathal saw his Garden as so very perfect when these were the alternatives.

The elevator lurched as it settled awkwardly on the bottom, pulling Shaleigh from her thoughts. The doors opened and she saw that several magicians were watching them now. There were at least double the number than had been down here before, and none of them looked very pleased to see them. At least they didn't crowd the doors or spit on the ground.

Daphne turned and gave them a small smile. She looked a little concerned by the crowd but kept a straight posture as she stepped out of the lift. "I'll see what I can find. If you two could stay here for a moment."

Teagan glanced her way, his eyebrows raised. "I'm not sure if we should stay in the lift considering the audience we've somehow gathered." He pursed his lips as she walked away without answering and turned to Shaleigh. "What's going on?"

"This place weirds me out." Shaleigh crossed her arms, working to relax her jaw. It probably only made her look more suspicious. "The Council, or rather just Druce since he pretty much *is* the Council, probably set them all up for this."

Teagan nodded, his gaze moving toward the magicians. Shaleigh looked too and blinked. Had she imagined it or were there even more now? Why did it suddenly feel like they were trapped?

"Perhaps we ought to go back up..." Teagan whispered, taking a step backward.

Shaleigh looked around again for any kind of lever. "How? I don't even know what she did to get us down here."

More magicians joined the others. What had happened to make all of them suddenly despise them? Before it was all about harvesting vegetables, reading books, and enjoying the fireplace. Now they looked like they wanted an excuse to add them to the pyres outside.

The young woman who had dropped a book earlier pushed her long, brown hair out of the way and stepped forward. "You're the one the Faerie is searching for, aren't you? The two who brought the Garden to its knees."

Teagan gave a polite smile. "I think you must be mistaken. We are friends of Druce who was kind enough to spend time talking with us just now, and-"

"I don't think you're helping," Shaleigh whispered,

maneuvering her way over to the fake buttons and pushing one just in case it worked this time. It didn't.

"Aye, Druce said he just spoke with you," a young man in gray robes called out, pointing an accusatory finger at them. "He said if we gave you over, then they would leave us be!"

"Give us... over?" Teagan said, blinking in confusion.

Shaleigh slammed on the wall. "Come on, take us back up!"

The doors closed at her command: that was the spark the idling mob needed.

REUNION

Shaleigh

The doors to the lift slid closed smoothly, but through the cracks they could see the outrage caused by their supposed escape. Where could they possibly go, though? The Sanctuary was as much a prison as the lift itself.

The lift started to climb upwards without any fuss or difficulty. Shaleigh couldn't help but wonder if Daphne feigned her aloof attitude the whole time. Something had happened, something had changed them.

A woman's angry cry reverberated through the building and just as the lift began to reach the first ring of the stairwell something slowed it to a stop. Shaleigh looked through the cracks around the door to see green leaves waving in the breeze. Enormous vines had emerged from a potted plant and looped around the bottom of the lift. The lift tried to rise again but the vine kept it tethered, making the floor tilt. Shaleigh slid, nearly falling into Teagan.

"What kind of plant is that?" she cried, but Teagan didn't answer. When she looked over, he was leaning against the wall, holding his head and panting. "Teagan?"

"She's in my head," he grunted. "How is she able to do that?"

Shaleigh remembered the eerie way Laurel, the guard, knew exactly who they were when they walked in. Clearly, she saw Teagan as the bigger threat of the two of them, and even though Laurel couldn't see them, it didn't prevent her assault.

A loud *bang* erupted as something hit the doors, and Shaleigh jumped. Then came the massive wave of heat, that made her hold her arm up to shield her eyes - that's when she saw the fire. It looked like someone had literally lobbed magma at the wooden door. It wasn't much, but it was enough to start a smoldering fire, and the smoke was spreading rapidly.

She glanced through the crack on the other side of the door and looked down just in time to see Daphne below them with an angry expression on her normally kind face as she prepared to lob a second ball of fire.

Shaleigh knew that whatever was happening now, it wasn't their fault. This wasn't the woman who had stood helplessly upstairs as a doormat for the Council of Elders moments ago - even if she had seemed mildly concerned earlier, she wasn't capable of this level of violence. It wasn't the same woman who offered to get supplies for them under the table just to spite her boss.

Something had happened, but Shaleigh couldn't figure out what.

A second ball of magma landed on the door. The smoke was getting thicker; Shaleigh's eyes were watering and her throat itched. A small fire had formed on the outside of the door, but she couldn't reach it to put it out. If they didn't get out of here soon, they would die of asphyxiation.

Teagan was sitting on the floor, cradling his head.

"Teagan, I need you to focus. I need you to help me get us out of here."

"I can't... think... she won't let me."

Shaleigh couldn't see through the cracks in the door anymore. The smoke was too intense. It was getting to the point where she could barely see Teagan through her tears. First, she needed to find a way to cover their noses against the smoke. They might be able to get out if there was an opening, but they had to survive the smoke first.

She was trying to figure out if she could pull off a strip of Teagan's tunic when she froze for a moment as the words stumbled out of her lips, "The Scáil flower. It must be in the Sanctuary somehow, maybe as a gas. It must have been brought in through the bottom."

Teagan nodded. "That makes... sense! She's just screaming into my mind, it's difficult to—" He broke off into a coughing fit.

She wasn't sure why the flower wasn't affecting them, but someone was clearly controlling the magicians. She didn't have time to be curious. Quickly, she tore off a piece of Teagan's tunic and wrapped it around his nose and mouth. The door was beginning to collapse as the fire spread outwards and toward the metal of the rest of the lift. She could already hear the groaning of metal as it was heating up and the pop of splintering wood where other areas burst into flame. It may not be a normal elevator, so it may not fall, but it was still a death trap.

Shaleigh pulled Teagan into a corner and hoped that the makeshift mask would help as she pulled off a second strip. She could barely keep her eyes open now and was mostly having to work by feel alone. The heat was becoming unbearable, her skin felt singed. Even with the mask she was getting tired; it was getting harder to move.

She wrapped her arms around Teagan, burying her face against his back as tears streamed from her eyes. He put an arm around her, attempting to be comforting, but then lost the strength. His arm dropped away like dead weight and she squeezed him tighter.

This was it. This was how she died. Not on some grand arena in the Garden, not in the belly of an abandoned building, not even in the Slumbering Forest getting eaten by Shadow Wolves, but in a freaking burning elevator. She would have laughed if she could've stopped coughing.

She thought of her father and how upset he would be that he never got to see her again. He would probably assume she had left him like Kristen did. There was no telling what he had done to himself by now.

Then there was Kaeja, and the pain that tore through her chest was more than just her lungs needing oxygen. The thought of her alone and scared, searching for Shaleigh and crying herself to sleep at night, believing it was her fault that Shaleigh disappeared, made the tears come faster.

Screams pulled her mind away from her thoughts. The door was engulfed in flames, and she didn't trust herself enough to try to push through it yet. She didn't even know if she could.

There was something bright red against the door. She tried to focus to see through the smoke. Was it another blob of magma thrown at them, or some other kind of magic?

Something picked her up. She tried to hold onto Teagan as her feet left the ground, but she didn't have any strength left. Her hands felt like they had fallen asleep and she found she couldn't hold onto anything. Then, she was flying through the air. Lights flashed in her eyes, too bright and painful. She tried to shield them, but she couldn't move her arm. Instead, she gave a groan of frustration.

She was placed on the ground and the blurry figure standing above her put a hand over her mouth. Oh great, was asphyxiation by smoke not good enough? They wanted to do it the old-fashioned way? When the hand pulled back away, every inch of Shaleigh's lungs screamed in pain at once. She cried out against it. It felt like dozens of knives were being pulled through her insides and up her throat.

A thick blackness escaped from her mouth. Her lungs felt empty, desperate for air, and she sucked in a deep breath, crisp and clean. Her body shook as her vision cleared and she was finally able to see who the mysterious figure was in front of her: Talek.

~

IN ONE HAND Talek held a ball of dark smoke that was almost black with flecks of red liquid. It took Shaleigh a moment to realize that it was the smoke that had clotted her lungs only moments ago. The red liquid? She assumed it was blood – her blood. The realization made her wince.

He was grinning at her, almost the same way he had when he first met her in the Slumbering Forest when he dropped out of the trees to rescue her. Only, this time his violet eye was vibrant and mocking. Here he was again, thundering into her life to rescue her. And once again she wasn't sure why.

He took the ball of smoke and blood, squeezing it between his hands until it condensed down to a pebble and threw it over his shoulder. "It's good to see you, Shaleigh. It's been too long. I bet you didn't think we would find you, did you?" He grinned wider as though this was supposed to be a happy reunion.

She was lying on one of the stair landings. Above her the stairway continued its spiral upwards. She could see the thick smoke from the fire. Her skin still felt raw from the heat and suddenly her eyes went wide. Teagan was still in the lift. How could Talek know that though? The smoke too thick down there.

"Tee-," she croaked, her throat raw from the smoke inhalation. She broke out into a coughing fit, and Talek furrowed his brows at her.

"There's no need to thank me, you're very welcome." He bit his lip. "If my master knew I had rescued you he would have a fit! But he's too busy with his Scáil smoke to be bothered with me at the moment. It's kind of fun!"

Her coughing fit wasn't letting up and every part of her body hurt. "Tee-" she tried again as Talek placed a hand on her shoulder. There was a burst of warmth, every part of her body shivered, then her throat cleared completely. She put a hand to her neck, her mind trying to keep up with so many things at once.

She gulped in a deep breath. "Teagan!" she cried, "Teagan's down there! You have to save him!"

Talek's eyes went wide and despair wracked across his face. Without a word he leapt off the stairwell and down to the lift. Shaleigh rolled over onto her side. Her body was healed but everything took so much effort: she felt tired from head to toe and all she wanted to do was sleep. Was it another bad reaction to Talek's corrupted magic? She wasn't sure, but she didn't have time to rest, not when Teagan was still down there. Instead, she pulled herself up to her feet and looked over the edge of the landing.

Talek was in a frenzy. The fiery lift had been pulled to the ground and he was flinging pieces of it everywhere in his attempt to find Teagan. He tossed pieces of the flaming door backward, and everywhere the boards hit, the flames spread as well. Fires sprouted up all around the ground level of the Sanctuary. The magicians, who she now knew were under mind control, were standing there completely unaware of the flames. One young man, who she recognized as one she had seen upon entering, was completely engulfed in flames and dying on the ground. Their horrid controller, who had to be Keriam, must have had no use for them any longer because they stood there frozen with glassy eyes. She caught a glimpse of a robe before one magician was yanked away; someone was dragging them out.

Shaleigh leaned against the wall as she descended the stairwell. Her limbs felt heavy; she couldn't walk as fast as she wanted at first but gained speed as she went. She couldn't see Teagan. All she saw were magicians and fire; all she heard were the desperate cries of Talek and the spreading of crackling flames.

"Leave him!" a deep voice reverberated through the Sanctuary and Shaleigh paused as she searched for who had spoken.

Keriam the Magician leaned on his staff in a corner not far from the rubble of the lift. He looked annoyed and sounded impatient. His order, despite the Faerie pact that Shaleigh knew they had, was ignored. Talek continued throwing around the fiery pieces until there was nothing left. Then, he gave a terrible scream causing Shaleigh to rush down the remaining stairs. If Teagan wasn't in the lift, where was he? Had he been thrown from it when it hit the ground? Had she blacked out at some point and not seen it?

When she reached the main floor, she saw Colin dart in from the front door. He grabbed hold of the woman who had summoned vines earlier, the one standing now like a mannequin despite the fires climbing ever higher beside her. Slowly he dragged her to the door where Mawr waited. Shaleigh wanted to call out to them. She wanted to see the look of happiness on Mawr's face, she wanted to give Colin a hug and apologize for this horrible mess she caused, but then Talek gave another howl.

"I said leave him!" Keriam roared, slamming his staff onto the ground and shaking the entire building. Shaleigh put a hand against the wall to steady herself. Up above a loud groan echoed and a piece of the metal ceiling fell. Shaleigh darted to the side as it fell only a few feet from where she had been.

She took a deep breath but knew this was the beginning. The place was built of metal and would soon turn into a furnace. Most of the ground level of the Sanctuary was on fire and even though Colin and Mawr had gotten almost all of the magicians out, the tower was no longer stable. Up above the ceiling swayed side to side, far more than it should have been way at the top of the staircase. The chimney, which had extended from the large fireplace to the top, had collapsed to the side, funneling more hot smoke up to the roof.

"Oh no," she whispered, backing away. There was no telling how much wood and metal stood above them. There was no magical barrier here to keep people safe like the Garden had once possessed. This building was already structurally impaired just by design, this was too much stress for the supports to withstand.

"Of course, you would be here," Keriam shouted from across the room as another metal panel fell from the roof between them. Shaleigh looked up to lock eyes with him. "I knew it! I knew you would come here!"

Shaleigh swallowed the dryness in her throat, glancing to the exit door only briefly but immediately regretting it when Keriam laughed.

"You think I'll let you escape from this? You think you could dare?"

The gem of his staff gleamed violet in the room and, again, another shudder tore through the building. He headed to the exit where Colin and Mawr were trying to get the last person out, but Keriam ordered them both inside with his gleaming staff aimed at them. Mawr had to hunker down to get through the doorway and Colin had his arms up as he followed behind.

"No!" she shouted even as Talek screamed again in agony. No. She had already lost Teagan, she couldn't lose them too.

She got to her feet and sprinted toward them even as Keriam closed the doors shut with a wicked smile. She tripped over some rubble and fell hard on her knees. The pain flared up hot against her skin and she winced at her own clumsiness. She used to have such good footing when she'd been exploring abandoned buildings ages ago, and now she couldn't get her legs to move like she wanted them to.

She pulled herself back to her feet when a flash of red on the ground caught her attention.

It was a swath of red hair.

It was Teagan.

He was covered in pieces of broken benches and tables. He must have been thrown from the lift when it crashed and landed here. She had spotted a bit of his hair beneath a broken chair leg and when she pulled it off of him, it came away red with his blood. She pulled off the makeshift mask she had wrapped around his face and he groaned. The more furniture she pulled off of him, the more she realized he was in terrible shape. His left arm was bent at an impossible angle, and she was pretty certain his right leg was also broken.

"Teagan, can you hear me? Teagan!"

His eyes flickered open, his dark eyes searching her face. "Shaleigh, you're alright," he whispered with a pained smile. "I was worried about you."

Tears burned her eyes and she swallowed back the sob that wanted to break free. "I'm going to get Talek. He can help you. He helped me."

She was about to get to her feet when Teagan grabbed her wrist with his good arm. "Please, be careful. He doesn't mean what he does." There were tears in his eyes. "He's good under there, I promise."

He was delusional. That wasn't good. She thought about the blood she had spotted on the chair leg. He might have hit his head hard when he landed. "I know, it's okay." She looked up to Talek in the distance, bracing herself for what would come next. "He's here!" she cried, waving to him. "I've got him!"

Talek was beside them in a flash, his eyes that of a wild animal, crazed and intense. He was trembling from head to toe as he leaned over him. "Teagan, oh my dear, what happened to you?"

Teagan gave a small chuckle. "I think you know the answer to that. Can you help me?"

"Of course, I can. What good is all of this if I can't help you?"

Talek reached out to place a hand on Teagan's chest, the same thing he had done to Shaleigh earlier when she couldn't speak without being in pain. She saw the pain tear through his body as Talek mended everything.

"It's okay," Shaleigh said, patting his good arm. "Just let him work."

There was a woman's loud cry and Shaleigh turned just as a ball of heat whizzed past her face. Teagan gave a horrid scream. Shaleigh turned back to see that a ball of molten lava landed right on his chest. Teagan's body went limp as his eyes rolled up. Talek stared down at him in absolute horror and Shaleigh had to back away from the sheer heat.

She heard a wicked laugh and turned to see Keriam standing in the doorway, Daphne standing beside him, her eyes glassy like a doll.

The doors closed on his smirk.

Shaleigh looked back to Teagan, her eyes burning. The fiery ball had blazed a hole in his chest, and the fire still smoldered within the cavity. Tears streaked down Shaleigh's cheeks.

Talek stared at his love in horror. "My darling," he whispered, and the words hung in the air.

PART IV
THE TOWER

LIFE AND DEATH

Shaleigh

Teagan's eyes were open, but Shaleigh couldn't look at them again. However, she still reached out to take his hand in hers. She lifted it, noticing it was nothing more than dead weight and growing colder by the second. Teagan's mouth was open, but Shaleigh didn't want to see that either. Instead she stared at his hand, at his long fingers and his open palm. She didn't want to believe it. Couldn't believe it. Teagan was too strong to be dead, too powerful, too full of life. It couldn't possibly be real.

She willed her own body heat into his cooling hand. Her eyes burned as tears fell. The room was too hot, but she couldn't pull away.

How much magic had Teagan done with his hands? From making the High Castle at the Garden defy gravity, to bringing night to the Slumbering Forest, to giving her voice power at the Games. She could still remember the warmth of his hand on her throat and the tune on his lips. She remembered his powerful grip on her as they fled to escape the minotaurs through the trees. She remembered holding his hand in the Dark Lands. Now his hands would be cold forever.

Someone was pulling at her shoulder, but she didn't want to let go. She held Teagan's hand tighter, gripping it like a lifeline. She couldn't leave his side. He needed her still, even if he was gone.

"Let go of me!" she cried at another tug, and turned her head to see Colin standing there, his clawed hands around her shoulders.

"We can't stay!" His eyes were wide and red. That was when Shaleigh noticed the fire all around them. Pieces of timber and metal were falling to the ground, covered in flames. Something cold touched her other arm, and she looked around to see Mawr standing at her side with his nose to her skin. His cheeks were dark with tears and his glasses gleamed in the firelight.

"If you want to stay here, Shaleigh, I won't let you stay alone." He pushed his enormous body closer to hers as a piece of the wooden stairway landed behind him. He was shaking from muzzle to tail, but his eyes stayed fixed on hers in determination.

"*Please*," Colin urged, pulling at Shaleigh's shoulders again, but she stood still and stared into Mawr's sad eyes.

"I don't have a home to go back to anyway," Mawr said, even as his heavy purrs made the ground vibrate around her. "I came to help you. If you want to stay here, I'll stay too. It'll be okay." He licked at her arm, gravel on her skin, and Shaleigh shook her head.

She let go of Teagan's hand and leaned against Mawr's body, cooler than the hot air surrounding them. She felt Colin's grip release from her shoulders and heard him sob behind her. The place would collapse, but the smoke would kill them before the fire would, and soon she would be as still as Teagan.

Mawr might survive it, though. Another lonely survivor wandering and looking for more friends to help and protect; looking for a library to call home.

She closed her eyes and his deep purrs helped calm her. His claws dug into the wood under her feet, betraying how frightened he was despite his purring.

She turned around to Colin and took his furry hand in hers. His face was wet with tears.

"I'm sorry," he whispered. "We just wanted to save you. We just wanted to help."

She reached forward to give him a hug and, for once, Colin permitted it. He even hugged her back. "I'm sorry I destroyed the Garden," she whispered.

"And I'm sorry I kidnapped you," his voice broke and she squeezed him tighter.

That's when she realized someone else was crying. She released Colin and they both looked over to see Talek on his knees, his face cradled in his hands, rocking back and forth over Teagan's body. He was wailing at such a high pitch that it reminded her of the banshee from the Dark Lands.

"Talek... I'm so sorry..."

He shook but lowered his hands. "I did it. It's all my

fault. I killed him." He looked up at her with tears streaking his cheeks, both eyes now that striking violet color swirling with black. Colin gasped behind her and Shaleigh felt a knot of terror form in her stomach.

Here she was worrying about the fire consuming them when Talek could thrust them all into a wasteland like the Dark Lands at any second. He would become another Masked King, blighting the land with his fury and madness.

Shaleigh bit her lip as Colin moved closer to her, his tail whipping anxiously around her leg. Mawr still purred on her other side. She had led them all here; Talek included. She was responsible for all of them and if they died today, if Talek blasted them all to bits or cursed them to wander his wasteland at his side for eternity, it would be on her shoulders and no one else's.

The thought gave her a strange calm. It made her control her breathing and the urge to sob diminish. A new determination built up inside of her, forcing her to stand taller despite the fire spreading closer. She would not cause her friends to get killed. She refused to let that happen. She had already lost one friend, and she wasn't about to let it happen again.

Sure, Talek might be about to blast the entire place to dust, but he could also get rid of all the destruction in the same breath.

She pulled away from Colin and Mawr to step around Teagan's body. She put her arms around Talek's chest and pulled him into a tight hug. To her surprise, he didn't struggle or even try to pull away. Instead, he leaned against her, even as he gasped for air with each sob.

Shaleigh rubbed his back, crying with him. "I'm sorry," she whispered. "I'm so sorry about everything."

Eventually, Talek's sobs quieted and she rocked him gently, staring off into the flames, watching the black smoke rise into the tower above them like a chimney.

"I did this for him. I did all of this for him."

"I know you did. I should have seen that from the start. I should have tried to help you instead of running away all the time."

Another sob broke through him and Shaleigh shut her eyes as she held him. Colin came over to crouch beside her, and Mawr moved to block them all from the creeping flames, digging his claws into the wood and vibrating the ground with his deep purrs. The fires had spread throughout the level, but for some reason hadn't reached them yet. Was that Talek's work, she wondered? Even as he mourned, did he protect them?

"You can still stop this," Shaleigh whispered, hoping that somehow there was truth to her words, hoping that it wasn't too late to give him the help that he so desperately needed.

A shudder tore through him. "I can't do anything right. Everyone I try to help gets destroyed. Every time I try to help, I only make things worse!"

Shaleigh squeezed him tighter. "You can still try. It's not too late to save us."

He hugged her back now. "I'm sorry for all the pain I put you through. I never meant to hurt anyone. I just wanted Teagan to be happy again like he used to be."

"I know."

The black smoke from above hovered down toward

them now. The back of Shaleigh's throat tickled and a rough cough tore through her. Talek had to let go of her as she pulled away and the cough racked her body.

He stared at her for a moment, his face painted with regret. "If Teagan were alive," he winced as though about to break into tears again, but pushed it away, "he would know what to do."

Colin coughed next to her and Mawr dug his claws into the wood moving to nuzzle against her shoulder.

"You know what to do already, Talek. You're just afraid to do it on your own," she said, then coughed again. "But you're not alone. We're all with you. We all want to help you." She wiped at her eyes.

Talek stared at her, the violet in his eyes piercing through the dark smoke.

"Please help us," Colin added, his voice small and sad.

Talek stared at him and turned to Mawr as though just realizing they were there. There was a change in him, a shift that gave her a small glimmer of hope. This wasn't just about her and Talek, it was about all of them. Even Teagan.

Getting to his feet, Talek raised his palms into the air. He sang a sad lament into the sky; one she would've expected to hear in the City of the Fae. There were no words, just his voice and it pulled at her heart - made her think of watching the stars at night with Kaeja by her side. It made her think of weeping willow trees and birdsong.

Slowly the smoke pushed away; the fire dwindled. As his voice moved upwards, the stairs far above them at the top of the tower, which had looked about ready to collapse, mended themselves and reformed. The smoke was pushed out through the cracks and holes, through the open windows and out the chimney, anywhere it could find a way to escape.

He went silent and his violet gaze fell on her and Colin. That familiar pain ripped through her chest as the smoke and particles were pulled out from within. Shaleigh gulped down a big breath of clean air, and then another, until her breathing was normal again. Colin was beside her, spitting out black liquid.

"What was that?" he gasped.

Talek gave a small smile and looked up to give another push, getting rid of any last remnants of smoke with a few more notes of his song. Then, it ended and he lowered his arms, looking exhausted. "That was something I learned with Shaleigh a little while ago."

Mawr pushed his face against Shaleigh's arm. "I'm so glad you're okay! You are okay, aren't you? Oh gosh, I'm so glad!" He rubbed his face on her, chaffing her skin, but she didn't care. She pulled his muzzle into her arms and gave him a big hug, letting his deep purrs rattle through her.

She turned to Talek. "Thank you for helping us."

Talek took a deep breath as he stared up through the cracks in the tower, up into the blue sky. Morning must have come because dusty beams of sunlight broke through where smoke used to be. Talek crouched down to Teagan and placed a hand on his stomach, dragging his fingers gingerly around the terrible wound in his chest.

A shudder went through her. It felt disrespectful

somehow. "What are you doing?" He didn't respond. "Talek, he's dead."

"I've learned so much with this power. I've learned how limiting death can be." He hummed a tune and Teagan's chest pulled together until the flesh showed no sign of damage.

Colin got behind Shaleigh, his fingers gripping her arm as he looked over her shoulder. "Oh no, not this again!" he whispered, terrified.

Teagan's mouth clamped shut and his eyes closed. Shaleigh jumped causing Colin to grip his claws further into her arm. "What - Talek, what are you doing?" she asked again, not wanting to believe her eyes.

Mawr shook his head and crouched down to the ground, dragging his big paws over his eyes. "Colin, please tell me what happens!"

Talek gave a wide smile. "I worked too hard to make sure Teagan was safe. I'm not about to leave him here to rot." He got to his feet. "Teagan, stand please."

Teagan's corpse pushed up into a sitting position, his eyes glassy and emotionless, staring off into nothing. But he got to his feet despite the fact that he wasn't breathing. His body was painfully pale, especially contrasted against his brilliant red hair. Talek took Teagan's hand in his own and squeezed despite how limp it was.

Talek wiped a stray tear away. "It's not perfect, but it'll work for now."

Shaleigh approached Teagan, reaching out to put a hand on his cheek. His skin felt as cold as marble. She winced and went back to Mawr's side. "This isn't right," she whispered. "You're desecrating him."

"No, I'm going to save him," he snapped, his violet eyes flashing in a beam of dusty sunlight. "The Masked King gave Keriam immortality. He can give Teagan life; I know he can."

Shaleigh gaped. "Keriam told you that?"

"Oh yes." He gave a disturbing smile. "I also know the cost of that immortality, though that part he didn't tell me."

"Oh no..." Colin backed away. "Not the Dark Lands. We can't do that. You saw what happened to those soldiers. We can't go back there. No way!"

Talek glanced to him, a cruel expression fleeting across his face. "If you don't believe it's possible, then don't join me." He turned and cupped Teagan's jaw. "If he can extend life, then he can bring back my love. I just want to apologize to him for everything. I don't even care if he never wants to see me again." Despite the confidence of his words, his voice shook. "I just want him back. I just want him happy."

Shaleigh stared into Teagan's dead gaze. Only she and Teagan had been able to convince the Masked King to let them live last time. She knew that Talek was in no position to barter with anyone. He would walk into the Dark Lands and the Masked King would claim him and Teagan as his property, just as he had tried to do with her and Teagan.

She closed her eyes and took a deep breath, already regretting the decision she would have to make. "I can't let you go alone, Talek. You're in no position to deal with the Masked King right now. He would destroy you."

Talek glanced to her with surprise. "You're concerned about me? Even after all I've done?"

"Teagan and I have already had to deal with him once. And I don't want him to trap either of you in the Dark Lands. Though I don't think he'll want to bring Teagan back to life."

"The Masked King deals in death, not life," Mawr whispered.

"Life and death are the beginning and end of everything. They are the same," Talek insisted. "If he can slay life and extend it indefinitely, then he can help my poor Teagan. He can bring him back."

Shaleigh sighed. She couldn't allow the Masked King to have Teagan's body. He already tried once to claim him, and she wouldn't let him get his corpse instead. That was just too much. She had already failed Teagan once; she couldn't fail him again.

She turned to Mawr and Colin. "Neither of you have to come with us if you don't want to. I understand. I wouldn't want to go either, but they both need my protection."

Mawr nuzzled her arm. "I'll go where you go, Shaleigh. I don't want to lose you either."

"I mean," Colin started with a sigh, "I don't want anyone to get hurt or anything, but I'm not too keen on going into the Dark Lands. Mawr and I can stand outside of it, if that's okay?"

Mawr shook his head, his golden-rimmed glasses sliding slightly down his nose. "No, I'm going with her."

"What? I thought you were scared of the place!"

"I am scared, but I'm more scared of losing my friends."

He nuzzled Shaleigh's arm again and she reached out to rub one of his ears with a small smile.

"You don't have to prove yourself to me. I know you care. It's okay."

But Mawr shook his head again. "I'm not leaving you again, Shaleigh. Each time I do, something terrible happens to you. Please let me stay."

Shaleigh's heart hurt at his words and she put her arms around his neck in a hug. "Okay, if you're sure. I just don't want to put you in danger...again."

He put a big, rough paw around her shoulder. "I know, but at least we'll be together."

Colin sighed again. "I still think this is a really bad idea, but I don't want to stay in those woods by myself, especially that close to the City of the Fae. I'll come, but I'm staying on top of Mawr's back the whole time."

Shaleigh pulled Colin into a hug. He tensed for a moment then pulled away. "I know, I know," he muttered and gave an awkward laugh. "I just can't believe Mawr's suddenly braver than I am."

THEY STEPPED out of the Sanctuary, half expecting to see all of Keriam's troops waiting for them with Lieutenant Varg: the only people there were the magicians. Many of them were sitting on the ground and, as their group passed, several of them backed away.

She spotted Druce walking towards her; then, he saw Talek's violet eyes and froze. His mouth dropped open and the anger in his gaze melted into sympathy. Shaleigh couldn't risk going to talk to him. It was too dangerous to bring Talek's attention to him or to any of the magicians. She wanted to tell them their plans, to apologize for what happened in the Sanctuary, but considering her group consisted of a walking nuclear bomb and a walking corpse, she didn't think that was a good idea.

She braced herself as they passed, wondering if they would be angry at them for Keriam's actions, but they didn't say a word. Instead, they backed away for them to pass.

"Where are all the troops?" Mawr asked in a quiet voice.

"I don't know," Colin said, glancing around. "They were supposed to be waiting until after Keriam had burned the place to the ground."

"Master Keriam left," Talek said simply. "He summoned me multiple times, but I refused to go to him. So, he took the troops and fled back to the Garden. I believe he assumes I died."

"Wait," Colin said. "How do you know what he did?"

"I have a pact with him. I know his thoughts. I know what he wants, and I know his plans." He held up his wrist to show the purple ribbon that was tied there. "We are still bound together, even if he no longer wants me. I am his servant so I can't cause him harm, but I know where he is."

"But he made that poor lady attack Teagan. It wasn't her fault. It was that bad air," Mawr whimpered.

"That was the Scáil plant, wasn't it?" Shaleigh asked. "That's what he used to control people before, that's what Teagan told me when we were in the City of the Fae."

"Yes, I filled the first floor with its spores. It had

mostly dissipated by the time you came down, but I made sure to give Daphne a dose as well because she was so powerful. Master Keriam demanded it." He paused a moment before adding, "Then, I understood why."

"I'm sorry," Shaleigh said, but Talek didn't respond further. Instead he readjusted his grip on Teagan's hand and continued onward.

They walked along the path that she and Teagan had taken only hours before. There weren't as many magicians out here, but there were still a few who had come out farther to escape the blaze. Each one drew away as they approached. Shaleigh dropped back to walk with Mawr.

"I feel bad," he whispered as an older woman backed away so quickly she nearly tripped. "They're all so frightened of us."

"I know." She kept her voice low, not sure if Talek could hear them or not. "I can't really blame them, though. We're a pretty frightening group." Her gaze fell on Teagan's limp, cold hand clutched in Talek's grip.

Mawr lumbered closer to her, leaning his head to the side to try to keep his voice low. "It isn't the first time he's made them walk."

Shaleigh narrowed her eyes, "Who, the magicians?"

He shook his head. "No, the dead."

Shaleigh swallowed down the dry patch that formed in her throat. Colin turned his head back to them and dropped back to walk on Shaleigh's opposite side.

"Talek used that magic on the minotaurs before," Mawr said, his nervous eyes darting forward to Talek every few paces. "He made their bodies walk over and lay down in the fires. I never thought he would do such a thing to Teagan. I thought he loved him."

Shaleigh rubbed at her eyes. "Love makes people do strange things," she said and thought of her father spraying an empty room with perfume. "Teagan told me before he died that he didn't mean what he did. He said Talek was a good person deep down." She sighed. "I thought he was delusional at the time, but now…"

"Clearly he's lost his mind," Colin said. "We're probably not far behind since we're walking into the Masked King's land like this."

"I'm just exhausted. It's hard to believe he's really dead when he's right..." Shaleigh trailed off as her throat constricted. Her gaze was pulled to Teagan again, walking ahead beside Talek. He shambled along without any grace, frequently tripping over brambles or wandering off to the side only to wander back again. It was like he was sleep-walking and Shaleigh wanted to go shake him awake, but that wouldn't do any good. Hot tears threatened her tired eyes and she wiped them away with the palm of her hand.

Mawr lowered his head. "You can sleep on my back if that would help." He licked at her hand when she sniffed. "You knew him better than I did."

"I'm okay. Thanks though," she said and rubbed his ear.

Shaleigh glanced over to Colin, who looked about as close to bursting into tears as she was. She knew Teagan well, but Colin had known him for years. She reached over and took his furry hand in hers. He blinked at her as though being pulled from his thoughts and gave her hand a squeeze.

"I'm okay," he said.

"No, you're not. None of us are."

He looked like he wanted to argue but the words wouldn't come. He took a deep, shaky breath instead. "My mind keeps making excuses. Like maybe he's not dead but in some kind of other state like with Faerie magic. Maybe he's just trapped inside and he can't get out, you know?" He swallowed hard. He sounded a little bit like her father talking about Kristen, trying to come up with alternate reasons about what happened to Teagan when he was right there in front of them. They had all seen him die, all had seen what happened to him, but still there was that need to find another explanation.

Her father had been given many pamphlets over the years each time he went to therapy or tried to talk with a psychiatrist. Most of them ended up on the kitchen counter, hidden by piles of junk mail and bills, but Shaleigh had pulled them out a long time ago to try to understand what was happening to her father. It was back when she thought she could help him, when she wasn't bitter about how stubborn he was in his delusions. Back when she had hope.

That seemed like another lifetime ago.

The pamphlet had talked about the stages of grief: denial, anger, bargaining, depression, and acceptance. She tried to talk with him about it many times, but he always had a reason why he didn't want to discuss it, always had excuses. He would bounce around between every stage - except for acceptance. That one he refused to look in the eye.

A long branch raked against Teagan's arm, but he didn't even react or pull away. This was what festering denial looked like when it was left out on the counter for too long. It was a level unlike anything she had seen with her father.

"No, he's dead," she stated. "Don't make it harder on yourself, Colin. It's already hard enough as it is."

Colin gave her a stricken expression. "You don't think maybe there's a chance, then? A chance that the Masked King could bring him back?"

His question hit her like a blow to the chest and Shaleigh winced before shaking her head like she had with her father countless times. "No, I don't. I'm sorry."

Colin blinked a few times before pulling his hand away and clenching his jaw. "I'm not giving up on him. I've seen magic do the impossible. You're just used to the limitations of the Human World. If you knew the possibilities—"

"Magic can't do everything," Mawr whispered, his voice low and rumbling. "I saw amazing magic users in Aife who tried to fight the Pello Pines, but they had to sleep eventually. No magic is perfect."

Shaleigh rested her arm on his side. "You know what I mean, right?"

Mawr's glasses glinted in the morning light as he turned his head toward her. "I've seen many people die, Shaleigh, but none of them have ever come back," he glanced to Teagan, "not really."

Shaleigh wiped at her eyes as they continued along in silence.

～

THE MORNING AIR was heavy with fog. The forest was waking up with the sounds of birds. When Shaleigh and Teagan had passed through the area before, they had thought the Sanctuary would protect them. If they had only known what awaited them in that enormous tower, Shaleigh would have demanded they never go there. The woods were so peaceful now, not the threatening dark places they were the night before. Then she smelled the familiar scent of burning wood and felt her stomach drop.

Colin glanced her way at her sudden tension. "What's wrong?"

"We're getting near the bonfires again."

He shook his head. "Oh, don't worry about those. They've all burned out by now I'm sure."

"Yes, but that's not what I'm worried about."

Talek and Teagan must have crossed the boundary line of the Sanctuary because suddenly several minotaurs were heading toward them, running in a steady rhythm, the ground rumbling with each thundering step. Colin leaped up to Mawr's back and was about to pull Shaleigh up to join him, when the minotaurs emerged through the trees. There were five of them, bigger than Shaleigh remembered, and giving a call that sounded almost like a horn. They must have been waiting for them to return, maybe choosing to strike at the smaller party instead of the army that must have passed through already.

They had their sights aimed on Talek. All five were aiming for him, ready to break him, but Talek held up his hand at the last moment. The minotaurs fell forward, landing on their faces or on their sides. Shaleigh didn't know what had happened at first until she saw the weeds that had grown up out of the ground and the branches that had reached out to grab hold of them. He had made the very vegetation bend to his will.

"This is quite the welcoming party," Talek said with a grin, releasing Teagan's hand. "Not exactly what I had in mind though." The vines whipped around the minotaurs, wrapping around their legs and moving up their bodies. They were screaming.

Mawr crouched down to the ground, his eyes wide. Colin watched in absolute horror. Shaleigh had seen what had happened to the Pello Pines in the Slumbering Forest and didn't want to see what happened to a bunch of minotaurs. She couldn't just stand there and watch him kill them, even if they would have killed her and Teagan just hours before.

She ran to Talek and wrapped her hands around his arm. He was humming a wild tune to himself but paused when she grabbed him. The vines froze around their victims, waiting for orders. Each of the minotaurs had already a leg engulfed in them. Talek looked down at her with violet, swirling eyes, questioning and outraged. "What are you doing?"

"Don't kill them, please."

He gave a high-pitched laugh that sent a shiver down her spine. She had to be careful. She didn't want to end up losing her mouth like Madam Cloom. "Why ever not? They were about to kill me, as you saw."

"They're just trying to protect those they love."

He narrowed his eyes. "Why do you think that?"

She took a deep breath, taking a moment to think, trying to ignore the minotaur in the back that was crying and begging. "Because you killed a bunch of their family last time and they're afraid you want to kill more of them. You're doing exactly that. They think this is what they have to do in order to keep their loved ones safe now."

His smile faded. "That was not my decision, that was my master's decision, and he has since taken leave of me. That is not who *I* am."

She gently pulled his arm down. "But this time it is your decision. You are choosing to kill them. Keriam has nothing to do with this, only you."

He blinked and looked around as though realizing he was the one wielding magic. The vines fell from their captives and the minotaurs were free. One gave a quick thanks to Shaleigh, but she kept her gaze focused on Talek. He needed that kind of emotional connection, needed something to keep him grounded.

The minotaurs limped away, but she didn't want to let go of him yet, not until she was certain it was safe.

Talek looked confused and concerned. "That's not at all who I am. I wouldn't do such a thing. I'm not a monster."

"I know you're not," she said, willing her heartbeat to slow down. "I think you lose yourself sometimes, don't you?"

He blinked again and glanced at her, briefly looking like a frightened child. "Sometimes," he muttered.

"It's okay. We can help, but you have to let us know when you're losing control of yourself, okay? You have to communicate with us. You can't just get lost in your head because you might accidentally kill us too."

"*What?*" he scoffed. "That's ridiculous. I wouldn't do

that to you." He looked like he knew otherwise, and his hands shook as he lowered them to his sides. "However, if you insist, I'll try to communicate better with you all."

He turned to see Mawr and Colin looking terrified, and sighed. "Don't worry, I'm not killing anyone right now. You can stop with your cowering already."

Shaleigh widened her eyes at Mawr, gesturing with her fingers for him to stand back up. He glanced from Talek to her and back to Talek again, before reluctantly standing, still keeping his claws extended and firmly dug into the earth.

"We were just getting ready for battle," Colin muttered, sitting up from behind Mawr's head. "That's all."

Talek pursed his lips. "Of course you were." He reached out and took Teagan's hand again. "Come along, we're not far from the Masked King's land."

Shaleigh took a moment to breathe as Talek and Teagan walked ahead. Mawr came up beside her as she started walking. "I'm sorry, I panicked!"

"It's okay. It's not your fault. You didn't do anything wrong."

"You say that," Colin said, "but he was a few seconds away from smiting us both. What were you thinking grabbing him like that? He could kill you in an instant, or did you miss the piles of dead minotaurs burned in the distance?"

Shaleigh watched the two Faeries in front of them silently before putting a hand on Mawr's mane. "We can't look at him like that, Colin. We have to try to help him. I think he's just as scared of himself as we are of him."

Colin gave a bitter laugh. "If you say so."

ARISE

Shaleigh

Shaleigh could tell they were close when the sound of birds began to dwindle, even with the sun still high above them. The air felt colder now, and she wrapped her arms around her elbows for warmth. The trees were spaced out farther than they had been and more of them looked dead.

They were definitely nearing the Dark Lands.

"Are you all still sure about this?" Colin asked, his whisper jarring in the still, cool air. "What if he can't do anything? What if he won't?"

Talek turned to him, his violet eyes vibrant and cruel. "He'll have to do something. Otherwise, I'll destroy him. He has the power; I know he must."

Shaleigh reached out to put a hand on Colin's furry arm. His muscles felt rigid, either from him being scared or out of anger. He looked like he wanted to say more, but she shook her head. This was not the time. Talek sounded like he was near a breaking point and she really didn't want that. He was too angry and desperate to be rational. Colin didn't always have a good notion of when to stop talking, and if he wasn't careful, he would end up like those minotaurs, either dead or running away, lost in the woods.

Colin nodded meekly at her and Shaleigh took a deep breath.

Fog was rolling in, the moisture clinging to her skin and making her shiver. The light that had been so comforting earlier was nonexistent here. They had to be getting close. She wished she could tell where the boundary line was for the Dark Lands, maybe she would be able to prepare herself somehow.

She dreaded dealing with the Masked King without Teagan at her side. They were anchors for each other amid a torrent of confusion and delusions, and this time Shaleigh would need to be the anchor for so many. Colin didn't even want to be there, and she was worried about Mawr. He feared so much and yet here he was at her side despite being in the most frightening place in the land. She considered turning around and letting Talek take Teagan's body to the Dark Lands alone, but then she spotted the red eyes of a Black Dog.

It stood only about ten feet in front of them, wafting in and out of a fog that wasn't really a fog. Its teeth were bared, thick saliva dribbled down its muzzle. Its fur was all matted in places and sticking out in other patches. She could even see red blotches of matted blood on his skin. It almost looked like it had rabies, if it had still been alive, that is.

"Over there," she said, pointing to it. Her voice trembled and she wished it hadn't. She wanted to look like she had more strength than she did. Teagan had been so good at that.

Talek came to a halt, laughing under his breath in a crazed manner. "So many... he must have known we were coming."

She stepped up to Talek's side, keeping Colin and Mawr behind her. She didn't want them to get close if possible... She gasped. There must have been twenty of them, standing in a semicircle, black dogs of various heights and breeds. Some looked similar to greyhounds, others were closer to Irish wolfhounds. They snarled and bared their fangs, each ready to pounce, or worse yet, drag them into the fog where their minds would be lost for good.

Shaleigh swallowed down the lump in her throat as the fog rolled in quickly behind the dogs, and although they each stood their ground, they seemed to drift in and out - all except their red eyes, which glowed regardless.

Heart hammering in her chest, Shaleigh wasn't sure what to do. She and Teagan had barely been able to handle one of these creatures before, and now they had to deal with twenty of them. They didn't speak like the Shadow Wolves of the Slumbering Forest either, they only did their master's bidding. She knew there was no reasoning with these creatures; they were attack dogs. If the Masked King wanted Shaleigh and her group to be killed here and now, or to lose their minds, she had little doubt that he could cause it.

Without thinking, she took Teagan's hand in hers, despite it being cold and lifeless. He might not be here any longer, but she was.

She heard the familiar shifting of silk and the creaking of bones. A scent of decay made her wince. The Masked King stepped out of the fog from behind his Black Dogs, his bare feet silent as they settled on the dark earth, little more than skin and bones.

He passed through the line of dogs to stand only an arm's reach before Talek and Teagan. Instinctively, Shaleigh waved back to Mawr and Colin, urging them to move behind her. She didn't want him to notice them, even though he would have to be blind to not see Mawr crouched down behind them.

"You are not wanted here, Talek, the Mad," The Masked King said, holding his golden mask in place. "You have no business in my land. Turn away and hope that I forget your face."

Talek was trying to keep his laughter under control but wasn't succeeding. Soon he threw back his head and laughed into the dull, empty sky. The sound was loud and garish against the silence.

The Masked King snarled, before cocking his head to the side, moving his mask along with it. "Clearly you don't value your life any longer. That is one of the final stages, you know, forgetting your need to live. If you're looking for a place to destroy, I hear Queen Mab always welcomes back her own. Well, unless you create your own pocket of reality.

That seems to stretch her patience." He laughed and reached forward to stroke Teagan's cheek. Talek's laughing fit finally subsided at the gesture. "Your work, I imagine? Trying to fix what you've lost. It's a bold attempt, but faulty nonetheless."

Talek's eyes were hard. "All I ask is for you to bring him back to life. You have it within your power." He gestured to the Black Dogs. "Clearly, you create life on a regular basis."

The Masked King blinked at him from behind his mask. He had a completely different demeanor with Talek than he had with Teagan and Shaleigh. Was the Madness what frightened him or was it something else?

"What good would he be if he were alive? He would only break your heart again."

Talek clenched his jaw. "It will be different this time."

"Oh?" The Masked King pushed a hair out of Teagan's face. "Do you think I can bring him back to love you again? I'm afraid no magic in the world could permanently force someone to do that." He gave his creaking laugh. "And I don't think he would ever do that now that you've killed him, do you?"

Talek gasped as though physically struck by his words. "I didn't kill him. That was my master's doing."

"Yes, but you are his servant, aren't you?" He twirled a bit of Teagan's hair between two grotesque fingers. "So, in a way, you did."

Talek shook his head. "That's not true!"

Shaleigh was done. It was one thing to banter back and forth with Talek, but she didn't like this creature putting his grubby hands all over Teagan.

"Stop it," she said, and the Masked King cocked his golden mask toward her.

"You don't like me being so close to him? He's dead. He doesn't care about anything anymore."

Talek let out a shaky breath and shook his head. Shaleigh stepped toward them. "Don't touch him."

He dropped the tendril of Teagan's hair, and instead reached out to grab a whole clump of his hair, pulling down hard enough to yank his head down. Shaleigh rushed forward, placed two hands on the Masked King's chest, and pushed him back as hard as she could. There was a hollow sound, like a decaying tree stump getting thumped. He let go of Teagan, lost his footing, and fell to the ground in a crouch, stunned.

"I said, don't touch him!" she snapped.

Talek took the advantage and lifted a palm to the sky. A violet aura appeared around the Masked King and he was lifted up off the ground. He seemed more annoyed by it than frightened as Talek drew him close to his face.

"You can do it. Why don't you? You made a damn magician live forever, but you can't do anything for your own kind? Is it spite? Revenge? What is it?!"

Talek shook him in the air and the Masked King's mask fell from his hand, revealing the grotesque mummified face of a long dead corpse. His nose was reduced to thin slits for nostrils, and his mouth was a thin crack amid the pockmarked landscape of his face. He threw an arm in front of his face to shield it.

"Don't look at me!" he cried, wheezing. "Don't look!"

Talek smiled and his violet eyes pulsed. "I will make

them all look, every last one of them if you don't give him the gift of life again."

"I can't!"

"*Lies!*" Talek shook him again, and the Masked King cried out, begging him to stop. Shaleigh looked from Teagan to Talek to the Masked King.

Teagan was a walking corpse and Talek was a mad Faerie bound for the same fate as the Masked King. As cruel and heartless as the Masked King was, he hadn't always been like this, any more than Talek had always been this level of cruel. It wasn't that hard to imagine Talek as a mummified version of himself, being shaken into submission by someone more powerful.

There was *always* someone more powerful.

"Please, enough," the Masked King groaned, sounding exhausted as he tried to reach for his mask before being shoved to the side.

Talek laughed again into the empty sky and Shaleigh walked quickly to his side.

"Shaleigh, don't!" Mawr urged from behind, but she didn't listen. She grabbed Talek's arm with his hand glowing violet and urged it down again like she had with the minotaurs.

Talek glared at her. "Do you want to be next, Shaleigh?" His eyes pulsed.

"You've got to stop it. I hate him too, but..." she stopped and shook her head, trying to find the right words to keep from getting killed herself. "You're not that different from him. If you keep on this path, you'll be just like him soon. Haven't you killed enough?"

Talek was silent, his face full of outrage, and Shaleigh held her breath, but he didn't turn his attack on her.

"Teagan wouldn't want you to do this. He wouldn't want you to become this." She leaned forward, keeping her gaze locked on his and trying not to let him see her fear. "You're better than this."

That seemed to hit hard, and Talek finally looked away and shook his head. "If he hadn't died, I wouldn't be here."

"Yes, but he did. Do you know what his final words were to me? He said you don't mean what you do. That you're good. I want to believe that."

Talek shook his head. "I'm not... as good as he thought I was."

Shaleigh pressed, "He wanted to help you. He felt guilty for how he treated you when we were in the Faerie City and he wanted to apologize. I know that because he told me."

Talek winced and shut his eyes.

"Please, put him down. Despite what Keriam has done to you, you aren't a monster like him. You're better than you think you are."

With a deep sigh, Talek nodded, and dropped the Masked King to the ground in a heap.

Talek looked around at the Black Dogs and the dead wasteland all around them. Tears came to his eyes. He turned to the crumpled Masked King. "You know everything that happens in this land. You bring about life all the time. Why can't you do it for him? What makes him different?"

The Masked King was doubled over, holding his mask like a precious heirloom to his face. "I ask for life from a greater being than any of us, and she grants it to me. She understands my purpose, approves of my plans. She grants me the gift to create these shadows, to steal these lives. I cannot grant life, not in the way that you ask, but she could. She could grant you anything."

"Is this another lie?" Shaleigh asked noticing Talek was staring at him in stunned silence.

"No lies, not this time, child. I merely want to go home. I'm tired of these games."

"Yeah, me too," she said, crouching to the ground near him. He turned away from her, ashamed, and he reminded her of the homeless she and Kaeja had found on the streets. She didn't put a hand on him, but she did keep her voice calm as she asked, "Who is she, then?"

The Masked King gave a long rattling sigh.

She didn't move, but patiently waited for him to find the answer. To be honest, she wasn't sure if she really wanted to know. She wasn't sure if she could stomach giving Talek another target to go rattle in the air like a broken doll. She wasn't too keen on traveling with Teagan's walking corpse either. Looking down, she realized just how exhausted she was. She also realized how much she missed home.

"She will slay you all on sight," he said at last. Talek stepped forward, his foot raised, likely ready to kick him in the face. The Masked King huddled down again and Shaleigh held her hand out to Talek.

"No, stop it! What you doing?"

"He won't talk to us!" Talek cried. "What else am I supposed to do?"

"Let me work with him! All you're doing is making

things worse. Go — go stand with Teagan." She stared down those violet eyes with as much fury as she could muster. Eventually, he took a couple of steps back, not as far as she wanted, but it would have to do.

She leaned over to the Masked King's ear, trying hard not to smell him, but of course failing. "If we don't bring him back, Talek will kill us. If Keriam finds us, Talek will kill us. I think my friends and I would rather try than give up."

The Masked King turned to her and she had to move her head back, she was too close to that grotesque mask. "I am a monster, child, but she is far worse than anything I could be."

Shaleigh felt her mouth go dry and understood it logically, guessed as much at least from his tone, but at this closeness she could see the fear in his eyes, and it had nothing to do with Talek. She suddenly understood his reluctance, and almost wanted to take back her question. The words were on the tip of her tongue, but she pushed them down.

"The dragon, Tanwen, who lives up in the peaks of Gwern. She who lives in fire and is swathed in hatred. She is who you must reach. She is the mother of us all."

Talek kicked dirt into the Masked King's face, making him cough up a storm.

"Talek!" Shaleigh shouted. "What was that?"

"Tanwen isn't some sort of god, she's a dragon. She eats people, she burns villages, and she hates to be bothered. She isn't going to be able to help. He's just wasting our time again."

The Masked King snarled. "I'm not lying! I speak the

truth, even if it is a truth you don't want to hear!" He spat black goo to the ground and Shaleigh stood and took a full step backward, grateful to breath clean air again.

"Do you have proof?" Shaleigh asked. "He doesn't trust you, and neither do I."

"I have no proof. Her voice comes to me in smoke and flame, ethereal elements that vanish quickly. If you want your true love back, Talek the Mad, then Tanwen is the only key. Otherwise, I suppose you'll have to let him rot." He broke into a bitter laugh and Talek looked like he wanted to strangle him.

The Black Dogs moved forward as one, each of them taking a bit of the Masked King's robe into their teeth and dragging his body back into the fog. A blast of wind whipped at their fur and the Masked King's silks, but his laughter continued, even once he had disappeared.

"I don't think he was lying," Shaleigh said finally, stepping away from the fog. Something caught underneath her foot, and she tripped, falling hard onto her butt. "Ow!"

Colin and Mawr were at her side in an instant.

"Are you okay?" Mawr asked, his voice a whine from his pent-up fear. His rough muzzle pushed into her shoulder and she grabbed hold of it so he could help her to her feet. Colin meanwhile fished something off the ground.

"What is this?" He held up a jar covered in dust and cobwebs that looked like it had just come from some forgotten attic. "It looks empty, was this here before?"

"I don't think so," Shaleigh said, climbing to her feet. "Want me to look?"

He handed it over, eying the fog warily. "We should get moving though, I don't like being so close to that thing."

Shaleigh took the jar and turned it around. Cobwebs came off onto her fingers. It was a large mason jar that looked like it came from the Human World, but it was empty. Somehow, she doubted it and tried to turn the lid, but it wouldn't budge.

Mawr's rough muzzle pushed against her shoulder at her hiss of frustration. "I don't like it. We should leave it here."

"No, I think we should bring it. There's nothing like this out here."

"It could be the Masked King's way of tracking us or something," Colin offered, crossing his arms.

"Or it could just be a jar," she insisted, turning to Talek. "I guess we're going to find this dragon, then?"

It was then that she noticed that Talek was still on guard. He was staring into the fog, tracking movement of things that Shaleigh couldn't see. His eyes were wide, and he had a death grip on Teagan's arm.

"Talek?" she tried again, but he didn't seem to hear her.

Another minute passed and she put a hand on his shoulder, and he jumped, staring down at her as though she was one of the Masked King's banshees. Slowly he relaxed, trailing his hand down from Teagan's arm to entwine their fingers. "We should leave this place," he whispered, backing away.

"Finally, something we can all agree on!" Colin added.

Shaleigh wasn't sure what he saw that was freaking him out so much, but she could take a few guesses. Why was he only now getting alarmed? If he could see the creatures living in there, why hadn't he seen them before? Was his Madness getting worse?

They turned and walked back through the sparse trees, following Talek's lead. There was a nervousness in the air that they all felt after Talek's sudden fear of the place. He had attacked the Masked King as if he were nothing more than the weak, dead thing he appeared to be, not the disturbing magic wielder he truly was. What had changed his mind?

When the first bird call rang out in the woods and Shaleigh found the first sprout of a weed, vibrant and green in the middle of the ugly landscape, the anxiousness broke. It was of course Colin that broke the silence first, but only after they heard a few more bird calls.

"Are we really going to find that dragon?"

Talek glanced over his shoulder, his violet eyes piercing against the backdrop of the sparse trees. "We are going to bring Teagan back," he said, as though it was as simple as picking him up from school.

"You're assuming she is actually going to want to work with us, or that she even can bring him back," Colin said.

"It doesn't matter," he stated flatly, "If that's who can do it, that's who we'll go see."

"Tanwen the Ancient!" Mawr said with a strange mixture of awe and excitement that she hadn't expected him to have about a deadly dragon.

"Friend of yours?" Shaleigh teased.

"Oh no, I've never met her. I never thought I would ever meet her. She's so terrible, no one even ventures into the mountains of Gwern anymore. They're too afraid of her. She's probably still angry after Flidais attacked her."

Colin shook his head. "That was two centuries ago!"

"Dragons have a long memory. They live forever."

Shaleigh had felt better after leaving the Masked King's land, but now with all their talk of the dragon they were heading to meet, fear was taking hold of her again. She hoped she had done the right thing by allowing the Masked King to talk, by preventing Talek from attacking him further.

As Mawr and Colin exchanged stories about the villages that used to pepper the mountains, and about how they had, one by one, been eradicated by a dragon made of flame, Shaleigh second guessed her actions over and over again.

THE FOREST slowly became hilly before they finally found themselves climbing what certainly felt like a mountain. Shaleigh was tired, her feet were sore, and her stomach was growling. The sun had risen to the highest point in the sky and she was sweltering in the heat. She was burning up, but Colin had a full layer of fur all over him that kept him far warmer. He nearly passed out at one point and Shaleigh had insisted that he get on Mawr's back. He hadn't stayed awake for long after he climbed up and wrapped his tail around himself. He was fast asleep with his nose buried in his tail.

They needed to find water - soon. She knew that much, but it was difficult to convince Talek that while he had unlimited stamina, none of them did. Teagan of course walked at his side completely unfazed by anything.

She was pretty sure a tree could fall on his foot and he would keep walking regardless.

They reached the top of the hill and Shaleigh had to lean against a tree to catch her breath. It felt like the steps of the Sanctuary all over again.

She leaned her head against the bark of the tree, feeling the prickly texture against her sweaty skin and breathed in the scent of the wood. She had no idea what kind of tree it was, but she appreciated the shade.

Talek let go of Teagan's hand, the first time he had done so since they left the Dark Lands, and stepped out to the grassy clearing that formed at the top of the hill. Shaleigh's curiosity got the better of her and despite her exhaustion, she went over to see what he was looking at.

The hill gave them a perfect view into the mountain valley. Greenery blanketed the hillsides and a flock of birds flew overhead. A warm breeze went by that felt amazing to Shaleigh and she caught the distant smell of flowers on it. The hills all around them nestled a thick forest below and ahead stood what she assumed was the peak of Gwern. It was the largest mountain that Shaleigh had ever seen and the size of it was overwhelming. She looked to the top to see a trail of smoke getting carried away by the wind.

"That's where Tanwen lives?" she asked, unable to keep the fear from her voice. There was something so grand and inescapable about the mountain, the way it dwarfed everything else out here, and the way it loomed made her feel like it was watching her. Perhaps that was what the dragon was doing, watching them and waiting for the right time to strike.

"Yes," Talek said. "It's beautiful, isn't it?"

Shaleigh blinked, trying to figure out how to respond. It was beautiful, but also terrible too. She wondered if this was a similar feeling being at the base of Mount Everest, knowing all the people who died trying to climb it. It was one thing to look at it, to admire it, to be impressed by its size and majesty, but knowing that they were going to be climbing it? That they were going to be dealing with the fierce dragon above? That was terrifying.

"We should camp here tonight," Talek said, speaking to Teagan as though he would be able to answer back while Teagan simply stood there, staring blankly, unimpressed and unmoved. Shaleigh felt an ache in her chest at the sight of him, his glassy eyes and vacant expression exposed by the bright daylight.

She used a big leaf to wipe away some dirt that was stuck to his face. She almost got him in the eye accidentally, but he didn't flinch or even blink. He just stood there, staring at nothing. She wanted to scream at him, to shove him, to force him to do something, but she knew it was fruitless. There was nothing she could do, and deep down, she doubted there was anything the dragon Tanwen could do either. Talek needed to let him go. He needed to move on. Instead he was dragging Teagan's corpse everywhere he went, putting them all in danger by his mere presence. The arrogance of it frustrated her and she had to turn away, unable bare the sight of Teagan any longer.

Colin approached her, one hand hovering in the air as though about to reach out to her. "Are you okay?" He glanced to the edge of the hill with concern.

"Yeah," she muttered, wiping at a tear she hadn't known was there until then. "I'm just tired. Everything is so much worse. And I have a bad feeling we're going to get killed on that damn mountain."

Colin put a warm, fur-clad hand on her shoulder and gave it a squeeze. "Hey, it's okay. Maybe you should have taken a snooze on Mawr's back instead. I feel better." He gave a lopsided smile that didn't meet the worry in his eyes.

Shaleigh glanced over to Teagan, who was still unmoving. His red hair whipping in the wind and into his unblinking eyes. "I just... Teagan is so..."

"I know," he said, giving her shoulder another squeeze, his claws almost reaching her skin through the fabric in his distraction. "I can't bear to look at him much, to be honest. It's like someone's walking around in his skin, and I just can't deal with it." His voice became shaky, as he continued, "I keep hoping Talek will change his mind and just put the poor man to rest, but I know he won't. He's determined to do this. I just don't want us to get dragged down with him."

She nodded and lowered her voice to reply, "We can't exactly leave. He would find us." She watched Talek for a moment before glancing at Mawr, who had found a soft patch of dirt in the shade to dig in his claws. "Maybe you and Mawr could get away. He doesn't care about you two as much."

Colin pushed back a laugh. "Yeah, I know. I'd be dead before I got ten feet away, and I don't even want to think about what he would do to Mawr."

Shaleigh considered that for a moment. Mawr was a

Living Statue and seemed indestructible, but she had noticed the dark, smooth spot on his back and was pretty certain either Talek or Keriam had something to do with that, though she couldn't bring herself to ask about it. If Talek could put out the Sanctuary when it was engulfed in flames with just a few notes and hand gestures, she could only imagine what he could do to Mawr if provoked.

She bit her lip. "I'm sorry, I didn't even think about that. I keep overlooking things. I don't mean to; it just keeps happening." Her throat constricted and she swallowed, not wanting to burst into tears here, not in front of Talek who was glancing her way. She felt that they were at a level of mutual respect since she helped him with the Masked King, and she didn't want to lose that. It could be that the only reason Talek hadn't killed them yet...was because of her.

Colin smiled. "At least we're together, right? Trust me when I say it was way worse when you weren't with us." Mawr came over to join them, pushing his muzzle under Colin's hand for pets. Colin scratched absently at Mawr's nose.

"Oh goodness, Colin, you're still too warm to be in the sun!" Mawr warned. "Come back into the shade with me."

Colin gave Shaleigh a shrug. "He's turned into a complete nursemaid."

She couldn't suppress a smirk. "You mean he stopped being one?"

Their conversation was cut short when Talek spoke, "Teagan, make sure everyone gets some food if they want it."

They all turned to see Talek crouching beneath a large

tree. All around his feet was a campsite that hadn't been there just a few minutes ago. He had conjured a blanket, a couple of picnic baskets, and even cups of water for them all. Colin and Shaleigh gaped when Talek pulled out an apple from one of the baskets and bit into it.

He looked at them oddly. "Aren't you two hungry?"

"How did you do that?" Colin asked, gesturing to the whole spread.

Talek smirked. "I stole it from the Garden, just now."

"That's amazing," she whispered. Then a piece of fruit was pushed into her hand and she turned to see Teagan beside her handing her an orange. His eyes were completely empty of emotion and when his fingers brushed against hers, they were cold despite the heat of the day. She watched as he carried his basket over to give Colin some food.

There was something terrible about seeing him do something so normal, so Teagan, when he was still so clearly not alive. His feet had no coordination. He stuffed his hand into the basket without being able to really see or care what he was doing. It was like somebody else was making his limbs move. She gripped the orange and went over to sit at the campsite in the shade, not wanting to watch Teagan, but unable to look away.

Colin sat down beside her and Mawr spread out behind them on a shady patch of grass, watching them eat. His purrs made the ground rumble beneath where they sat. Shaleigh realized she hadn't heard him purr since the fires at the Sanctuary and she reached back to put a hand on one of his big, outstretched paws. He opened his eyes and smiled at her, purring harder and digging his claws into the rocky soil, before closing them again.

Colin offered her a pitcher and she guzzled at least five cups of clear, crisp water, followed by two sandwiches and several oranges. By the end, she was full and very tired. She leaned back against Mawr's side and stared up at the sky. The sun was now on a downward path, and although the heat was worse now than it had been before, she didn't mind it so much. It felt like a lazy, dreamy afternoon, and if she shut her eyes, she could imagine Teagan was with them still. Soon Colin was snoring and Mawr's purrs eventually lulled her to sleep.

SHALEIGH DREAMED OF TEAGAN. She was sitting at the Overlook in High Castle at the table beside Madam Cloom who was talking about something with dramatic arm motions, but Shaleigh wasn't listening to her.

Across the table sat Teagan, relaxed and smiling with calm happiness. But... he was dead and Shaleigh had the sense that she needed to study every part of him, she needed to remember every section of his face: the way his eyes crinkled at the corners, the golden flecks at his temples, the way he cocked his head to the side when he smiled. She studied him like she would study a map because she knew she would never see him again, and she wanted to remember everything good about him before he died.

She woke slowly; her eyes sticky from sleep and tears. Her cheeks were cold and wet, and she wiped at them, pushing away the crushing despair in her chest. Mawr was no longer behind her and she was laying down on a blanket that she knew hadn't been there before.

The sky was dark, but there was still light and warmth near her - someone had started a large fire. She pushed herself up with her hands, feeling the rocky earth through the blanket's fabric and wondering how the heck she had been able to sleep on such a hard surface. Her back ached as she moved into a sitting position and she stretched it uncomfortably. Feeling someone stare at her, she looked across the fire to see glassy eyes fixed on her - Teagan.

She froze on instinct, the feelings from her dream flooding through her again along with that painful despair she fought against upon awakening. He sat with his knees beneath him in what would normally be a very uncomfortable position on the stony soil, but it of course didn't bother him at all. One of the big trees was behind him, a black shadow against his red hair.

It was creepy to see him so alive and happy and full of joy in her dream and then waking to see him so very different. *Dead*, she reminded herself. Dead was the proper word to use because that's what he was. It didn't matter how much Talek made him move, or how he had fixed his lethal wounds, Teagan was still dead. There was no heart beating in his chest. He didn't breathe air or need to eat or sleep. He was frozen; forced to look as alive as possible on the outside.

He was a time capsule, she realized, and thought of her father. She thought of her mom's room back at the house, and how meticulously he kept it. Shaleigh had watched him swap out the dress that was laid out on her bed, how he moved the shoes around, how he fluffed the pillows and sometimes even changed the sheets. She had watched him spray perfume and go out to purchase more, usually once a year. It wasn't cheap either, but he still did it like clockwork.

He was determined to make Kristen feel alive again, even if she wasn't around. If he had been in the same position as Talek, he probably would have done the same thing to Kristen, and that realization made Shaleigh shudder. In a way, her father had done that to Kristen, making her feel alive and present even when she wasn't. For Shaleigh, that only served as a constant reminder of her absence, and of her father's delusions.

The fire crackled, but Teagan never blinked as he stared across the fire. Shaleigh wiped away tears from her eyes. Teagan lingered after death, and all it did was remind her of his absence. He infiltrated her dreams, he stood on the outskirts of conversation, he watched as she slept, but it wasn't really him. It only made letting go of him so much harder. It made coming to terms with his loss so much more difficult.

She got to her feet and stepped around the sleeping forms of Colin and Talek to reach Teagan. He didn't even turn to look at her, his eyes instead fixed on the fire. She wrapped her arms around his shoulders and pulled him into a hug.

His skin felt slightly warm against her, another lie brought on by the fire that was only a few feet away. She pressed her face against his shoulder, imagining him hugging her back even though his arms were lifeless at his sides. Teagan would know what to say to make her feel better. Even if he was a jerk at times, he would still be there for her. Even if he had to order her to be beaten by a skilled soldier in a fight to the death, he would be there if she survived it, a constant presence despite everything. It was ironic that even in death, he was still a constant presence.

She squeezed him tight, then let go, staring into his face. "I'm sorry for everything. I've screwed up so badly. I don't know if there's a way to fix it this time." She sat beside him, bringing her knees up to her chest. "I miss you. Even though you and Colin were ordered to kidnap me and bring me here in the first place. You still tried to help me. You were still there, even when I yelled at you. I don't even know why. But I'm sorry I let you down." Her throat constricted and she didn't fight the tears this time. She let them flow and sobbed at his side. She cried for Teagan, but also for her father and mother. She cried for putting Mawr and Colin into this horrible situation, for making Talek even worse off than before. She cried for Kaeja who she hoped had found another friend by now because thinking about her waiting for her to come back only made her cry harder.

"Shaleigh?"

The voice made her jump, and it took a moment for her eyes to adjust to the darkness outside of the firelight. Mawr walked over from the cliff edge and his golden spectacles caught the light of the flames. She wiped at her tears and nose.

"Are you okay?" he asked, moving closer to her. He was too big to get around the tree without waking Talek or bumping into Teagan, so he sat down and wrapped his tail around his feet.

"No," she admitted.

Mawr looked to Teagan and folded his ears back. "I'm sorry, I didn't mean to eavesdrop."

She got to her feet. "It's fine, it's not your fault." She walked over to him, trying to get herself under control again.

Mawr watched her for a moment. "Do you want to sit with me? I know I'm not very comfortable, but I want to help."

Shaleigh wrapped her arms around his muzzle, hugging tight. "Mawr, you always help."

His tail thumped happily against his feet. She let go and sat down beside him. Mawr reached a paw over to grab her old blanket with a single claw and used it to cover her. She pulled it around her shoulders and neck. "Thank you."

Mawr laid down on top of his feet beside her and she leaned against him. He was already purring.

"For what it's worth, I don't think you let Teagan down," he soothed. "I think he'd be proud of you."

Shaleigh squeezed her eyes shut, feeling the tears threaten again. "I don't really want to talk about it right now, if that's okay."

He nodded slowly and she took a deep breath to steady herself.

"I love looking at the stars," he whispered a minute or two later. "When I was in Aife I had a lot of nights to stare up at them and think. Some nights I tried to count them. Other nights I tried to see shapes. And then sometimes I even talked to them. I don't know why, but it helped." He shook his head. "It didn't matter how upset I got, the stars were always there for me."

Shaleigh looked up and noticed how absolutely incredible the stars were, spread out like a blanket above them. She hadn't even noticed them. She snuggled against him, his stone body warming slowly from the heat of the fire.

He looked down at her, his golden spectacles shifting on his nose. "I want to be your stars, Shaleigh. I want to be there for you regardless of what happens. You can talk to me when you can't talk to anyone. You can come sit with me when you can't talk."

"Oh Mawr," Shaleigh whispered, wiping her nose again. "I don't know if that's a good idea. I'm not worth that."

"Yes, you are," he insisted, glancing down at her, his head cocked at an angle to see her better. "I know you're upset now, and we don't know what's going to happen to us, but you're important to me. If you ever feel like you're alone and don't have anyone who believes in you, remember I'm your stars. I will always believe in you."

Mawr was going to make her start sobbing all over again. She laid an arm against his side. "I don't deserve your friendship, you know that?"

He shook his head. "No, I don't deserve yours." He purred harder.

Shaleigh couldn't help the fresh tears that fell.

They grew quiet as the sky began to brighten, and she knew that the sun would be coming up soon. Shaleigh took a deep breath and snuggled closer to Mawr. She still hurt inside, but not as much. It helped to cry out her frustration, her sadness, and her fear. It helped to have someone like Mawr who cared for her regardless of what she did. As dawn came, the shadow of the mountain in the distance loomed. Somewhere on that mountain a dragon stirred.

Together they watched the sky come alive as the sun slowly peeked over the horizon. The stars were chased away, and light flooded across the valley. The birds awoke, chirping in early morning excitement and Shaleigh breathed in the crisp, cool air.

Oddly enough, she was more hopeful now about encountering the fierce dragon Tanwen. It didn't make any sense, but Mawr reminded her that even though she couldn't reach her father or Kaeja back home, even though Teagan was lost, she still had friends here who needed her. They were practically a family at this point, if perhaps a disjointed one.

She had somehow negotiated with Madam Cloom, Queen Mab, the High Council of the Sanctuary, and the Masked King — twice even. Maybe Teagan would be proud of her. One thing Shaleigh was certain of, she would do whatever it took to make sure her friends didn't suffer from her mistakes again. She couldn't lose her stars or anyone else.

~

EVERYONE STARTED WAKING as the sun moved higher into the sky. Shaleigh found some leftover fruit and used some of the drinking water to wash her face before they continued the journey. Her eyes felt puffy from crying, but she felt better after talking with Mawr.

Talek got to his feet and with a hum and a wave of his hand, the fire extinguished. Colin stretched and yawned, his fur sticking up in weird places.

"Anybody else sleep horribly?"

Shaleigh considered admitting that she had barely slept at all, but didn't want to mention what she dreamed about, or her conversation with Mawr, so she remained silent.

They gathered their things, and Talek got rid of their blankets and baskets before they headed out, backtracking a little. They wanted to take a more winding path to get down the hill than the sheer cliffside they had been at earlier.

Colin looked ahead at the mountain that seemed to grow taller as they wound their way closer to it. "What do you think, another two days before we'll reach the top?"

"Oh no," Talek said with a grin. "I don't think it'll take that long. We get to the base and I should be able to fly all of us up there."

"All of us?" Mawr's voice was small and frightened, and Shaleigh slowed a bit so she could put a reassuring hand on his mane. "I don't like flying, Shaleigh," he whispered to her in a loud voice.

"I know," she said. "But I don't think we're going to have much of a choice unfortunately."

He nuzzled her as they continued through the valley.

Shaleigh expected the area to be a dense forest, but it was clear that this place hadn't always been so isolated. Husks of burned out buildings stood as scaffoldings for ivy, and the fallen pieces of scorched timber were the perfect bed for sprouting moss. At one point they had to step around a large metal door that had somehow burst inwards in the middle showing ripped pieces of metal that stood up in dangerous spikes where the heat must have turned it into putty for something to tear through. Shaleigh couldn't help but crouch down beside it, gently dragging her fingers along the edge of the metal bits, marveling at the sharpness despite the rust that was slowly corroding it.

"What happened here?" she asked.

"This place used to be littered with little towns and villages," Colin said, crouching down beside her. "Slowly, one by one, Tanwen destroyed all of them. She went on a rage for some reason."

Mawr shook his head adamantly. "One of the first things I did when Master Teagan gave me access to the library in the Garden was look up all the history on Tanwen the dragon. There was so much more that had happened that I didn't know! Not that I would read any of that to the children, they're far too young to learn about dragons. It's too scary."

Shaleigh couldn't help but smile. Mawr trying to keep children from getting frightened, when he was probably frightened of more than they were, was absolutely price-less. "So, what happened?"

He pawed at the ground in excitement. "Flidais the Fierce was one of Master Cathal's friends. She came up to the volcano to try to build a land despite the danger. She didn't know that this was where Tanwen lived, nobody knew she lived here. She hadn't been seen in centuries.

Many thought she was dead, but I never believed that because dragons don't die.

So Flidais built her castle out of smoke and then Tanwen found out she was building right on top of her house! I'm sure she was terribly angry.

Supposedly they fought because the blade that Flidais made out of molten rock was found, but she never was. Everyone knew Tanwen was angry because she found every town in the mountains and destroyed it: burning everything to the ground and killing everyone she could find. The City of Gwern used to be at the base of the volcano, named for the lady who founded it centuries ago, but they were the first to be destroyed."

Colin stared at him with a grimace. "So, does anybody know if she's still angry?"

Mawr shook his head. "No, nobody comes here anymore. It's too dangerous."

"And, um, we're going to ask her for a favor?" Colin turned to Talek looking uneasy. "Um, you did hear that, right?"

Talek stepped forward. He had been listening from a distance. Teagan moved beside him. "We aren't here to build on her land. We aren't here to claim her mountain, or to fish in her rivers. All we're asking for is Teagan's return. Then we will leave her in peace."

"And if she refuses and wants to fry us all into crisps? What do we do then?"

Talek shrugged and turned away. "That won't happen," a pause, "that can't happen."

Colin gave a nervous laugh and turned to Shaleigh,

lowering his voice, "Can I get a slice of that denial he's having, 'cause it sounds delicious."

Shaleigh sighed and looked to Mawr. "You know the most about Tanwen than any of us. Do you seriously think we have a chance?"

"I mean, I like her, but I don't know what she thinks of lions. Especially stone lions. There have been people to talk to her before, but that was centuries ago, and some people thought they were crazy."

"Great," Colin said. "Just like crazy eyes up there. I'm seeing a pattern."

Talek stopped in the distance, a bright shadow amid the trees. "Are you all coming?"

Colin rolled his eyes as they hurried to join up with him and Teagan. "What do you think he would do if we said no?"

"I wish you wouldn't say things like that. He can probably hear you," Mawr whispered.

Colin's ears flattened back, and he frowned, looking forward to Talek, who turned around and gave him a creepy stare before continuing on. Colin shrank at the sight, putting two hands on Mawr's side and leaping up onto his back.

"I think I need to shut my mouth," he whispered, now terrified, and held onto Mawr's back with all his claws extended.

"I think so too," said Mawr. "I don't like how he looked at you."

Shaleigh kept silent. Talek was playing a game with those two, and she didn't like it. It reminded her of a cat playing with mice, and that never ended well for the mice.

TANWEN THE FIERCE

Shaleigh

It wasn't long before they began following the steady incline that lead up the side of the mountain. Shaleigh couldn't see the peak anymore with its ominous smoke trail, but the pain in her legs told her that they were climbing rapidly. Sweat broke out on her brow and she was breathing hard. They reached a clearing that overlooked where they had just come from, but it didn't look as far as it felt. She gave a frustrated sigh as she leaned her back against a tree trunk.

"Can I carry you?" Mawr asked. He wasn't the least bit bothered by the climb.

Talek walked out on the edge, looking up to the peak, probably gaging the distance to fly.

Shaleigh laughed softly to herself. Of course, she would be the only one suffering for no reason. Why hadn't she asked for help already? Mawr had asked her over and over again if he could carry her, and she always refused. What was she proving, other than that she was stubborn?

"Sure," she agreed with a smile. "I don't know why I didn't think to ask."

Mawr smiled and started his deep purrs before dropping to his belly so she could climb up. "I just figured you were thinking..." His tail twitched nervously.

Colin had a hand out, but she leaned over to see Mawr's face better. "And?"

"Well... I thought maybe you didn't want to ride on my back anymore after the ride through the Slumbering Forest. I thought you were afraid I might run off a ledge or something."

Shaleigh blinked. She hadn't even considered that. Yet looking at Mawr she could tell that it had clearly been bothering him for a long time, ever since their first adventure together.

"I mean, I wouldn't blame you!" he said quickly. "I could tell it scared you and I really don't like scaring people. I just thought you didn't... trust me as much after that."

She patted the stone fur along his cheek. "That wasn't it at all. Of course, I trust you! You're sweeter than anyone I've ever met, Mawr. You weren't thinking straight, you were terrified. Plus, you couldn't see! It's okay." She wrapped her arms around his neck and gave him a tight squeeze. Mawr's purrs rattled her teeth together, but she didn't care.

"Besides, you're my stars now, remember? I can't be scared of you."

He purred even harder.

When she pulled away, Talek was staring at them, his gaze unreadable. Teagan stood at his side; their fingers entwined. "If you two are done," he stated dryly, "I think we're close enough to fly."

"Oh no," Mawr muttered. "Can I just walk please? I really don't like flying!"

"Yeah," Colin agreed and patted Mawr's side. "I'll go with him. We can meet you two at the top if you want."

Talek gave a long sigh. "No, that's out of the question. What's to keep you from fleeing completely?"

"Our loyalty?" Colin tried. Shaleigh couldn't help but wince. If he was trying to convince anyone, he wasn't doing a very good job. Colin was much better at sneaking around than trying to straight out lie.

Talek gave a disturbing laugh and Shaleigh shivered. Colin thankfully didn't instigate him any further, probably guessing from the evil laughter that he was very close to being flung over the edge. Shaleigh quickly stepped forward. Colin had no tact, but that didn't mean he ought to be punished for it.

She held her hands up. "It's okay, we'll fly. It's fine, we'll deal with it." She glanced back to them. "Right, guys?"

They both nodded anxiously.

Talek still had a cruel smile that made her nervous. He started humming a tune that was strangely soothing, and a purple glow formed around each of them, similar to the one she had seen on the Masked King.

Shaleigh held up her own hand, seeing her skin as

though through a purple, digital filter. "What the heck is this?"

"Flying," Colin said, whimpering.

Then they were lifted off the ground, faster than Shaleigh expected. Limbs of trees snapped off as they slammed through them. The bubble of purple protected them, but she still jumped each time a limb snapped. Flashes of her fall through the trees and into the lake at Aife flooded her thoughts, and her heart pounded relentlessly in her chest. She crouched down, trying to make herself small.

When they emerged above the trees, she had to force her body to stop shaking. What was wrong with her? She wasn't hurt, and the leap from the ground to the air wasn't as terrible as some of the things she had dealt with. So, why was she shaking?

Shaleigh wrapped her arms around her elbows and hugged herself tight, looking over to see Mawr floating in almost a C shape, covering his eyes with his big paws and whimpering. Colin was the only one of them that seemed to take it sort of well. He looked surprised, but he was also trying to watch Talek.

That's when Shaleigh noticed that the violet in Talek's eyes was the same shade as the cocoon she was floating in. It was an extension of his magic, and therefore, an extension of his Madness as well. Suddenly her reassurances that they would all be fine flying felt hollow. A terror filled her; they truly were at the mercy of Talek. Worse yet, if his Madness did finally erupt into the destruction that had led to the Dark Lands and the Masked King, they would be annihilated on the spot. Or if they were truly unlucky, they could be turned into his mad little puppets.

Before she could say anything, they were floating quickly upward. Trees moved past them at an alarming rate, and she got the distinct impression that this is what it felt like to be in a plane crash just before impact. They were moving too fast and too low to really be able to stop. Her heart was in her throat now, pounding away in her temples.

"Shaleigh!"

She turned her gaze to Colin. Her head felt like it floated on her shoulders.

Colin's eyes were wide. "Close your eyes! Don't look at the trees. Just close your eyes and breathe."

She swallowed down the dryness in her throat and followed his orders. With her eyes closed, it was easier to deal with the motion. It was easier to listen to the whooshing of the wind around her than it was to see the landscape zooming past.

"Just breathe!"

She nodded, breathing deeply in and out, urging her pulse to slow down. Slowly her body started to calm, and her mind became clearer. The wind continued to whip around her bubble, almost a howl, but she didn't open her eyes. She kept them closed and concentrated on herself.

Then the wind began to die down.

"Can I open them?" she called out to Colin, blind and desperate.

"Hang on." His voice was shaky and Shaleigh's own panic tried to pick up again, but she pressed it back down. No, she wouldn't panic. She wouldn't lose herself. She had to stay focused and calm. When they landed, that would be the true test. *The final test*, she thought ominously. She needed to keep her wits about her.

"Okay," Colin gasped out. "Okay, I think we're good."

She cracked her eyes open, expecting to see the lush green trees beneath them again. Instead of trees, the ground was streaked in browns and grays. The earth was empty of any kind of life, and it reminded her of the Dark Lands with the Masked King for just a moment. She looked around and spotted a distant lava flow with alarm. She had seen the smoke trail, but she hadn't realized this was an active volcano. Surely Talek didn't expect to go all the way to the top. They wouldn't be able to withstand the heat.

Talek was lowering each of them down toward the ground. He had found an empty, relatively flat spot to put them on. When their bubbles disappeared, Shaleigh fell hard onto her shoulder and cried out, pushing up onto her hands and knees. "Ow..."

The place was very warm, she broke out in a heavy sweat almost instantly. It also felt like the air was thinner up here. She had to take deep breaths in order to breathe properly. The ground shook and she almost fell again. Mawr had landed on his rump, his big paws covering his eyes. "Is it safe to look now?" he asked.

She pushed up to her feet, rubbing at her sore shoulder, and went to his side. "It's okay, we're here." She pulled at his elbow, and he reluctantly uncovered one eye. Only once she had rubbed his mane and calmed him down did he finally remove the other paw and stand up.

"I don't like this, Shaleigh. I don't like any of this. I

think I like reading about Tanwen way more than I like visiting her."

"I know, this doesn't look safe at all, does it?"

Colin rushed over to them. "Are you two okay? I was worried you were going to pass out, Shaleigh. You looked really close."

"Yeah, I must have been. That was really rough. Thank you."

"Volcanos are dangerous," Mawr urged. "We really shouldn't go any higher, especially if there is lava around. Oh goodness, I don't even want to think about lava!" He pranced in place, raking his claws into the soft, dark soil. Wait, that wasn't soil…

She squatted down and picked up a handful and released it into the air. It was ash.

"Is that…?" Colin asked.

"Volcanic ash," Mawr said, sounding even more anxious. "That means sometimes the volcano spews up ash and everything gets covered. That's why birds don't fly up here often. They could get their wings covered or they'll breathe it in and suffocate. Oh goodness!"

Shaleigh wiped her hands off and looked to both of them. "I'm so sorry, you two. I'm sorry I got you both into this."

"Look, it's not your fault. We're all in this together, okay? If we stick together, we may have a chance here," Colin said. "Maybe if Talek distracts the dragon we can get out of here."

Shaleigh shook her head. "I can't leave, Colin. I can't leave Teagan like that. I just can't. You two can go. I want you to be safe, but I can't."

Colin's face went serious. "Shaleigh, Teagan is dead. He's gone. Nothing Talek does now is going to help him. He's going to lose his mind for good and he's going to decimate anything in the vicinity. You don't want to be here when that happens." He reached out and took her hands in his. "I really hate to say it, but I will kidnap you again if you insist on staying here. I won't let you kill yourself over him."

Shaleigh gaped, hardly believing her ears. Was he seriously threatening to kidnap her? Again? She dropped his hands, a retort on her lips, when suddenly a voice drowned them all out.

"Tanwen the Ancient, Tanwen the Fierce! I wish to have council with you!" Talek roared to the cloudy sky. A flash of lightening tore through the dark clouds and Shaleigh felt the ground shift. It wasn't a vibration or even something she could really describe, but something moved. He had gotten the attention of something, and it didn't feel good.

"What is that?" she asked, her voice sounding small and insignificant.

"That's the dragon Tanwen," Colin whispered, all his fury from earlier lost.

Mawr dropped down to his belly, trying to flatten himself out on the ground as best he could and Shaleigh understood how he felt. She also suddenly felt the indescribable urge to not be seen, to not be noticed, and was second guessing all her decisions all over again.

The air seemed to crackle around them, and Shaleigh wondered if this was what it felt like before being struck by lightning.

THE GROUND VIBRATED SO hard that Shaleigh fell against Mawr's side as Colin fell to the ground and Talek fell to his knees. Only Teagan seemed to be able to keep his footing. Then it sounded like a firecracker went off as the ground pulled apart near where Talek stood. He backed away, grabbing Teagan's hand and pulling him back as well. The chasm grew wider and Shaleigh winced at the wave of heat that washed over them. It wasn't painful, but it was close.

Then the rumble of earth ended even as the chasm remained. Shaleigh had a feeling it wasn't on accident that it should form just when Talek called out to the dragon.

Talek held an arm in front of him, having trouble seeing due to the heat, and he and Teagan had to fall back to where Shaleigh and Colin were huddled near Mawr.

"Please," Talek pleaded. "I merely want council. We are not here to claim your land, great Tanwen. We are not here to fight you. We do not wish to harm you. I only want your help."

For a moment Shaleigh wondered if the silence meant that she wasn't coming. Perhaps Tanwen was slumbering, or perhaps they simply weren't worth her trouble. That was the logical part of her hoping. Deep in her bones she knew that wasn't true. She could feel the dragon's gaze on them, could feel her fury. Shaleigh only hoped it wouldn't mean their deaths.

To be continued in:
Chosen

ALSO BY MARLENA FRANK

The Stolen Series
Young adult, portal fantasy, faeries
Stolen

Broken

Chosen

The Wolves of Kanta Series
Young adult, dark fantasy, steampunk, werewolves
The She-Wolf of Kanta

The Blood of Kanta

The Hunters of Kanta

The Fury of Kanta

The Howl of Kanta

Standalones
Young adult, horror, sci-fi, dystopian
The Seeking

Short stories, horror, dark fantasy
The Impostor and Other Dark Tales

Ocean horror, weird, short story
Undertow

Weird western, werewolves, vampires, short story
Night Feeders

Mystery, film noir, humor, short story
The Mysterious Disappearance of Charlene Kerringer

The Blade Filled with Stars

A kingdom is under siege from a familiar enemy. Families and friends are pitted against each other without reason. Slaughter is imminent while the winged Queen Khafil soars overhead. Desperate and terrified, Anna works with her sister, Lilah, to summon aid from their mother's ancient spell book.

Determined to save their people, the sisters

summon Death to help them, but Death is not easily swayed. Neither of the sisters are prepared for the consequences.

Want a peek behind the scenes?
Want to preview my books before they get released?

Get exclusive access to book goodies, giveaways, and cover reveals by joining my mailing list. Not only will you get notified of all my new releases, you'll get an exclusive copy of The Blade Filled with Stars.

Subscribe to the Mailing List at:
http://marlenafrank.com/mailinglist/

Support Me On

Ko-fi

Follow me on Ko-Fi for regular updates on my writing progress.

Monthly subscribers get access to sneak peeks at stories way before anyone else. They also get access to cover reveals, monthly shout-outs on social media, and thanked by name in the acknowledgements in my books.

http://ko-fi.com/MarlenaFrank

ACKNOWLEDGMENTS

Writing book 2 in a series is incredibly difficult. There are so many details to keep straight, so much consistency to consider, and so many decisions to be made. Broken wouldn't have come to life without the help of so many people.

Kelley, you keep me grounded as only an older sister can. Even when festivals and author events get harried or all the publishing tasks make me panic, you're always there to be a calming force. I appreciate you so much.

Mom and Dad, you support me in everything I do. You've always given me the strength to leap even when a safe landing is uncertain. Aunt Charmaine, you are an unflappable cheerleader for my work, and I'm always learning from you. Aryn, and Kyle, you all support me in every creative field I choose, and I thank you for inspiring me every day.

I'm grateful to The Parliament House who first published this series. For the few years I was with them, they guided me on this journey that was at times terrifying. I've grown as an author in the past few years more than I ever imagined.

To my fantastic editor, Rae, who I had the pleasure of meeting in person at BookCon in 2019. You know this book would be nowhere near as perfect without your incredible insight. And to my line editor, Emily, who saw how beautiful and clean this book could be.

Finally thank you to my fans. A book is merely a bound set of pages without readers. You inspire me to continue creating worlds, crafting characters, and writing stories. I hope you've enjoyed my words, and I hope you'll come back to read more.

Marlena Frank is the author of young adult fantasy and horror novels, short stories, novellas, and book series. Many of her books have hit the bestseller charts, including her debut novel, Stolen. Her work has been praised by Readers' Favorite and featured in De Mode of Literature Magazine. Her stories have appeared in anthologies such as Emporium of Superstition, Catstruck!, Heroic Fantasy Quarterly, Georgia Gothic, and The Sirens Call ezine.

Although born in Tennessee, Marlena has spent most

of her life in Georgia. She lives with her sister and two spoiled adopted cats. She serves as the Vice President of the Atlanta Chapter of the Horror Writers Association, is an active member of the Science Fiction and Fantasy Writers Association, and is an avid member of the Atlanta cosplay community.

She is also an INFJ, a tea drinker, and a wildlife enthusiast.

Support her on Ko-Fi: ko-fi.com/MarlenaFrank